BROKEN IN PLAIN SIGHT

A Story of Truth, Healing, and Love

BRIDGETTE *L* COLLINS

BROKEN IN PLAIN SIGHT
published by Origins Publishing Company
A subsidiary of Total Innovative Wellness Solutions, LLC

This is a work of fiction. The characters, incidents, and dialogues
are products of the author's imagination and are not to be
construed as real. Any resemblance to actual
events or persons, living or dead, is entirely coincidental.

ISBN: 978-0-9790932-3-4

Cover design by Steve Gardner, www.shootpw.com
Interior design and typeset by www.cover2coverbookdesign.com
Photography by Sirena Williams Photography

Printed in the United States of America.

For information:
ORIGINS PUBLISHING COMPANY
P.O. Box 542671
Grand Prairie, TX 75054-2671

To those whose lives have been broken by circumstance.
This book is dedicated to you.

Acknowledgments

*To Antonia Jones, Tess McCall, and Sharon Young,
whose personal stories of circumstance have inspired me
and who contributed significant content to this book.*

Special Thanks

*To Angela Collier and Private Chef H.D. Harris
for your contribution of healthy recipes*

In Memory of

*Diane Proud, an athlete with
courage and an amazing spirit to the end.
www.runproud.org*

Contents

The Gathering

"Lord, did I hear You clearly? Am I ready? Can I help Uncle Bert fulfill his mission?"

For nearly ten years, Trevor McElroy had traveled around the world, educating, encouraging, and empowering people to make healthy lifestyle changes. It was a passion he recognized in his early thirties that led him to help people evaluate all the things vying for their attention, to help people weed out those things that added no value, to prioritize the things in their lives that should be essential, and to explore their options for making small, healthy changes. He was noticeably changing lives. Through his message of choice and change, Trevor had become an up close and personal resource that influenced many to make a commitment to live happier, healthier, and with purpose.

Most impressed by the work Trevor was doing locally and abroad was his Uncle Bert, a well-known businessman and state representative in Houston, Texas. Uncle Bert knew that Trevor's motivating and persuasive skills were what he needed for a mission he was ready to pursue, a mission that included oversight of his business and distribution of his wealth to three of his great-nieces (Claire, Erin, and Melissa) and three of his great-nephews (Edward,

Thomas Wayne, and Dillard). They were the grandkids of his older sister, Saddie. Their mothers—Lucille, Wynona, Ruby, and Helen—were victims of the same hardships as Saddie, and now the cycle of hardships continued with the great-nieces and great-nephews. For years, Uncle Bert had carried around the guilt of not coming to the aid of his sister and her daughters when they needed him the most. Now, he wanted to correct his negligence through Saddie's grandkids.

Despite his good intentions, Uncle Bert knew there were some matters that needed immediate attention before he handed over his wealth and the leadership of his business. In the hopes of spurring continued growth of Spencer Security Services for years to come through his great-nieces and great-nephews, he knew that the content of their lives needed a major overhaul. Under their present condition, he was not willing release his life-building achievements until they could responsibly handle what he was offering.

Uncle Bert identified Trevor as his catalyst for instilling a new perspective. But Trevor's reluctance had delayed the movement of his mission. After numerous attempts, Trevor agreed to meet his Uncle Bert for dinner. Trevor imagined putting an end to his Uncle's appeal for support.

During their dinner at Rudee's Seafood Grill, Uncle Bert asked Trevor a question, "Is your mission really to change lives?"

Surprised by the question, Trevor looked down at the half-eaten grilled salmon on his plate and thought to himself, *Why me?*

"For months, you have dismissed my text messages and telephone calls," Uncle Bert said. He looked both angry and disappointed. "You spend so much of your time giving precedence to building your forum for educating and empowering individuals to live healthier, mind, body, and spirit, but you've ignored my motives for helping your own blood relatives."

Trevor mumbled to himself, "With good reason."

"What did you say?" Uncle Bert waited for a response.

Reluctantly, Trevor said, "As much as I hate to admit it, Uncle, over the years, I have consciously avoided my cousins."

"Why?" Uncle Bert was anxious to hear Trevor's response.

"You know why."

"I want you to tell me."

"The last thing I want to do is expose myself to the resentment they have harbored against me ever since our childhood. You know how they are."

"I know they haven't all made the best decisions in life."

"They are a bunch of nasty, mean, critical, complaint-driven, and ungrateful adults."

Uncle Bert looked disturbed as Trevor continued talking.

"To pretend that me and my cousins have a healthy alliance and a love for each other as family… you know I'd be lying." Trevor paused, "Right now, I find it difficult to make an unwavering commitment to you."

Trevor started to pick at his steamed broccoli. "I know that's not what you want to hear."

Uncle Bert hesitated, and then he said, "If anyone knows firsthand what it's like to be bruised, battered, and broken in spirit by decades of chaos and pain, it's you."

Uncle Bert took a bite of his filet mignon. His eyes opened wide, disturbed at Trevor's attitude.

Trevor switched his attention to a table in front of them. He observed a plain-looking, full-figured lady drinking a large margarita.

"I need for you to focus on me and this conversation."

Trevor put on his charming smile and looked at his uncle. He thought, *Not me. Not now. How do I respectfully get Uncle Bert to understand that?*

"Trevor!" his uncle shouted.

Trevor chuckled while he picked up his glass of water and took a sip. He quickly said, "No, I'm sorry, Uncle Bert. I can't help you on this one. I simply can't."

Uncle Bert looked around the restaurant, took a deep breath, and said, "You 'simply can't'. Now what does that mean, Trevor?" He continued to emphasize his desire to offer Trevor's cousins a second, third, fourth, or even a fifth chance to reconcile and restore their lives.

"I understand what you're saying, but it's not my problem to help them fix their lives," Trevor said harshly.

"Of all the people I would expect to respond so negatively, I never would have considered you, especially when I think about the person you credit for helping you to change your life."

Trevor shrugged while lowering his head to eat the remainder of his grilled salmon.

"For the last four years, my surveillance team has tracked the height of your cousins' reckless decisions, destructive lifestyle behaviors, unhealthy relationships, drugs, alcohol, and impulsive spending habits."

"Uncle, they've been pretty reckless and destructive for decades," Trevor frowned.

Trying to hide his distress, Uncle Bert continued talking, "At the age of seventy-five, I have realized how emotionless and irresponsible I have been with the family God has paired me with. God has blessed me with prestige, money, cars, homes, investments, and a lucrative business, but I have shared my success with none of my family members."

Trevor nodded, thinking about his busy schedule and his new girlfriend.

"I've had to do some deep soul-searching. I feel terrible that I have avoided communicating with your cousins."

Trevor sighed and said, "Unfortunately, I don't share your sentiments. But, just as you have focused your life on becoming a prominent political figure and a wealthy businessman, I have done the same."

"And that saddens me even more." Uncle Bert admitted mistakes that he wanted to correct before his life ended. He had a responsibility to truly make a difference, and this was his last opportunity to do so.

"I need you, Trevor, to help me make that difference."

Trevor exhaled, looking astoundingly grateful as he stared at his Uncle Bert. If his cousins were going to have a chance at change and to meet Uncle Bert's expectations for acquiring what he wanted to offer them, he would have to disband his negative thoughts and feelings to reach out to and reconnect with his cousins.

❖

Chapter 1

❖

An Appointment with Destiny

To move beyond what was difficult for him under the circumstances, Trevor initiated a meeting between himself and his cousins. It was now mid-June, and the time for the long-anticipated gathering had arrived. They were the cousins who Trevor had grown up with, but had limited communication with for the past twenty years. He had accepted the notion that they needed his immediate attention. All he needed to do was get them together under one roof. The perfect place for the gathering would be where they all found refuge and had felt protected as children. That was Grandma Saddie's house.

"Trevor!" a loud, fearful voice shouted from outdoors.

It was nine o'clock on a cloudy Saturday morning. Trevor was deep in thought, adding a 24-inch leaf to a traditional dining table that Finger's Furniture had delivered the day before. Startled by the loud cry, Trevor stood straight up from his bent over position and hurried across the buckled wood floors to open the front door. He paused on the front porch to pinpoint the direction of what he'd heard. At the edge of the narrow driveway stood his cousin, Erin, watching a familiar scene.

"Hey, Erin, what's wrong?" Trevor yelled.

"Look! Down the street by Ms. Bettie's old house."

From a distance, he could see Erin's brother, Dillard, walking fearfully on the shoulder of the street with a Home Depot bag in each hand. His ex-wife, Veronica, was driving behind him in a white 2000 Toyota Tundra with the car window rolled down, honking the car horn and yelling out obscenities and profanity.

Trevor was stunned in disbelief. Shaking his head and laughing uncontrollably, he thought to himself, *Man, I can't believe this. This is insane.*

Erin looked back, "Do something, Trevor! Do something before she runs him over. She's crazy!"

"Get in the car, stupid!" screamed Veronica, as she leaned out the window. "Hey, stupid broke man! Too afraid of your wife?"

Trevor jumped off the porch, ran down the driveway, and onto the street. Erin trailed behind him in her flip-flops with her large breasts bouncing. Trying not to trip or lose her balance, she slowed down her steps. She held on tightly to her bag of Cheetos.

Trevor raised his arm and motioned to Dillard, "Man, jump in the ditch!"

Just as Veronica increased her speed to hit Dillard, he leaped into a deep and narrow ditch that was filled with rainwater from the night before. He was still holding onto his bags.

Veronica yelled out of the car window as she watched Dillard wading in the ditch, "You better pay that child support, muddy man! I'll hit you for real next time. Look at you! Looking like something from *The Swamp Thing*. And take this old piece of luggage." She threw an old suitcase into the ditch and sped away, leaving tire lines on the blacktop street and a trail of white-gray smoke smelling of burnt rubber.

As Trevor and Erin approached Dillard, nearby neighbors were watching the commotion from their yards. The cloud of white-gray smoke caused them all to choke and cough.

From the moment Dillard and Veronica had wed, his life had been in constant turmoil. The death from Leukemia of their ten-year-old daughter had caused unbearable discord in his marriage. Then, never-ending bickering and fighting had led him to divorce Veronica a year ago. Now, she was limiting his contact with their other two children, Tiffany and Walter, ages ten and fifteen.

"Man, you alright?" Trevor asked. He extended his hand to help Dillard balance himself as he walked out of the dark, muddy water. When he looked down, he noticed worms clinging to Dillard's right pant leg.

Distracted by Erin's labored breathing, Trevor turned and asked, "Erin, are you okay?"

"Yes, I'm okay, and, no, he's not alright. And get those worms off him!"

"I'm alright, guys," Dillard said. He reached down to pick the worms off his blue jeans. His sneakers were soaked with mud.

Erin handed her opened bag of Cheetos to Trevor and wrapped her arms around Dillard. She pulled him close and said, "Come on; let's get you out of those muddy clothes."

Trevor looked at the bag of Cheetos, shaking his head. He positioned himself carefully at the edge of the ditch and picked up the mud-covered suitcase and Home Depot bags. The bags seemed unusually heavy, so he looked inside. One bag was filled with cleaning products Trevor had asked for so they could clean Grandma Saddie's house. In the second bag, he noticed materials to repair the door locks and something enclosed in foil paper with a familiar smell. He placed the bag of Cheetos inside.

"What's in the foil, Dillard?" Trevor inquired, as he walked quickly to catch up with them.

"Just a couple of pork chop sandwiches I purchased at Old Joe's Smokehouse."

"Pork chop sandwiches? Don't you have high blood pressure?"

"Not now, Trevor! Everybody has high blood pressure," Erin glanced over at Trevor with a cold look and shouted, "Dillard, did you get the potato salad and peach cobbler?"

"Yes, I did."

As they neared their grandmother's house, an old neighbor stood at the edge of his driveway, waiting for them to get closer. With a breathing tube in his nose and an oxygen tank trailing behind him, when he was a few feet away, he asked, "Are you Saddie Johnson's grandkids?"

"Yes, sir," Trevor responded, as they approached the man.

"Wow! What on Earth happened, son?" the neighbor asked, looking with confusion at Dillard as they stopped at the edge of his driveway. "Looks like that lady was trying to kill you."

Trevor looked at his watch and thought, *I knew this reunion would be anything but calm and pleasant.*

Dillard smiled at the man who he remembered from their youth and told him, "Everything is okay, sir. My ex-wife stopped taking her anti-depressant medication." He explained her steady downward mental spiral since the death of their daughter a few years earlier.

"So sorry to hear about your ex's mental state and the loss of your child." Holding a lit cigarette in his right hand, the man managed to pick something out of his nose. "It's great to see you all, though. I don't know if you remember me, but I'm Mr. Whitehouse. I know I look much different, at least one hundred pounds heavier. I've been plagued by a number of health problems. After over fifty years of smoking, I guess I should have expected *some* problems."

Erin stared blankly at Mr. Whitehouse and thought, *Why is he telling us all this? Who on Earth cares?*

Dillard looked at Mr. Whitehouse and nodded through a perplexed daze.

Mr. Whitehouse said, "I have chronic obstructive pulmonary disease (COPD), and my boys have abandoned me. They blame me for their mother dying from lung cancer."

As he rambled on about his medical condition, Trevor smiled and interrupted him, "I remember you, Mr. Whitehouse. You'd always take Grandma Saddie to get fertilizer for her roses."

"Absolutely! She was the nicest lady I've ever met; that is, next to my wife of fifty-five years—Mindy. She died about five years ago. I don't know if you all remember her and my three boys. They blame me for their mother's death, you know," Mr. Whitehouse restated. He paused for moment, and then continued, "Your grandmother's house has been vacant for a while now. The people who lived there a few years ago really made a mess of it—always fighting, breaking out windows, and puddles of oil from raggedy cars."

The one story, three bedroom, and one bathroom house was over sixty years old. Out of love for the house and his grandmother, Trevor had recently purchased the foreclosed house for $65,000.

"Mr. Whitehouse, we don't mean to be rude, but we need to get my cousin in the house and out of his dirty clothes," Erin said, pointing at Dillard's shoes and pant legs.

"I'll be here through tomorrow," Trevor said, "and I will stop by before I leave."

"Did you all buy the house?" Mr. Whitehouse asked as they walked away. "Um… I didn't think anyone would ever buy that house again. Such a mess!"

"Yes, sir, I did."

Mr. Whitehouse looked curiously at Trevor. "My, you turned out to be good looking chap. I remember you being a round, pudgy something."

Erin and Dillard looked at Trevor. He was a tall, handsome, well-built man. They could see his six-pack through his T-shirt top.

Staring at Erin's form-fitting dress, as he took a puff on his cigarette, Mr. Whitehouse said, "You need to change out that flimsy front door now that you're back. Burglaries are bad around here. Someone broke into my shed the other day and stole all of my lawn equipment. My sons could get me out of here if they wanted to. Total desertion!"

Mr. Whitehouse turned around, looking at the houses in the neighborhood with obvious distaste.

Trevor, Erin, and Dillard walked silently back toward Grandma Saddie's house. After what they had just witnessed, they were at a loss for words.

Trevor thought, *I knew it was going to be an interesting weekend, but I could never have imagined a beginning like this. What has Uncle Bert committed me to? This is going to be crazy.*

Standing at the end of their grandmother's driveway were Melissa and Edward with frozen faces and gaping mouths. They were waiting for Trevor, Erin, and Dillard and were desperate to find out what had happened to Dillard.

A noticeable blackish-blue bruise consumed Dillard's right eye.

Shaking his head with disgust, Edward asked, "What's up with you, cuz? You have more drama in your life than anyone I know. We're going to create a website in your honor—Dillardsdrama. com."

Erin leaned toward Dillard's ear and whispered, "Just ignore him." She knew that Edward's spirit was more than Dillard could stand up too.

"Seriously, man, what happened? You look a mess!" Edward shouted louder. "And what's up with the black eye? Veronica still beating that ass?"

Erin shouted, "Shut up, Edward! Just shut up!"

Ignoring Erin, Edward continued, "She just uses you as a punching bag. Such a worthless, weak man, still battered physically and mentally at forty-four years old. I'm embarrassed to call you my cousin. What are you, around 6'2", 300 pounds? Just a damn shame!"

Dillard was immune to the insults, having grown up with relatives who routinely verbally abused and physically beat him.

"Leave him alone, Edward," Trevor said, walking between the two.

"What happened this time?" Edward insisted while laughing. "And, how on Earth did you end up in the car with her?"

"Edward, just get out of my way," Dillard said, giving him a slight shove as he moved past him to greet Melissa.

"Hi guys," Melissa said to Dillard, Erin, and Trevor.

"Dillard, I hate that I didn't pick you up," Erin said apologetically.

Dillard looked embarrassed beyond embarrassment.

"My brother's car is not working, and Veronica offered to pick him up from work, trying to get money out of him as usual," Erin said.

"Damn shame!" Edward said facetiously.

Dillard looked back at Edward with clenched fists.

"We're pretty used to this drama between Dillard and Veronica," Edward said, looking at Trevor. "You've been so far removed from the family that you wouldn't know it, Mr. Fitness! I can't believe you lost all that baby fat."

Edward stared at Trevor with amazement.

"You were always a big, fat kid. Look at you now, all buffed up! What did you do Atkins, liquid, pill, or grapefruit diet?"

"No dieting, my cousin Edward." Trevor took a deep breath. "Once I discarded the garbage inside weighing me down, I was freed up to move out of a stagnant state and implement the sort of habits I needed to live healthy—mind, body, and spirit."

"Um… guess you're Mr. Spiritual now, too," Edward said, mocking him.

❖

Standing in front of their grandmother's house, the cousins listened to Erin recount Dillard's horrid experience with Veronica, "It's no laughing matter, Edward. She's a maniac. He should have left her years ago," Erin said, standing nervously.

"Man, you're just weak! You were weak as a kid, and now you're weak as a man!" Edward shouted at Dillard.

Dillard started to walk away.

"Dillard, wait up!" Erin said. "Ignore stupidity. Let's get in the house so you can get cleaned up."

"You are so insensitive," Trevor said, as he shoved Edward's arm with his hand. "Still a bully at forty-eight years old."

Edward laughed and said, "Uh, you know that whole incident was crazy."

"Hey, guys, wait up!" Trevor said, hurrying to catch up with Dillard and Erin. "I sure hope the neighbors don't call the cops on us."

"Don't get mad at me for telling the truth!" Edward shouted.

"Come on, Edward," Melissa said, as she started to follow Trevor.

Seconds later, they were distracted by the loud sounds from a black Cadillac Escalade. The SUV drove up and blocked Grandma Saddie's driveway.

The long, narrow driveway was already filled with Trevor's Lexus 330, Erin's Ford Escort, Melissa's Honda Accord, and Edward's Ford Mustang.

"I know that's not Thomas Wayne in that black Caddy," Erin looked back.

They all turned back to walk toward the edge of the driveway.

"Probably so. You know my li'l brother has always been a showoff," Edward said. "But, at least the good ole' deputy sheriff can help you press charges on that ex-wife of yours," he said to Dillard with unconcealed coldness.

A short and stocky man exited the SUV wearing a brown hat with an orange and black plaid headband, brown khaki shorts, a white long-sleeve polo shirt, python snake-skin sandals, and Tag Heuer sunglasses.

Edward's brother, Thomas Wayne, was known for flaunting his elaborate cars, Tiffany jewelry, and flashy clothes.

"Said it ain't so," Trevor said as he walked up to Thomas Wayne. Maneuvering around the suitcase and bags in his hands, Thomas Wayne embraced him with a big hug. "It's good to see you, T-Wayne."

"Why do you have on that hot shirt? It's ninety-some degrees out here?" Edward asked.

Thomas Wayne ignored his brother and said to Trevor, "It's good to see you in the old neighborhood. Wow! You look great! Where's that chubby kid I remember?"

Thomas Wayne squeezed Trevor's right bulging bicep. His nose was noticeably runny.

Trevor was wearing an athletic, grey, short-sleeve shirt and cargo shorts that highlighted his muscular body.

"Take off those shades, man, so I see you," Trevor said, as he reached to remove Thomas Wayne's shades.

Thomas Wayne motioned for him to leave them on. He looked at their grandmother's house. "Seeing all of us here together at grandma's house brings back some happy memories of growing up on Kittridge Street," Thomas Wayne said, nodding quickly.

"Maybe good memories for you, but definitely not for me and my brother," Erin replied, as she moved to hug Thomas Wayne.

The house that was once beautiful and vibrant, filled with love and a family well-connected, was now damaged and in need of restoration. Like the lives of Trevor's cousins, there was no paneling or paint on the walls in the house covering up the problems underneath, and the problems that needed fixing or replacing were transparent. A change in the interior and exterior of both the house and his cousins meant shared responsibility and sacrifice for Trevor and his uncle. Trevor was ready to help his cousins gain a new perspective on life to position them on the path to a happier, healthier, and purpose-filled life.

Chapter 2

❖

Beyond the Brokenness

It had been over thirty years since Erin, Melissa, Dillard, Edward, and Thomas Wayne had been in their grandmother's house together. Walking up the steps, they first noticed boarded windows and the outdated air conditioning unit partially hanging outside the window. Entering one by one through the front door, they walked almost reluctantly across the large living room that had hosted many family gatherings.

Still harboring ill feelings from their childhood, they were curious about why Trevor had summoned them to their grandmother's old house. All victims of their parents' unhealthy behaviors and devastating decisions, Erin, Melissa, Dillard, Edward, and Thomas Wayne had suffered the consequences at an early age. Decades later, their inability to extinguish their anger, blame, resentment, and lack of forgiveness had caused them to experience their own endless stream of impulsive and reckless decisions.

Trevor knew that the only way his cousins could experience real and meaningful change in their lives was through transforming their mind, body, and spirit. He thought that a good way to start the transformation process was by reconnecting them through the renovation of their grandmother's house.

"Walk around, guys," Trevor suggested. He set the suitcase and Home Depot bags on the floor in the living room area.

Melissa pushed Edward in the shoulder and told him, "Walk around down the hallway."

"Walk around for what?" Edward asked. He jerked his shoulder away from Melissa. "This place reeks of mold and mildew. I'm not trying to end up with some lung disease. We'll be walking around with tanks like that old man down the street."

Thomas Wayne followed behind them with his nose continuously runny.

"For once I agree with my brother," Thomas Wayne said.

"Me too," Erin echoed from the kitchen.

"Man, wipe your nose," Edward said. "You look like some snotty-nosed kid. And take off those shades. You look crazy with them on inside."

To hide his embarrassment, Thomas Wayne opened the bathroom door and walked in.

Dillard picked up his suitcase. "I'm going to change clothes. I'll be in Grandma's bedroom. Trevor, is the refrigerator working?"

"It's on," Trevor answered.

"Can you put my food in the refrigerator?"

Edward overheard Dillard's question and asked, "What food?" He brushed past Melissa to go back into the living room.

"Our pork chop sandwiches, potato salad, and peach cobbler," Erin replied. "Anything else you need to know, nosy. Trevor, put my chips on the table."

Thomas Wayne walked out of the bathroom. His eyes were distinctly glassy. He and Melissa started to walk from room to room. The 1,000 square-foot home brought back memories for the two. Walking through the rooms once referred to as the boys' room and the girls' room, they were saddened by the sight of damaged sheetrock and peeling paint.

"I remember the twin beds. At any given time, there may have been two to three boys in a bed," Thomas Wayne said.

"Yeah, the girls' room had one big queen-size bed where us girls would sleep two at one end of the bed and two at the other end of the bed."

Erin walked up behind them and said, "On occasion, one or two of the girls would get to sleep with grandmother in the big bed. We loved her bed, because it stood high with three mattresses."

In the small house, it was easy for Trevor to hear the varied conversations.

"Uncle Bert will be here soon," he announced abruptly, as he opened the blinds near the dining table.

"What?" Edward asked.

He stepped quickly in front of Trevor, looking at him in open-mouthed astonishment, but Trevor continued to pull on the string to open the blinds.

"Why is he coming here?" Edward asked.

He stood there staring steadily at Trevor with his shoulders stiff and his fingers trembling as though he wanted to hit someone.

"Just wait and see," Trevor said calmly. "It's all good, cuz."

Trevor walked into the living room. He began to remove the items from the Home Depot bags and placed them on the living room floor.

"I don't know why we had to meet here," Erin said. "Everything is filthy. I need my sanitizer."

Melissa scooted past Erin and said, "I bet the bathroom tub, the sink, and the medicine cabinet look a lot smaller than when we were kids."

"One of the things Uncle Bert wants to talk to us about is fixing up the old place," Trevor said, speaking loudly.

He didn't want to steal Uncle Bert's thunder by sharing his true intentions.

"For what? It's a dump!" Edward said. "Plus, it's your house now. Why would we help you fix up your house?"

Trevor made no reply.

Edward walked up to Trevor and stood there, waiting.

Determined not to answer Edward, Trevor lowered his eyes and walked away.

"He's right. I don't know why you bought it. The floors are rotted. The walls have holes. In the boy's room, the roof is leaking. The ceiling has fallen in," Dillard said, walking into the living room area. "Plus, the neighborhood is nothing like I remember."

"Mold!" Edward blurted out.

"This place has been abandoned for years. It's falling apart and will require too much money to make all the repairs and changes," Melissa pointed out.

"Trevor is a big time fitness guru. He's like Uncle Bert. They both have plenty of money," Edward said loudly.

One by one, they assembled in a large room that combined the kitchen and dining areas adjacent to the living room. Around the rectangular, double-pedestal dining table, Trevor had positioned ten Brandywine chairs that had beautiful splat backs, upholstered seats, and two front cabriole legs.

"Sit down," Trevor motioned to everyone.

Edward stood against the refrigerator with his arms crossed over his chest.

Melissa crossed the kitchen floor quickly, trying to sit in the chair with armrests. She loved their grandmother's chairs with armrests. With broad and excessive body fat in her hips and thighs and wearing a tight-fitting dress, she paused and stared at the chair. She positioned herself, grabbed hold of the armrests, and forcibly wiggled her lower body from side to side to squeeze into the chair.

Sitting uncomfortably, she was relieved that everyone was distracted and hadn't noticed her.

Edward leaned on the refrigerator and focused on reading text messages on his cell phone. Erin and Thomas Wayne seated themselves away from the table to make room for their oversized bellies. Dillard shifted a chair to sit facing Trevor who was seated at the head of the table.

Trevor recounted the needed renovations, but before he could explain the specific problems, Edward interrupted him, "Man, ain't no need for you talk about this stuff to us."

"Shut up and listen," Thomas Wayne blurted out. "You're always saying something that don't mean nothing."

Edward looked at Thomas Wayne as though he was going to hit him.

A wave of nervous tension resonated around the table.

Undeterred, Trevor talked about the outdated electrical wiring being a fire hazard, a new roof, the replacement of all appliances, the installation of a central air-conditioning and heating system, the rebuilding of the front and back porches, and new fencing around the yard.

Edward sat down next to Melissa and murmured to her, "Again, why are we here listening to him?"

"What did you say?" Trevor asked loudly. He was growing frustrated with Edward's negative remarks.

"Y'all listening to this fool like little kids being scolded and punished for something? The things he is talking about are his problems."

Thomas Wayne interjected loudly, scratching his right arm, "Edward, we're just as much in the dark about what Trevor is talking about and why. Clearly this is his house. For whatever reason, he wanted to purchase it and come back to the old neighborhood. Let's just hear him out, wait for Uncle Bert, and make the best of an uncomfortable situation."

Edward shook his head in disagreement and said, "Whatever, man." He clasped his hands behind his head and crossed his legs.

Erin got up from the table and walked over to the refrigerator. "Does anyone want something to drink?"

"Trevor, do you have any sodas?" Melissa inquired.

Erin opened the refrigerator door. "Grandma Saddie always kept her refrigerator filled with soda."

"Yeah! Big Red was my favorite. She'd always have some Big Red," Dillard said.

Erin looked inside. She glanced at Melissa and Dillard and said, "There's plenty of bottled water, but no soda."

"Figures," Edward murmured.

"Only water in the house," Trevor confirmed.

Thomas Wayne got up from the table and left the room.

Edward nodded his head back and forth slowly and said softly under his breath, "I bet he's having a hard time."

"Hard time with what, Edward?" Melissa asked.

"A hard time," Edward repeated.

"With what?" Melissa looked over at Edward with great interest.

"A hard time pretending that he's got it going on. Owes me a bunch of money. Don't know what he's doing with his money."

Erin yelled out, "Does anyone want a bottle of water?"

"Not really, but I'll take one anyway," Melissa said, while pushing herself sideways to get out of her seat.

"I'll get it, Melissa," Erin said, motioning for Melissa to remain seated.

Trevor was quickly distracted by a vibration on his cellular telephone. After taking a moment to read it, he got up from the table and headed toward the front door.

"I guess it's intermission time," Erin said, while placing several bottles of water on the table.

"Where is Trevor going?" Edward asked, while hitting his fist against the table. "I've got things to do. I don't have time to sit here all day waiting on massa Trevor."

"Man, just chill!" Dillard shouted out.

Edward pointed at Dillard and said, "I got your chill."

"Come on, guys; can't we stay civil with one another?" Melissa pleaded, as she picked up her bottled water. She took a long time to swallow.

"This is entirely too much hostility in one room," Erin said.

Thomas Wayne walked back into room and sat down. Sniffing, he inconspicuously tried to wipe his red and raw nose. Unknowingly, he had some white powder across his nostrils.

"What's up, Thomas Wayne. You can't stomach hanging out with the family rejects? And why are you sniffing like that? Why is your nose runny like that? You have a cold or something? What's that white stuff on your face?" Edward asked boldly. "You weren't in the backyard doing drugs now were you?"

"Man, you crazy!" Thomas Wayne chuckled. "It must be flour from my pant pockets. I made pancakes from scratch this morning for my wife. Between mixing the ingredients and retrieving my cell phone from my pocket this morning… it's the residue of flour. No drugs, my brother. I put drug addicts in jail."

Edward looked around for Trevor and said, "Don't tell Mr. Fitness you had pancakes. I'm sure that's a no-no."

Thomas Wayne, rubbing his nose, changed the subject. He sat down, looking nervous, and starting to sweat as he fumbled for his cell phone. "Have you all seen the rooms we slept in as kids? They look exactly the same."

"Memories of the ghetto," Edward said sarcastically. He clapped his hands. "What's the point? The neighborhood is pitiful, vacant lots filled with old furniture and trash, people with parked cars on their front lawns, houses painted with all sorts of psychedelic colors."

"He's right; Kashmere Heights Park looks terrible, broken benches in the park where we played as kids, the fencing around it is hanging on the ground," Erin said.

"I saw a washing machine and dryer on the porch down the street," Edward said, shaking his head. "I'm trying to figure out if they wash and dry their clothes on the porch."

Edward laughed uncontrollably. Melissa joined in.

"Hey, I still live in this neighborhood," Erin said.

"So sorry," Edward apologized. "I even saw a sofa on Ms. Carol's curb. Looks like it's been there for weeks."

"He's right," Melissa added. "People back in the day took pride in the upkeep of their homes and neighborhoods. We never saw a house with debris laying around in yards."

"That's why I live in a gated community," Thomas Wayne responded. "We don't have these sort of issues—just beautiful homes, green lawns, sprinkler systems, and amenities comparable to the rich and famous—and a homeowner's association to keep everyone focused."

"I don't live in a gated community like you, li'l brother, but my neighborhood is decent," Edward said. "By the way, where is that money you owe me? You need to stop living an extravagant lifestyle and pay back the people you owe!"

Thomas Wayne stood up, placed his hands on the table, and stared at Edward.

Dillard tried to ease the tension, "I remember us playing cops and robbers and popping wheelies on our bikes."

Ignoring Dillard, Edward jumped up and said, "Look at my brother, the little, short, stubby man. Deputy Sheriff! Fat as a kid and fat as an adult. Guess you've eaten more than your fair share of donuts and crawfish. What you want to do, little fat man? How you going to catch a criminal? Looks like you need to be on Trevor's diet plan."

"Man, I've lost 30 pounds. I'm down to 210 pounds."

"Are you serious. You're still fat. I'm sure Mr. Fitness can confirm that!" Edward exploded with laughter. "You could stand to lose another 40 pounds."

Erin looked mortified, and the group sat in silence, but just as the tension became unbearable, Trevor walked in to announce, "I have a surprise for everyone."

Great-uncle Bert entered the living room, wearing a three-piece, chocolate-brown, pinstripe suit with a tan shirt and brown tie. He stood 6-feet-3 inches tall and weighed 230 pounds. Uncle Bert was their grandmother's baby brother who had never married or had any children.

For the past forty years, Uncle Bert had devoted his life to the business and political arenas in North Houston. He was known in the community as a hardworking, honest, generous, caring, and funny business man with the ability to transform little into much while providing assistance to his low-income constituents. He sat on many boards and was an adviser to several business colleges. He had served as a state representative for nearly twenty years and was a vocal advocate for the underprivileged. But, with all of his achievements, he knew he was about to take on the biggest challenge of his life.

"Hi, Uncle Bert," Erin said. She was the first to greet him with an intense embrace.

Dillard and Thomas Wayne followed behind her.

"It's good to see you all after so many years," he said, as he hugged Dillard and Thomas Wayne.

Edward and Melissa lagged behind, watching the greetings. Gulping down a bottle of water, Edward was clearly not moved by the emotional exchange. Melissa sat there looking disgusted.

Uncle Bert looked over at Edward and Melissa and asked, "Aren't the two of you going to give your uncle a hand shake, hug, or something?"

Edward walked toward his uncle and said, "Well, if it isn't the infamous Bert Spencer!" He clapped his hands. "Business mogul! State Representative! Impressive!" He clapped his hands again. "So what's the big mystery? Why did you have Trevor lure us to this old house? You sold this house years ago after our grandmother died. And, I thought, good riddance. Contrary to what my cousins believe, for me there is nothing here but a bunch of bad memories," he paused, looking disappointedly at his uncle. "You haven't made time for me in over twenty years. When I asked you for money to go to college, you said no. So, what's up now? I hear you're helping kids in the hood get jobs and have scholarship programs. All of a sudden, we're just supposed to welcome you with open arms."

The others stood listening to Edward's rant while Melissa remained seated.

Uncle Bert asked them to sit at the family table. Everyone took a seat except Edward. He went to lean against the refrigerator.

"Where is Claire?" Uncle Bert asked, as he looked around the room. He turned to Trevor for an answer.

"She's in the hospital," Trevor responded.

"Claire is in the hospital?" Melissa shouted. "Why didn't you tell us? What's wrong with her? Why are we here? We should be at the hospital."

"Girl, you don't even like Claire," Edward said, propped alongside the refrigerator. "Stop pretending. Your fake concern is stupid."

"Stop it! Just stop it right now!" Uncle Bert demanded.

Trevor explained to everyone that Claire was in the hospital undergoing tests for diarrhea, abdominal cramping, fever, and a severe rash. She had recently been diagnosed with Sweet's Syndrome.

Uncle Bert sat in the chair at the head of the table and said, "In response to Edward and all of you, we have some family issues that run deep and now cross generations. I love you all and our family too much to leave things where they are. For you all in particular, it's good to remember the past and learn from it. But, you all have settled into the past, and doing so has affected your lives tremendously through the years. It's time that you stop looking behind and start looking ahead. If you hang onto anger and resentment, you're only hurting yourself and your families."

"For once I agree with Edward. Where did this Uncle Bert come from? What's with the dispensing of sincere sounding and caring comments?" Melissa asked. "I, too, asked you for money years ago when my husband left me. I was evicted from my home with two small kids. We had to go live in a homeless shelter. All I wanted you to do was help me get caught up on my mortgage. Today, after raising two kids, I'm fifty years old, still trying to play catch-up from how my ex left me with nothing but a bunch of bills."

"In a homeless shelter?" Edward repeated.

"Yes," Melissa said.

"Who goes to a homeless shelter?" Edward asked. "That's like for people on the streets. Prostitutes and drug addicts."

"It's for people who don't have folks in their lives to care enough about them to take them in or give them money to help them get on their feet," Melissa responded.

"Edward and Melissa, I deeply regret not being there for you, or better yet, not telling you why I couldn't help you," Uncle Bert said apologetically. "Frankly, at that time, I saw in front of myself a damaged family. And I didn't want to be associated with it. So I put my sister, your mothers, and everything else behind me and didn't look back."

"Every time I see you on TV talking about your youth-to-work program and your medical assistance for the poor, I get sick. I say to myself, *He's such a hypocrite*," Melissa said.

"Uncle Bert, we weren't your responsibility. We should have been able to count on our parents. They were negligent. Their own personal problems took them away from what should have been their focus," Dillard said.

Uncle Bert reminded them of a troubling and tragic past that had caused them to either conceal or act out their feelings of anger, bitterness, pain, resentment, and discontent.

"Don't let your anger toward me or an inability to resolve and settle the memories of your childhood prevent you from fulfilling God's plan for your life. A prayer I have for all of you is to be free from the demons haunting you. It's time to reconcile your past. If you believe, you can overcome the twists and turns of life. And that is the sort of strength and resilience you want to pass down to your children and our family's generations to come. I learned late in life that to resolve the existing thoughts and feelings of a tumultuous past, you sometime have to sit with the past before you can walk away from it," replied Uncle Bert.

He paused so that he could choose his next words carefully.

Edward groaned loudly to let Uncle Bert know he was bored. He sat down next to Erin.

"Man, what's wrong with you?" Erin whispered. "Listen, and you might learn something."

Edward ignored Erin and started to slouch down in his chair.

Uncle Bert continued, "You have persevered, and you have achieved. Although you've accomplished this and that, you're living a life that is empty and defeated. And, you don't even recognize it. Oftentimes, it's the pain of one's past that stifles the progression of a healthy life: mind, body, and soul."

He paused again and said, "I'm seventy-five years old. My days are numbered. I've been in business for forty years, and now it's time to hand it over." He smiled and nodded again. "For those of you who have been affected most by your parents' mistakes and life's anxieties, I want to bless you."

Melissa looked down at her watch and sighed, as her uncle continued to speak, "As my political counterparts often say, 'You can't keep kicking the can down the road. At some point, you have to pick up the can and take action.' Well, I want to position all of you to take action."

They all looked bewildered.

"It's going to be up to you, the chosen ones, to carry out the building of a healthy infrastructure for the next generation so that they will live a life of spiritual, physical, financial, and emotional abundance. I have selected the five of you plus Claire to follow in my footsteps."

He paused and reached into his suit jacket's pocket. He continued, "In my hand, there is an envelope for each one of you. Inside is a piece of paper that contains a simplistic directive."

"A simplistic directive!" Edward said. "What sort of game are you playing with us?"

"Not a game, Edward. You, Erin, Dillard, Melissa, Thomas Wayne, and Claire have lived silently far too long while dealing with rooted pain. If you don't deal with it now, you never will."

"He's right, guys," Trevor paused. "I know what you are going through, being trapped in your childhood, holding on to... I can tell you because I've been there myself. I know how easy it is to gravitate to the wrong things for comfort. For me, it was food, alcohol, and sex, and in that order. After hearing my pastor preach a message one Sunday, 'From a Junkyard to a Pick-A-Part Mentality,' I made a decision to do things differently."

"What in the world does that mean?" Edward blurted out.

Trevor looked at Edward, stared at him for a second, and replied, "I'm sure all of you remember Mr. Jerry's junkyard on Hirsch Road. Just like any other junkyard, his was a place where people took their trash, things to be discarded, like cars, secondhand items, or broken items that could be bought and sold, like a refrigerator. Most people didn't view junkyards as something useful. Then the title 'Pick-A-Part' surfaced. The sales pitch changed: 'We've taken junkyards to a new level. We have fresh inventory arriving daily, arranged efficiently on stands, ready for your picking.' Both the junkyard and Pick-A-Part offered the same set-up, but there was a different presentation to change a negative perceptive to a positive one."

Uncle Bert smiled as Trevor expounded, "With a junkyard mentality, your thoughts are filled with trash. Feelings have been broken and discarded, and actions are not useful. But, if you change your mentality from junkyard to one of Pick-A-Part, you'll be able to recognize and sift through the fresh inventory arriving in your minds daily. You will learn how to manage your feelings and add value to your actions. A Pick-A-Part mentality enables you to sift through your thoughts, feelings, and actions, and then pick out the good and leave the bad."

Noticing Trevor's teary eyes, Uncle Bert interrupted him and said, "Thank you, Trevor."

Trevor thoughtfully smiled.

"I'm not playing a game with you at all, at least not the sort of game you're probably thinking about." He looked directly at each of them individually. "There is an inheritance, though. It requires all of you to be in agreement with satisfying my stipulations. Otherwise, the acquisition of my wealth and the continued success of my multi-million-dollar security business will be non-existent to you. So, for now, I'm going to leave you. Trevor has been given the task of helping each of you satisfy my stipulations."

Uncle Bert stood up from the table and handed the envelopes to Trevor who was sitting to his immediate right. Trevor took the envelopes and stood up to hug his uncle. As he did so, his cousins stood nearby for their turn to hug their uncle. Edward shrugged off the family moment as though it didn't matter to him.

Melissa walked out the back door.

Chapter 3

The Truth Revealed

M elissa returned after she was sure Uncle Bert had left.

"So, what's up with the envelopes, Trevor?" Edward asked. "Are we going to get them or what?"

"He's right. I think we've all had enough of this suspense drama," Melissa said. "Either Uncle Bert is going to give us some money, or he isn't. I'm not going to grovel. I did that twenty years ago and ended up empty-handed."

"To me, it's the least he can do. He was never there for us when we were growing up," Erin stated.

"And what is he talking about—he'll see us soon?" Edward demanded.

"Okay, guys! Here are your envelopes," Trevor said, and he handed an envelope to Erin, Melissa, Dillard, Thomas Wayne, and Edward.

Each one opened the envelope and read the words, 'To live healthy, mind, body, and spirit, and with purpose.'

"What!" Edward shouted.

Everyone started talking loudly over one another. Trevor couldn't follow what was being said.

"Okay, everyone," Trevor commanded. He walked to the center of the adjoining kitchen and dining area. "Calm Down."

Erin looked at him intensely. "So, what's the real deal?"

Melissa walked toward Trevor, waving her envelope back and forth.

Trevor took a deep breath and said, "There are two requirements that each of you must successfully fulfill together before you can gain access to Uncle Bert's fortune. However, to meet his expectations, you'll need to find your solution for letting go and letting in God so you can live healthy and do so with purpose."

Erin reached for her envelope from the table and asked, "Letting go of what?"

"For each one of you, it's different," Trevor responded. "It could be letting go of anger, resentment, bitterness, blame, hurt, sadness, discontent, unforgiveness—all or a combination of thoughts, feelings, and actions that have led to unhealthy lifestyle choices."

"Ain't nothing unhealthy about the choices I make," Edward insisted.

Melissa muttered, "I agree with Edward."

"Like Melissa said, I think Uncle Bert wants us to grovel for his money," Erin said.

Nudging Edward in his side, Thomas Wayne whispered, "Big brother, just stay cool. We can fake whatever we need to get our portion of the business and money. Then I can pay you back."

Edward looked at Thomas Wayne, confused.

"So, Trevor, what are Uncle Bert's specific expectations?" Thomas Wayne asked, scratching his right arm.

"To live healthy and to live with purpose," Trevor said softly. "But, before that can happen, you have to let go and let God lead you."

"I told you," Thomas Wayne whispered to Edward. "Easy."

Trevor explained to his cousins that they would not inherit what Uncle Bert wanted to offer them until they proved they had mended years of tension and conflict stemming from their childhood. Uncle Bert's expectations would prove challenging to fulfill: to remove all obstacles standing in the way of their emotional well-being and team up in a way that would continue the growth of the business.

Erin rubbed her forehead, looking puzzled. She frowned and asked, "What are we expected to do to live healthy? Exercise? Eat fruit and vegetables? Cottage cheese? Lose weight?"

"I sure hope not. I'm definitely not eating cottage cheese. And exercise! At the end of the day, the only thing I plan to continue to do is watch TV. That's the only thing I'm inspired to do after all of extra jobs I work," Thomas Wayne said.

"I know that's right. I simply don't have much energy after dealing with the highs and lows of a bipolar boss and backstabbing co-workers," Melissa said, laughing.

"Living healthy is much bigger than eating right and becoming physically fit. It's also the inclusion of your mental, emotional, and spiritual health," Trevor responded.

"What?" Edward shouted. "You're somewhere in la-la land."

Before Trevor could respond, there was a knock at the front door.

"I'll get it," Dillard said.

As he approached the door, he could smell the aroma of something freshly cooked.

When he opened the door, there were two middle-aged men standing in chefs uniforms with large bags in each hand.

One of the men spoke gently, "We have a delivery for Mr. McElroy."

After Trevor paid the gentlemen, his cousins began taking the containers and eating utensils out of the bags and placing everything on the dining table.

"Thanks, Trevor," Erin said with a smile. "I'm famished. The Cheetos weren't enough to do the trick."

"It's the least he could do after dragging us all here," Edward said, rolling his eyes at Trevor.

"Grilled salmon, baked chicken, whipped sweet potatoes, steamed broccoli, and mixed green salad. What is all this?" asked Melissa.

"Man, you know how we eat. Where is the fried chicken, dirty rice, macaroni and cheese, and biscuits?" Thomas Wayne commented while rubbing his hands.

"I think I'll just eat my pork chop sandwiches," Dillard said, as he turned away from the table and walked toward the refrigerator.

"There's no cheese sauce for the broccoli and no gravy for the potatoes. No butter! No dessert! No soda! No thousand island salad dressing!" Erin added with disappointment.

"You should have left this stuff wherever you got it," Edward said and headed toward the front door. "I've had enough. I'm out of here."

Thomas Wayne walked quickly after Edward. He placed his hand on Edward's shoulder and said quietly, "You need to stay. I want my share of that money. You heard Uncle Bert. It's a group thing. I'm not going to let you mess this up for me. He owes us!"

Edward shoved Thomas Wayne's hand off his shoulder in annoyance.

"Come on back," Thomas Wayne pleaded. "For once, we need to unify for a common goal."

"Hey, guys, are you going to stay and eat, or what?" Trevor asked, looking at them.

Edward's hand was on the knob of the partially opened front door.

Thomas Wayne looked at Edward and they both turned around.

Everyone sat around the dining table and ate. Dillard ate one of the pork chop sandwiches, while his cousins picked over the grilled salmon, baked chicken, whipped sweet potatoes, steamed broccoli, and mixed green salad.

"So, Trevor, tell us more about Uncle Bert's requirements," Thomas Wayne said while smiling faintly.

"For the next twelve months, you will be required to engage in a variety of activities together," Trevor revealed.

"What sort of activities?" Edward asked.

"Well, as you all know, I'm a fitness coach, so you'll be invited to a number of my fitness sessions, seminars, 5K walks, volunteer activities, and we will probably even have a couple of so-call family retreats together."

"Just stop! Hell naw!" Edward abruptly shouted. "I ain't doing all of that touchy feely stuff. Not my style."

Trevor disregarded Edward's comment and continued, "Uncle Bert has arranged for us to spend time together at his lake house in Conroe, Texas. The first gathering will be in a month, and we will spend an entire weekend together."

Erin interrupted Trevor and asked, "What about my kids? I'm a single parent with a irresponsible ex-husband. Do they get to come along? Brian needs constant monitoring because of his diabetes."

"Arrangements will be made for your kids. Uncle Bert will hire a nurse to come and stay with Brian," Trevor responded. "This time together is just for all of us, and Claire, if she's well enough."

"I just started a new job as an accounting clerk. I can't ask those people for time off so soon," Melissa said. "This job will give me the experience to become an accountant one day."

"I think you need to go to school to become an accountant, Melissa," Edward quickly interjected, "and that takes real smarts, not clerical smarts." Edward started to laugh.

"Ladies, please," Thomas Wayne said. "I don't know how much money is at stake, but I'm sure it's a lot. Get with the program. No one is going to mess up me getting my share. And, what's the deal with Claire? Does she need to be present? I'm not trying to work three and four jobs for the rest of *my* life."

"Uncle Bert has given you all one month to get your affairs in order. Erin, he's arranged for Aunt Libby to care for Chanitah and Brian. Thomas Wayne, don't worry about Claire."

"Aunt Libby is eighty years old. My ten and twelve year olds will run all over her," Erin said.

"The nurse will be with her," Trevor emphasized. "Keep in mind, everyone, that the only way this deal will work is through the cooperation of all of you."

"That's what *I'm* saying," Thomas Wayne chimed in.

"I just don't know," Erin said with reluctance. "We're still trying to figure out this diabetes stuff."

"Erin, Aunt Libby will do fine taking care of your children," Thomas Wayne said. "And Melissa, when the time comes, just make up a story for your supervisor. If you're sick or something, they can't do anything about that."

Trevor continued with the expectations, "Along with all of our activities together, we will eventually start restoring Grandma's house."

"Erin, slow down; you've already eaten half a chicken," Edward said, as Erin reached for another piece of chicken. "I see why your bottom is so big. I forgot how we used to call you 'Thunder Thighs' and 'Bulging Belly' as kids."

Erin squirmed as she pulled her fork back and placed it on the side of her plate.

"Shut up, Edward!" Dillard yelled.

"What in the world would we do together for a weekend?" Melissa asked. "We can't even get along together for an hour."

"The only thing I can say at this point is that the focus will be to discover your strategy for living healthier, mind, body, and soul, and with purpose," Trevor said.

Chapter 4

❖

On the Brink of Eruption

The Saturday before their first weekend get-together, Trevor invited each of his cousins to attend a fitness talk he was conducting at his church, Golden Hill Missionary Baptist Church, at 10:00 A.M. He would be speaking to individuals about an upcoming wellness challenge at the church on Thursday evenings. He also wanted to introduce his "Meet Me: Morning Fitness on Your Corner" fitness initiative.

Erin, Melissa, Claire, Dillard, Edward, and Thomas Wayne were given instructions to meet Trevor in the main vestibule of the church.

Erin and Dillard were the first to arrive.

"You know what, Dillard?" Erin asked.

"What?" Dillard returned the question.

"I haven't been back to church since the incident with Nick," she confessed. "After the incident with the child, everyone treated me so badly, as though I knew what he was doing. Talk about forgiveness."

"You leave every Sunday going somewhere," Dillard commented.

Erin dropped her head, embarrassed, and said, "Actually, I go Starbucks for my favorite Peppermint White Chocolate Mocha."

Just as Dillard was getting ready to respond, Melissa walked up.

"Hey, Guys," Melissa greeted them. "Have you all seen Trevor?"

"Hey, cuz," Dillard answered, "No, we haven't seen him yet."

"He's probably somewhere setting up his room," Erin said. "This is a big church."

Moments later, Edward and Thomas Wayne arrived. Thomas Wayne was wearing his brown hat with an orange and black plaid headband, black Khaki shorts, a long-sleeve beige polo shirt, black alligator sandals, and a pair of Gucci shades.

"Y'all been here long?" Thomas Wayne asked.

"We haven't been here long," Erin responded. "You jumped sharp today, Mr. T. Wayne. You love wearing your shades, don't you?"

While Erin was commenting on Thomas Wayne's look, Edward's eyes narrowed in on her skimpy blouse and tight-fitting tracksuit bottoms.

"Well, it looks like you're going for that 'Desperate Housewives' look," Edward smirked. "Now, I'm not a church-going person, but I think the sisters would find your attire offensive for the Lord's House. Between you and Thomas Wayne…"

Erin cocked her head with visible anger and said, "I don't need you critiquing what I wear. My attire is none of your business."

Melissa stood silent, becoming self-conscious about her brightly colored, tight, clingy low-cut blouse.

"Whatever," Edward said. "Mr. Fitness needs to come on so we can get this show on the road and get out of here. You know I ain't into the church thing."

"Man, you better tone it down before God strikes you down," Thomas Wayne said.

"Yeah, right," Edward said. "If anything, He's going to strike you down for wearing those shades like you're some celebrity. Better yet, for living off others and not paying your debts. I'm going to call Trevor."

As Edward reached into his jacket to get his cellular phone, Trevor and Claire appeared from one of the hallways.

Claire and her cousins hadn't seen each other in years. She and her husband Mark had recently moved back to Texas from Maryland after moving away nearly twenty years earlier. As she and Trevor drew closer, a disturbed look overshadowed their faces. Claire walked slowly toward them and was noticeably thin and fragile in a sleeveless summer dress. Tiny red bumps covered her neck.

"Hey, everyone. Look who I have with me," Trevor said, glancing over at Claire.

As Trevor and Claire walked closer, everyone hurriedly move toward them and one by one gave Claire a hug.

"Hey, cuz, are you going to take off those shades?" Trevor asked.

"I haven't had any sleep. I don't want anyone to see my bloodshot eyes," Thomas Wayne commented.

"Melissa, it's good to see you," Claire said.

Melissa gently embraced Claire. For years, Melissa had blamed Claire's mom for not coming to her aid when she needed her most.

"Mr. Fitness, let's get this show on the road. I've got things to do," Edward said, standing with his hand on his hips. "Take us to the room."

"Trevor, where are the restrooms?" Claire asked.

"They're down the hall and to your left," Trevor pointed.

"I'll meet you all in the room," Claire said.

Everyone else followed Trevor to a nearby meeting room. When they arrived, there were already thirty individuals seated. The cousins found scattered seats around the room and seated themselves.

"Greetings," Trevor said, standing before the group. "Thank you for coming out on a Saturday morning. Before we get started, I would like for everyone to say their name and tell us why you came today. Who wants to go first?"

A lady raised her hand.

Trevor acknowledged her. He then smiled and nodded for her to speak.

"I'm Monica," she said. "For some reason, my mother suggested I come to hear about the wellness challenge." She looked over at her mother who was sitting next to her.

Monica continued, "Sounds like it's going to be about eating rabbit food and exercising. If rabbits don't eat my regulars, like mocha madness ice cream, chicken fried steak dinners, fried calamari, cheese ravioli, and blueberry muffins, then I probably need to leave."

Trevor smiled and said, "Don't leave."

Monica's mother said, "My only concern is that Monica is going to experience some health problems real soon. She is forty-four, overweight, and a single parent of two kids."

"As usual, she's telling my business," Monica complained.

Her mother responded, "I'm just concerned because everyone is talking about this obesity, not just for adults, but the rise in childhood obesity. You're passing your unhealthy habits on to your kids, and it shows."

Edward whispered to Thomas Wayne, "If her kids look anything like her, she is a bad parent."

Trevor looked around and said, "Pastor is committed to helping our church family achieve a healthier, balanced lifestyle. It's no secret that when a human body is unhealthy, out-of-shape, and worn out physically and mentally, more than likely it does not have the energy to be an effective servant or contributor to the church body. Although you may have a desire to fulfill God's purpose for your life, a continuum of illness and disease will present ongoing roadblocks. Typically, if a person is chronically tired, feeling bad, and/or disease stricken, more than likely he or she does not possess the spirit, the disposition, or the capacity to enjoy life, to share the joy of life with others, or be all that God has called him or her to be."

"I know that's right!" Monica's mother shouted.

"That why he asked me to create to fitness ministry that will educate, encourage, and engage our church family to become physically active and to eat healthier while in the process of doing so. Your participation in this ministry will provide you with simplistic ways to create balance and build healthy lifestyle habits into your daily routine such as reducing your intake of unhealthy foods and reducing your overeating."

Another lady raised her hand and shouted out, "That's great. I need that something to spark me into sticking with a program. My name is Maya. I've recently been diagnosed with Lupus, and I don't know what to do."

"Eating healthier will be paramount to the management of your condition," Trevor said.

Maya continued, "I have gained over 30 pounds on my medication, prednisone. I can't wear any of my clothes, and I can't stand to look at myself in the mirror. Right now, I can't get focused on doing what I need to do. I'm always tired and fatigued. And have severe joint pain when I have a flare-up. My doctor has recommended water exercises and walking. But, once again, I can't get motivated. It's all so depressing."

Claire sat thinking about her condition.

Another lady chimed in, "I started working out in January. My goal was to lose 50 pounds by June. Well, it's June, and I have *gained* 20 pounds. I'm ashamed to admit that I lasted two weeks and stopped. Change wasn't happening quick enough for me. I just gave up. I'm thinking about weight loss surgery or this body wrap applicator a friend told me about." The lady got out of her seat and handed Trevor a brochure about the product.

A lady named Natalie sighed and spoke, "Coach Trevor, it's been a struggle the past few weeks. I've been traveling quite a bit, and life on the road has brought on some challenges. I'm unable to eat on schedule, because I'm in and out of meetings from the time my day starts till it ends. When the time does arrive to eat lunch and dinner, I have to eat with people who only want soul food, which makes it harder for me to eat right. Plus, I can't fit in any exercise."

One by one, the attendees gave pointed reasons why they were at the fitness talk. When it was time for Erin to speak, she stated that she and her relatives, Dillard, Thomas Wayne, Edward, Melissa, and Claire were there to hear their cousin speak.

Trevor glanced at the brochure the lady had given him and said, "Many years ago, I was like most of you. I knew I needed to do something. I was fat, depressed, in and out of relationships, and my perspective on the things that really mattered was out of focus. Following a voice I was intimately acquainted with, I often thought that if only I could change the way I looked and felt, my life could be different. It was a nice thought, but what I needed included much more. Now I know my life is different because of God's plot to free me and focus my attention. Little did I know, though, His plan for a healthy mind, body, and spirit would involve running."

Trevor looked at Monica, then at his cousins, and said, "Like so many others, the biggest challenge for me when I started reviewing my options for living healthy was eating. As I started researching the foods I had come to rely on for comfort, I recognized that some things had to change. One day, after reading the food labels for some of my favorites, I thought, '*This is going to be hard. Everything I love to eat is lacking in vital nutrients and is loaded with salt, sugar, and trans-fats.*' My discoveries prompted me to figure out how to make my favorite foods healthier and more beneficial to my body. For me, it meant no more all-you-can-eat buffets, no more guzzling the five cans of my favorite soda each day, and no more scarfing down cookies, cinnamon rolls, chips, and candy bars in the wee hours of the night. It also meant no more nachos and cheese fries and no more weekly happy hours!"

Monica blurted out, "And those are the sort of foods I'm not interested in giving up."

"If you're around me often enough, you'll hear me say this over and over; choices—life is about choices." Trevor stood firmly in front of the group and said, "Something that has always stuck in my mind is a statement an old boss often emphasized. He'd say, 'Winners are always in solution mode, and whiners are always in negative mode.' I want all of you to be winners who live in solution mode. Healthy people are winners who are always in solution mode. They don't curl up with excuses or give up when change is not immediate. They rely on God's infinite power to keep them in solution mode."

"Uh huh, not the 'God' stuff," Edward muttered to himself.

"God used running to elevate me to a position to live healthy and with purpose," Trevor stressed.

"I wonder if he'll dismiss us now. I have things to do," Edward said in a low voice. He looked back over his shoulder at Melissa. She was sitting behind him.

Thomas Wayne glanced at Edward and said, "Now, I've told you. You're not going to mess up this inheritance for me."

"Whatever!" Edward said ruthlessly, in Thomas Wayne's ear. "Who wants the old man's money anyway?"

In a harsh but low voice, Thomas Wayne exclaimed, "I do!"

Trevor looked strangely at his cousins as the sounds of their low voices became more and more distracting. He went on, "I realize that running is not for everyone. I also know of the personal challenges of becoming motivated to do something and the commitment to stay consistent once you get started. That's why I started the 'Meet Me: Morning Fitness on Your Corner' fitness initiative."

"What exactly is the 'Meet Me: Morning Fitness on Your Corner'?" Maya asked.

Trevor explained how he started running through his neighborhood at 4:50 A.M., "For years, while running through my neighborhood, I'd think about all of my neighbors who were probably still asleep, neighbors who could probably benefit from some exercise. So, I started the 'Meet Me: Morning Fitness on Your Corner'."

Neighborhood residents would be on a certain corner by a certain time. They would arrive at a designated corner and wait for Trevor and any other residents he had picked up along the way. Corner by corner, residents would fall into place to walk the sidewalks of their neighborhood. Many of his neighbors were taking advantage of the opportunity to become physically active before work, school, or the start of their daily obligations.

"This may be an initiative you can start in your own neighborhood," Trevor said. "If you're interested in doing so, I'll be happy to help get you started."

It was Trevor's version of an outreach service that would offer residents in various neighborhoods the opportunity to become physically active, to obtain tips for living healthy, and to seek assistance with any problems they may be having in implementing healthier lifestyle habits. He was beginning to introduce the concept to other fitness professionals.

Upon conclusion of Trevor's talk, the attendees approached him to ask questions that ranged from the benefits of strength training, flexibility exercises, to the difference between good and bad fats.

Trevor's cousins stood near the exit, waiting for him to finish talking.

A tall, slender, attractive woman in her early forties walked into the room and started to pack up Trevor's handouts. His cousins watched her curiously.

"Who is that?" Edward asked.

"She's probably a helper here at the church," responded Melissa.

"She sure is a pretty helper," Dillard commented.

"Nice fitness attire," Erin said.

"She can definitely help me any day," Edward said, laughing.

After Trevor finished talking, he walked over to the woman. They wrapped their arms around one another, and he kissed her on the cheek. He was beaming proudly. He proceeded to whisper something in her ear, and they started laughing.

"Guess she's more than a helper," Erin said.

Trevor grabbed her hand and walked toward his cousins.

"Everyone, this is Jenny."

Trevor's cousins waved, ad-libbing warm greetings. Trevor leaned toward Jenny and gave her another kiss.

"Where you been keeping her?" Edward asked.

"She's been around awhile. I'm proud to say that she's my girlfriend," Trevor said.

Jenny looked over at Trevor and smiled adoringly.

❖

Chapter 5

❖

Family Matters

After his talk, Trevor invited his cousins to lunch at Jamal's Healthy Kitchen. Based on his recent interactions with them, he knew they conducted a large majority of their eating in restaurants. He wanted to expose them to healthy options for eating out.

"That was a touching speech you gave, cousin. You make me want to go running," Thomas Wayne said, laughing. "Where is that waitress. I need some water? I am so thirsty."

"Man, you can barely walk ten steps to your patrol car. Don't they make you guys stay in shape?" Edward said.

"I've already lost thirty pounds doing nothing," Thomas Wayne said, as he wiped his runny nose. He had started to sweat profusely.

"Man, go get you a cold towel," Edward said, with a fierce look in his eyes. "You're starting to look like a wet dog or a woman having a hot flash!"

Claire, Erin, and Melissa locked eyes with Edward and stared at him with contempt.

"Hey, Trevor, why didn't your girl come along to eat with us?" Edward asked.

"He probably didn't want to expose her to his dysfunctional cousins," Dillard remarked.

"You're the only dysfunctional one I see," Edward said. He looked at Dillard and made a face.

"Come on, guys," Trevor said. "She had to get to a sorority meeting."

"Right! One of those snooty women," Edward said under his breath.

"She didn't look snooty to me," Claire argued.

Trevor interrupted and said, "A discussion on Jenny is off limits. Let's move on!"

"I can't be here too long," Thomas Wayne said. He looked worried and edgy about something.

Claire excused herself from the table to go to the restroom.

Trevor looked worried as he assisted Claire with getting up from the table. He was concerned about her health. He knew she needed her family more than ever.

"Is she okay, Trevor?" Erin asked.

"I hope she's okay. I'm sure she'll share her condition with you all when it's right for her," Trevor responded. He looked down at his menu.

"I sure hope that stuff on her neck isn't contagious," Edward said.

"What did you say?" Trevor asked, mortified.

"That stuff on her neck. CONTAGIOUS!"

"You are so ridiculous! No it isn't, Edward. It has to do with her medical condition that the doctors are still trying to sort through," Trevor said, staring intensely at Edward.

"A man can ask, huh?"

The waitress placed glasses of water on the table and informed them that she would be back to take their orders.

Thomas Wayne immediately took his glass of water and drank it without stopping. "I'll need a refill," he said and signaled to the waitress.

Claire soon came back to the table.

Trevor took a moment to assist Claire and then told them, "A huge part of daily food consumption comes from processed food because people don't take the time to prepare their meals from scratch. It's quick and easier for you to go to your favorite spot and order the two-piece chicken dinner with a biscuit and red soda, or a burrito supreme, or a personal pan pizza, or—" Trevor said.

Edward quickly interrupted, "Or a chicken fried steak dinner at Luby's where I can get some fresh vegetables, cuz."

"Or the Black Eyed Pea, where I can get Mom's Meatloaf with a side of macaroni and cheese, red beans and rice, and some peach cobbler," Melissa injected.

"Or Mimi's Chicken And Waffles where I can get the best smothered chicken with gravy and onions plus two waffles," Dillard said.

Everyone started laughing except Claire.

"Okay, guys," Trevor said with a smile. "The point is that you're relying on processed food for most of your meals rather than preparing nutritious, home-cooked food for most of your meals. Believe me, I understand that eating processed fast-food is necessary some of the time, but for most people it's all of the time. It almost goes back to what you all were saying at Grandma Saddie's house. As kids, we were programmed to eat unhealthy fried foods, soda pop, and lots of starches. The only good thing out of all of it was the fact that our meals were homemade. We didn't have the level of process foods your kids are consuming."

"Honestly, I try and cook more meals at home since Brian was diagnosed with Type 1 diabetes," Erin said.

"That's really good, Erin," Trevor commented. "I always tell my clients that if they want to reduce, eliminate, or better manage a disease or illness, then cut out the processed foods; the box dinners, frozen-food dinners, fast-food dinners, and pre-packaged dinners. My clients have been educated to look at the label of the food products they bring into their homes. After reading rows and rows of information outlining the ingredients, they are often amazed at how vague the information is."

"I'm sure that if there was something wrong with the ingredients, the government would prevent the manufacture, the distribution, and the sales of the food items to grocery stores and eating establishments," Thomas Wayne said suddenly, wiping his face with his napkin.

"It's not the government's job to monitor where, what, when, and how much we eat," Trevor said.

"I didn't say is was," Thomas Wayne commented forcibly.

"Be cool, brother," Edward placed his hand on Thomas Wayne's back and whispered, "Remember the money. Trevor is key to getting Uncle Bert's fortune."

Looking underneath the table at her cellular phone, Melissa revealed, "Hey, guys, did you know that the president sends you a letter when you turn 100? I just read a post about it on Facebook."

"I don't know if I want to live to see 100," Erin responded.

"I know I don't," Edward said. "All cracked and shriveled up."

Trevor stared, unblinking.

Melissa placed her cellular in her purse and said, "Sorry, Trevor. I love Facebook."

Trevor continued and said, "There are many preservatives and additives in processed food to give it a longer shelf life. That's why I like this place. Everything here is prepared from natural products with a three to five day shelf life, and not the one, two, three, or four year shelf life."

The waitress appeared and asked if they were ready for her to take their food order.

"Trevor, what do you eat here?" Dillard asked.

"I typically order the Build Your Own Salad that includes mixed greens, shredded carrots, cucumbers, roasted roma tomatoes, dried cranberries, and mixed beets with their red wine Dijon vinaigrette," Trevor responded. "That's what I'll get today. Thank you."

Trevor smiled and handed his menu to the waitress.

Thomas Wayne and Edward stared at one another, shaking their heads.

"Sometimes I'll get the Chicken Thai Green Curry which comes with chicken breast, lentils, chickpeas, sweet potatoes, peas, cauliflower, and brown rice," Trevor added.

"Well, li'l brother, I guess we're stuck," Edward said quietly to Thomas Wayne.

"We'll take the Chicken Thai Green Curry dish," Thomas Wayne said. He ordered for himself and Edward.

Suddenly, everyone heard a loud, buzzing vibration emerging from under the table. It was Thomas Wayne's cellular phone affixed to his waist. He looked at the cellular phone and said, "I need to take this call. I'll be right back," and he left the table.

"I'll order the Build Your Own Salad with the Grass-fed Beef Tenderloin and the mixed greens, shredded carrots, cucumbers, roasted roma tomatoes, dried cranberries, and mixed beets with the red wine Dijon vinaigrette," Melissa said.

"I'll have the same as Melissa," Erin told the waitress.

"Me too," Dillard also responded.

The waitress looked at Claire for her order.

"Off the Gluten-free menu, I'll order the Chicken and Butternut Squash pasta with walnuts, roasted garlic, and local goat cheese."

The cousins looked around the table at one another.

"I know I'm going to need some salt," Edward said. "I add salt to everything I eat."

As Trevor was getting ready to say something, Melissa added, "Now y'all know we grew up with folks who cooked with salt and added more salt when the food was done. That's what we do."

"Trevor, what can they use instead of salt when cooking?" Claire interjected.

"Paprika, parsley, ginger, basil, cilantro, dill, or lemon juice to name a few," Trevor said. "During our coming weekend together, we'll be experimenting with different seasonings."

"We'll be *cooking*?" Edward exclaimed.

"Yes, my cousin, we will," Trevor responded.

"What about the grass-fed animals," Dillard inquired.

"First, it's important for you to understand that there is a difference in how cattle are fed, either grass-fed or grain-fed, and how they are raised, in a pasture or in a feedlot. I'll send you some research I've done that talks about how grass-fed cattle produces meat that is more nutritious and lower in fat, with elevated levels of heart-healthy omega-3 fatty acids and elevated levels of another type of fat called conjugated linoleic acid, which has been tagged as a reducer of heart disease and cancer risks. Whereas, grain-fed cattle are fed grains, such as corn and soy that increase acid in a cow's stomach."

"Wow!" Melissa said. "Send that research to me as well."

"Me, too," Erin said.

"Beef is beef to me. Grass-fed, grain fed—who cares? If there is something hazardous floating around out there in the so-called feedlots, I'm sure we'd see something on the news about it," Edward said.

Trevor responded, "There has been quite a bit of information published about the two. I'll send it to you, Thomas Wayne, and to you, Claire, as well."

Thomas Wayne came back from his phone conversation and sat down.

Edward said, "I see this as just some high-polluting restaurant you wanted to bring us to. We would have been happier going to Joe's Smoke House. At least Dillard could have gotten his pork chop sandwiches, and I could have gotten some neck bones."

Everyone at the table was amused by Edward's comment.

"I know that's right. I could have gotten some of the baby back ribs," Thomas Wayne said, laughing. "And, I definitely don't care about where and what that hog was raised on."

While everyone was laughing around the table, the waitress and her helper began to place the food items on the table.

Melissa, Erin, and Dillard received their salads with Grass-fed Beef Tenderloin.

"Wow, this is a lot of salad stuff," Dillard commented.

The waitress placed Trevor's salad on the table, and the helper gave Thomas Wayne and Edward their Chicken Thai Green Curry dish. Claire was last to receive her Chicken and Butternut Squash Spaghetti with the brown rice spaghetti.

Trevor looked around the table and asked, "Who wants to give thanks?"

"You do it, cuz," Thomas Wayne suggested, picking at scabs on his face.

"Man, don't do that at the dinner table. That's disgusting," Edward said, upset at the sight of what his brother was doing.

Melissa managed to slip her cellular phone out of her purse without anyone noticing. She placed it in her lap.

"Okay," Trevor said, motioning for everyone to grab one another's hand.

Melissa was distracted by a message indicator on her phone.

"We thank you, God, for bringing together and reconnecting cousins. For those who have passed on and for Uncle Bert who is wanting to leave the family with a legacy to continue, we thank you for the protection you've given us as we have crossed the many paths of life. And, we pray for you to continue to do so. Thank you for this healthy food we are about to eat. We pray that it nourishes our bodies and becomes a starting point for future healthy meals—Amen."

Everyone responded by saying 'Amen.' They started to eat their meals, except Melissa who proceeded to read the message.

"Claire, what exactly does gluten-free mean?" Erin questioned.

"Gluten is a specific type of protein. It is found in wheat, rye, and barley," she replied.

Trevor added, "For the most part, she can't eat breads like white, wheat, marble, and rye. Also off limits are bagels, muffins, croissants, hamburger buns, and scones."

"What about pizza?" Erin asked.

"No pizza," Claire responded. "Now, there are a number of health food stores and some major supermarkets that carry gluten-free products. And they have an assortment of breads made with rice or potato flour instead of wheat flour. I just have to check the label to make sure it says '100% Gluten-Free'."

"What about cereals?" Erin asked.

"Y'all know we grew up on Frosted Flakes," Dillard said, reaching for his glass of water.

"Yes! We loved Frosted Flakes," Melissa added.

"Cereals are off limits as well for Claire. Our childhood favorites like Cheerios contain wheat starch, whereas Frosted Flakes use malt flavoring. She has to avoid any cereal containing wheat, barley, rye, or malt," Trevor said.

"What do you eat for breakfast?" Erin further inquired.

"Most days, it's just a banana and toast from gluten-free bread. I have experimented with some of the corn-based and rice-based cereals."

"So, I'm assuming that the pasta you are eating here is gluten-free?" Melissa asked.

"Yes, it is," Claire responded. "Since most typical pastas are made out of wheat, I'm very careful about eating spaghetti, macaroni, shells, and spirals. I have to make sure they're gluten-free."

"What the point of it all? And please don't gross us out while we're eating," Edward stated.

Claire eyes widened. She stared intensely at Edward.

"Claire has Crohn's disease," Trevor said, "which is an inflammatory bowel disease. It causes inflammation of the lining of your digestive tract, which can lead to abdominal pain, severe diarrhea, and even malnutrition."

"Wow! Sounds like you're in pretty bad shape," Edward commented. "Trevor told us you had something called Sweet's Syndrome."

"Man, do you ever think before you talk?" Dillard shouted.

"It's okay, Dillard," Claire said. "Yes, I have Sweet's Syndrome."

"What causes it?" Erin asked.

"I just know it's typically associated with leukemia and Crohn's," Claire responded.

"You sure know a lot about it," Erin said.

"When you're dealing with something that has changed your life the way this disease has changed mine, you want to know as much as you can about it."

Trevor could tell that Claire was having a hard time continuing to talk.

"Wow!" Melissa exclaimed.

"What?" Dillard asked.

Melissa answered, "A friend of mine on Facebook posted that she won a trip to Hawaii."

"Is she really a friend?" Edward asked.

"Well, we connected on Facebook," she responded.

"Not a friend. You'd probably get back in school and work on that accounting degree if you'd get off Facebook," Edward said callously.

Trevor shook his head, emphatically.

"Everyone, we will be meeting at Uncle Bert's lake house next weekend. Be sure to bring your walking shoes and exercise clothing," Trevor stressed.

"Do we need to bring anything to eat?" Erin asked.

"No, everything will be provided," Trevor responded.

Chapter 6

❖
❖

A Blessing in Disguise

One week later, on a Friday evening, one by one the cousins—Erin, Melissa, Dillard, Thomas Wayne, and Edward—met at Uncle Bert's lake house in Conroe, Texas. The three-story five bedrooms, four and a half bath townhouse was more room than any of them had imagined. The gated golfing community featured a state-of-the-art fitness center, three swimming pools, two putting greens, and they even provided fishing poles.

Dillard walked in with two bags filled with food selections from Mr. Paul's Chicken Shack. He placed them on the dining room table. Erin pulled out several boxes.

"WHOA!" Edward said, loudly.

He looked over Erin's shoulders into the bags.

"Where is Trevor?" he said, laughing. "You're in trouble."

"Quit tripping. I haven't eaten all day," Erin said.

"Trevor went to the store," Dillard told Edward.

Melissa and Thomas Wayne walked into the dining room.

"Did you get their famous biscuits?" Melissa asked.

"Here they are," Erin said. She handed Melissa a smaller bag.

Melissa walked around while eating a biscuit out of the bag.

"Wow, this place is stunning. Look at that view of the lake," she said, as she opened the back door to the deck area.

"Melissa, you're dropping crumbs on the floor," Edward said, looking at a trail behind Melissa.

She looked around for a towel.

"Uncle Bert definitely didn't skimp on the luxuries," Erin said, looking around at the sumptuous decorations and furnishings in the living room area.

Uncle Bert's modern lake house was decorated in a country style design. It was evident that brown was his favorite color. The wooden floor, the natural camel, tan, brown, and blue colors, and vintage and antique accessories added character to his house. The large living room area was furnished with a brown leather sofa and loveseat with a large leather ottoman separating the two, and three leather recliners were positioned throughout the area. A large portrait of his mother and father was mounted over the fireplace. One wall was lined with photos that depicted significant events in his life, notable awards, and honors; the first time he was sworn into office; the 2008 U.S. Small Business Person Award; and a Lifetime Achievement Award.

Trevor walked into the house carrying an ice chest.

"Hi, Guys," he greeted them. His senses were heightened. He frowned and said, "Is that fried chicken I smell?"

"Y'all in trouble," Edward said.

"Sorry, Trevor, I haven't eaten all day. On the drive here, I stopped by Mr. Paul's Chicken Shack."

"You did remember that we're cooking, right?"

"I haven't eaten all day," Erin stressed.

Edward stood nearby, amused.

"When we talked while driving up here, I asked her to bring me some of their biscuits," Melissa said.

"I haven't eaten all day, either," Dillard said, biting on a chicken leg.

Trevor opened the ice chest and placed some bottled water in the refrigerator. He turned around and said, "Downstairs there is a large entertainment room that includes a game room equipped with a pool table and a ping-pong table."

"Guess this is one of the reasons why he could never help us out," Edward stated, as he started to walk upstairs. "I heard he has a new home in Legends Ranch near I-45 and the Hardy Toll Rd. Has anyone been invited over? I'm sure Trevor has…"

"I know I haven't," Thomas Wayne responded. He walked up behind Trevor and continued, "The homes in that community are pretty expensive. Me and my wife checked them out when we were looking."

"Wonder why he's never picked up the telephone to invite us out here before now?" Melissa said, as she started to walk on the deck. She was noticeably irritated.

"Melissa, you know Uncle Bert. It's clear he didn't want to have anything to do with us. Years of no contact should be your clue," Edward shouted from the top of the stairs. "He has never come to any family events. Like he said, the big time state representative and prominent businessman was embarrassed by his family."

"Guess the same could be said of Trevor," Thomas Wayne said, glaring over at Trevor.

"Well, I'm just happy we finally got a chance to come," Dillard said sincerely.

Edward walked down the stairs and asked, "Who's going to get to sleep in the master bedroom. You can walk outside and sit on the balcony."

Trevor walked into the living room area and said, "There are plenty of bedrooms. Just take your pick. I'll probably sleep downstairs in the entertainment area. It has a sleeper sofa."

Dillard looked at his watch and asked, "What's for dinner?"

Trevor shook his head.

Thomas Wayne opened the refrigerator door. "Okay, guys, I know this is Uncle Bert's and Trevor's show, but I brought the food we like to eat. I didn't want to trust Trevor's food selections."

Trevor abruptly interrupted Thomas Wayne and said, "I've purchased food for the entire weekend."

"Yeah, I see," Thomas Wayne said. He moved items around. "All natural vanilla yogurt! Gluten-free coconut milk! Red cherries! Blueberries! Fresh-squeezed orange juice! Fresh Spinach!"

They were amused by Thomas Wayne's vivid account of Trevor's food selections.

"At least he thought long enough to get orange juice for the Patron," Edward said, laughing hilariously.

Erin leaned against the kitchen counter and asked, "What is Patron?"

"Premium tequila, my cousin, premium tequila," Edward responded. "And I've got a bottle in the car."

"In the Caddy, I have a lot for us to choose from," Thomas Wayne said, looking around at his cousins.

"Great!" Melissa cheered, as she walked into the living room area.

"What do you all want to eat this evening? Sirloin steaks on the grill? What about fried pork chops? Pork spareribs? There should be a roast prepared and ready to heat up," Thomas Wayne said.

"You got all of that in your SUV?" Erin asked.

"Yes!" Thomas Wayne said with excitement. "I even got baked Mexican macaroni and cheese. I think it has about four or five different types of cheese. After having greens with ham hocks at Mimi's Chicken And Waffles the other day for lunch, I had to get some for the group. So, we have collard greens, broccoli rice casserole, and cornbread dressing. And for breakfast in the morning, we have cinnamon rolls and muffins. I'm a great cook, and I'm prepared to make you a Mexican potato omelet served with bacon, sausage, chicken, and hash browns. Or, if you prefer pancakes, that's doable, too. For dessert, we have Blue Bell ice cream, an apple pie, and Mrs. Edward's key lime pie."

"Okay, let's help the man get the food out of the truck," Edward said, walking toward the front door.

"Come on, guys," Thomas Wayne said, heading for the door.

Trevor looked irritated as Dillard and Melissa followed behind Thomas Wayne.

Walking alongside Edward, Melissa said, "That's a lot of food, Thomas Wayne. We can't eat all of that in two days."

"It's okay. I'll get it donated to some charity or something. Or, we can just have whatever we don't eat thrown away. I'm sure Uncle Bert and Trevor will be pleased with the charity suggestion. Living healthy with purpose," Thomas Wayne started to laugh. "Trevor can take his food back home."

Trevor and Erin sat at the dining table while the others brought in the food and placed the items in the refrigerator and pantry.

"Trevor, your organic eggs are taking up room," Edward shouted from the kitchen. "And this low-fat milk and coconut milk is going to the back of the box."

Erin was bothered by Edward's comments. During the discussion, she moved to the sofa where a huge 52 inch plasma television was located. She started looking around for the remote.

"Guys, after dinner we'll have an exercise to complete," Trevor said.

"No games?" Thomas Wayne questioned. "At the family get-togethers, we play dominos and spades."

"No, just exercises designed to help us get to know each other better."

"I'm trying to find the TV remote. Do you know where it is, Trevor?" Erin asked in frustration.

Edward walked toward the front door to get another round of bags, "I sure hope you brought some beer, Thomas Wayne."

"Corona, Heineken, and Blue Moon," Thomas Wayne said, following behind Edward.

Trevor walked over to Erin and explained to her that they would be spending their weekend time engaging in getting-to-know-you exercises. There would be no television or computer access for the weekend.

"NO TV!" Erin exclaimed.

"Okay, guys, let's be clear about this weekend. It's about us spending quality family time together, reconnecting cousins, talking and sharing, none of which includes TV watching. Remember Grandma Saddie's favorite saying, 'The family that prays together, stays together.' "

"Clearly that saying didn't hold true for our family," Melissa stated. "Glad I have the Internet on my cell phone."

Thomas Wayne opened the car door and pointed to the beer. He proceeded to look in his glove compartment.

"What are you looking for?" Edward asked.

Thomas Wayne handed him a bag.

"This isn't what I think it is?" Edward said.

Thomas Wayne sat in the driver's seat and said, "I forgot my papers," and he began to light up a joint.

"You're smoking dope? You're a deputy sheriff!" Edward shouted, infuriated, as he threw the bag at Thomas Wayne.

Thomas Wayne brought the joint to his lips and inhaled.

After exhaling, he said, "Good stuff." He offered Edward a puff.

"No thanks. You're stupid, risking your job, your career, just stupid," Edward said. "Is this why you're borrowing money from me. I'm not giving you another dime."

Thomas Wayne brought it to his lips again and inhaled. "Chill, my brother," he said, calmly. "It's just an occasional thing. I need something to help me deal with Trevor and all this crazy stuff we need to do to get that money."

Edward looked at Thomas Wayne's behavior with disgust and walked off.

"Hold up, brother. I need to change my jacket. Don't want anyone smelling the smoke," Thomas Wayne said. "Oh, yeah, and my eye wash."

Edward and Thomas Wayne walked in with more bags and heard the tail end of Trevor's speech about the purpose of their weekend together.

"That is what we'll be working to change. Uncle Bert is looking for us to restore and elevate our relationships to the status of a family that does things together, interacts positively with each other, and fosters a close bond."

"Now I know we're going to be doing a lot of drinking this weekend," Edward whispered to Thomas Wayne and handed him a beer.

Melissa continued to arrange all the food in the refrigerator and pantry.

Erin walked into the kitchen. She wanted to see what healthy foods Trevor had brought. She had recently asked Trevor to help her get on track with implementing better eating habits for her and her kids. When she opened the refrigerator door, Thomas Wayne's whole milk sat front and center.

Erin thought, *All this meat—bacon, pan sausage, links, biscuits, cinnamon rolls, and cookie dough. Let's see what's in the pantry. Looks like more unhealthy stuff. There must be at least six different bags of chips. Dillard will be happy to see these chocolate covered donuts and chocolate chip cookies. Wow! Look at the cans of soda. This weekend is going to be hard, having all this tempting food staring at me.*

Trevor could sense that Erin was worried. He walked up behind her and said, "Don't worry. It looks like they placed all of the healthy foods in the back. There are some chicken parts to grill. I also have some sweet potatoes for us to bake, and fresh broccoli and mixed greens. We have some low-fat, low-sodium turkey and Swiss cheese from the deli."

"Guys, I've got the munchies. I can warm up the pot roast and baked Mexican macaroni and cheese, collard greens, and rolls I got from Tinsley's Chicken," Thomas Wayne said from the kitchen.

"Not rolls from Tinsley's Chicken," Melissa shouted.

"You've already eaten biscuits," Edward said.

"So," Melissa said, rolling her eyes at Edward.

"Yes, ma'am," Thomas Wayne confirmed.

"When is Claire coming?" Erin asked Trevor.

"Hopefully her husband will bring her in the morning," Trevor responded. "She had a flare up today and wasn't feeling well."

"I remember the lady at your fitness talk saying something about her Lupus and a flare up. What *is* a flare up?" Erin asked.

"When the symptoms worsen, that is, when the disease is said to be active, like joint pain, fever, diarrhea, rashes, and/or ulcers on her skin. A flare up can keep a person in bed or in a hospital for days or weeks at a time."

"What causes her to have a flare up?" Erin asked.

"Maybe something she unknowingly ate that contained nuts or was a high-fiber food. Maybe it was stress!" Trevor said.

"Hey, guys, I'm going to make some Margaritas," Thomas Wayne shouted.

"Great," Melissa said.

"Okay, guys, I want you all to be careful about drinking the alcoholic beverages," Trevor hesitated. He was unsure about springing his next statement on his cousins. "Our agenda on tomorrow will include exercise. Alcohol and exercise don't mix. You should be drinking plenty of water this evening to ensure that you're properly hydrated by tomorrow morning."

"Exercise!" Thomas Wayne shouted.

"Remember the money," Edward whispered to Thomas Wayne with a smile.

"I don't know how much water you all have drunk today, but you should be drinking enough so your urine is the color of light lemonade. That's typically around 100 ounces daily for men and 72 ounces for women."

"I'll be the first to admit that I haven't had any water today," Dillard said.

"Tomorrow will be hot and humid. It's critical that you start drinking your water now."

Edward, Dillard, and Melissa greedily ate the pot roast, baked Mexican macaroni and cheese, collard greens, and rolls. Meanwhile, Trevor and Erin ate a turkey sandwich with mixed greens and mixed fruit. Dillard and Erin made a conscious effort to drink water.

During their dinner, Trevor noticed that Thomas Wayne was not eating and was distant from the others.

"Hey, guys, I left something in the Caddy. I'll be right back," Thomas Wayne said.

"I need to go and check on Brian," Erin said. "We have to check his blood sugar four to five times a day."

Trevor walked over to assure Erin and said, "The nurse has all the instructions. He's in good hands."

After dinner, it was time for their first weekend group exercise. It was no secret that Trevor's cousins had allowed their childhood memories to consume them. A part of his plan for healing and deliverance included leading them back to the good parts of their childhood.

Trevor asked them to come and have a seat in the living room area. He took a stack of cards out of his bag.

Dillard and Erin sat on the sofa. Edward sat in a recliner, and Melissa sat on the loveseat with Trevor.

Thomas Wayne walked in as they were assembling. He sat in a recliner and asked with a sloppy grin, "Do I need to get a drink?"

"I'm thinking so," Edward said with amusement.

"No alcohol, and no cellular phones. I don't want Melissa sharing the latest posts on Facebook," Trevor answered back, staring intensely. He started to pass out the cards. "We had some great times as kids, a lot of good times to be revisited and thankful for, times that can determine your purpose at this point in your life."

"Is this some sort of therapy session?" Edward asked.

"No, not a therapy session, but an opportunity for all of us to look back and remember the fun times we shared as kids."

Trevor gave them the instructions for the exercise. Each of them had five cards with the name of a cousin placed at the top. Each card had a sentence that said, 'Describe your fondest memory of you and the cousin written at the top of the card. Include your age at the time.'

"What if you don't have any fond memories of the person?" Melissa asked.

Dillard quickly interjected, "I know that's right."

"Come on, guys. Here are some pens and pencils," Trevor said, as he placed the pens and pencils on the coffee table.

"I've repressed any fond memories that I may have had of you guys," Edward said, laughing.

Erin, Melissa, and Dillard started writing. Thomas Wayne stared at the card in deep thought. He walked out the front door.

Dillard flipped through the cards and asked, "What about Claire? Is she a part of this exercise?"

Trevor responded, "Yes, she is. Go ahead and complete a card for her. She'll have an opportunity to do the exercise and share her responses tomorrow."

Ten minutes had passed when Trevor asked if they were ready to share what they had written.

Thomas Wayne returned, again from outside, this time looking dazed and drunken.

"I'll go first, Trevor," Erin volunteered. She looked at three of the cards on top. "The fondest memory of me and Melissa was when I was nine. After a certain age, we only got to see you all on holidays and during the summers."

Melissa looked down because she knew what Erin was referring to.

"Grandma Saddie bought the girls an Easy-Bake Oven for Christmas, and the following summer, I had the best time making cakes with you."

Erin looked over at Melissa.

Melissa started laughing and added, "We'd argue over who would mix all of the products together—open the package of mix, add water, pour the batter into that little cake pan, and slide it into the tiny oven."

"Those were the best tasting little cakes," Erin said, licking her lips and smiling. "My next card says Dillard. My best memory of my little brother is him showing me how to dribble a basketball. We had the best time when he'd let me tag along with him to the park near where we lived with our dad's parents and watch him play basketball with the guys. After they'd finished, he'd give me the ball. I rarely got the ball in the basket, but I had so much fun trying to do so."

"You did develop good ball handling skills. I thought she might get better than me," Dillard smiled, as he hit Erin on her leg.

"How old were you, Erin?" Trevor asked.

"Probably around thirteen," Erin responded. "What I remember most about Edward and Thomas Wayne is riding our bikes in the summer to the nearby corner store, which was the best hangout for us in the neighborhood. You both taught me what it was like to be both bold and wild when we would do things like reach a high rate of speed and then stand up on the seat. Although I vividly remember our daring acts, I had forgotten those fun times until now. We were crazy, but it was breathtaking being unafraid and free from worry. I think I was around ten."

"What about Claire?" Trevor asked.

"I think because Claire was the oldest of all of us, she was the caretaker. She was smart and always took time out to help me with my math and reading when we'd visit Grandma Saddie during the summer. We rarely saw any of you after me and Dillard had to go live with my dad's sister, Mildred, after his parents died."

"Thank you, Erin. Okay, who's next?" Trevor asked.

Reluctantly, Edward said, "I'll go."

"Great!" Trevor said. He was surprised that Edward had volunteered.

"Guess I'll start with my brother, Thomas Wayne, since he and I shared our childhood together. I wanted to say smoking our first cigarette together or drinking our first bourbon and coke, but really it's probably me teaching you to shave for the first time." He glanced over at Thomas Wayne. "You were about twelve and I was fifteen. I lathered you up with my shaving cream. You were so excited. You really didn't have anything on your face except for a few dark hairs, but they were enough that you wanted to get rid of them. And you put a razor to your face for the first time."

"I remember that disposable razor," Thomas Wayne said while laughing. "I remember how patient you were with showing me how to shave down the right side of my face and chin. I couldn't wait to grow more and more facial hair."

Edward continued, "As far as my memories with Melissa, it's probably the time she took to help me write a love letter to Kelly, my first girlfriend. I was about fourteen and wasn't a good writer or speller. Since Melissa was the spelling bee champ and was always winning essay contests, I asked her to help me."

Melissa started laughing, "I remember that handwritten letter on Big Chief tablet paper, *'To my sweetheart, Kelly. This is the first letter I have ever written. And I am only doing so now because I want you to know how much I love and think about you. Every time I am with you, I feel like I am on top of the world. I think about you all day and every day. I wonder about what you are doing and where you are. I dream about you every night, holding and kissing you. I have never been with anyone who makes me feel like you do. I love you so much, and I am glad you are my girlfriend. Yours forever, Edward.'* It was great fun."

Chuckles consumed the room.

"Guess we all missed that soft side of you," Erin said, laughing uncontrollably.

"I remember Kelly. She started dating your rival, Coleman Strickland," Dillard replied with a sarcastic grin, flashing his white teeth.

"Anyway… mistakes of a young fool, is all I can say," Edward said sharply. "When I think of everyone else, I am reminded of the great times we had playing endless games of hide and seek, tag—you're it, Mother may I, and red light/green light at Grandma Saddie's house during the summer months."

"And don't forget about hide and go get it," Thomas Wayne shouted out laughing.

"Thanks, Edward. That was good. Who's next?" Trevor asked, laughing.

Edward stood up to walk into the kitchen and asked, "Anyone want something to drink." He opened the refrigerator and grabbed a cola.

"Bring a glass of that Margarita stuff Thomas Wayne mixed up," Melissa answered. "Sorry Trevor, I've got to have a drink."

Trevor looked irritated.

Melissa started waving her arms back and forth. "Although we all spent a considerable amount of time together, it was Claire who I was closest to. We were raised as the only kids, even though we had other siblings. We loved playing dress-up in Grandma's high heels and her elaborate hats. Grandma Saddie paid a lot of money for her church hats. Every time she'd catch us in her closest, Claire would manage to talk her out of spanking us."

"How old were you all?" Trevor asked.

Edward handed Melissa a glass filled with the Margarita mixture and sat down on the floor.

Trevor noticed the salt around the rim of her glass.

"I was around ten, so Claire must have been around twelve," Melissa responded, as she set the glass on the table. "Everyone else, I just remember the fun times at Grandma Saddie's house during the holidays. That is, before I had to move to California. I remember going to the roller rink with Claire and Edward and skating to our favorite songs, watching Saturday morning cartoons with the younger kids—Erin, Dillard, and Thomas Wayne, during our summers together."

"What about you, Dillard," Trevor asked.

"I would have to say, the hours we spent jumping on Grandma's mattress and having pillow fights. I just really don't have anything to share, Trevor."

Melissa began to lick the salt off her glass.

"Come on; sure you do," Trevor insisted.

Dillard hesitated for a moment and said, "I guess climbing trees with Edward before he got so mean."

Edward looked up with disgust and shook his head.

"Playing kickball with my sister and the neighborhood kids was fun. I remember one Christmas when Grandma Saddie bought us all skateboards, and Thomas Wayne showed me how to do tricks," he added.

"What about summers at Grandma Saddie's and vacation bible school?" Trevor added.

"I just remember that time I got a whippin' for being behind the church building with Lucy Taylor," Edward said.

"Hmm," Thomas Wayne said grinning. "I think you got a whippin' for what you all were doing."

"What about you, Thomas Wayne?" Trevor asked. "What are your favorite times?"

"I would have to say, the times Aunt Mertle would take us to the beach. A bunch of us kids piled up in the station wagon was too much fun."

"Yeah," Melissa agreed, "I still love to go to Galveston."

"Great! Thanks for sharing," Trevor said.

"Back in the day, relatives lived in the neighborhood, at least within a five mile radius of one another. For holidays, it was a given that the main event would be at Grandma's house, with all of us and our parents under one roof," Melissa added.

"And our great-aunts and uncles," Erin added.

"Yes, it was a great time," Trevor stated, "flying kites and climbing trees, no adult supervision, just the freedom to be kids. It's a shame that today's kids can't have that kind of freedom to play well into the night, as Erin stated."

"I remember us talking and laughing with one another when walking home from school, and walking home from the community pool with bare feet," Thomas Wayne said. "We were never bored."

"You're right. When you really think about it, we were never bored. And we didn't have video games, cellular phones, computers,

Internet, TVs with over 100 channels—just our cousins and our friends," Melissa said.

"Don't you dare pull out your cellular phone, Melissa," Trevor said quickly.

"Oh, yeah, and Grandma Saddie's homemade ice cream," Erin said.

"Now that's memories," Thomas Wayne replied. "I can visualize that old hand-cranked machine right now. Dillard and the girls would help Grandma Saddie make the custard. A few hours later, I would pour the cold custard into the canister and place it in the old wooden tub, put the lid on, and align the crank apparatus on top. After it was locked, Edward and Trevor filled the sides with ice and rock salt. Then we all took turns cranking the ice cream."

"We needed to take turns because Erin and Melissa couldn't go but a few seconds," Thomas Wayne said laughing.

"We did struggle quite a bit," Melissa said, also laughing, "but it was the best tasting stuff after all was said and done."

"I remember one of those times when Grandma made ice cream from snow," Erin said.

"You're right," Melissa confirmed. "It was one Christmas holiday. She told us all to gather clean snow. We watched her mix milk, vanilla extract, and sugar in a bowl, and then she added the snow to reach a thickness."

"Oh, my goodness, that was so much fun. It tasted better than ice cream our parents would buy at the store," Erin said.

They all relished the memory of Grandma Saddie's homemade ice cream.

"Don't forget about Grandma Saddie's infamous fig tree," Edward said. "We loved helping Grandma pick figs from the tree. We knew that within the next week or so our mothers would get fig preserves for breakfasts."

"What about helping Grandma Saddie hang clothes out to dry on the clothesline," Melissa asked.

"It was the little things that made us most happy," Trevor stated. "And I hope it's the little things that you will focus on with your own children and grandchildren."

Trevor's flash-back activity seemingly made a deep impression on his cousins. It helped his cousins recreate the feelings of good times and being around one another. It was apparent that they were pleased with being reminded of their personal happy memories. He hoped they would be inspired to embrace that inner playful child that loved to have fun. It would be the building block for helping them to foster a transformed life filled with love, new adventure, fun, excitement, and joy.

Chapter 7

❖

Breaking Through A Tough Interior

On Saturday morning, Melissa and Edward awoke to the smell of bacon and pan sausage. One by one, they entered the kitchen, where Thomas Wayne was preparing breakfast.

A few minutes later, Trevor walked through the front door, sweaty. He had gotten up early to run along the hilly country road that served as the entrance into the lake front community.

Thomas Wayne was hard at work in chef mode.

"Hey, guys, there's a fresh pot of coffee brewing—orange juice in the refrigerator, and fresh fruit, scones, and assorted muffins on the counter," Thomas Wayne said, as they entered the kitchen area.

"What are you cooking, Thomas Wayne," Melissa queried, smiling down at the counter.

"Hopefully, some of our favorites—pancakes, omelets, and hash browns, with bacon and sausage," Edward said.

Erin overheard the conversation as she entered the area. She frowned and asked, "Trevor, how was your run?"

"Just great!" he responded, as he sat down on the floor in the living room.

"Man, what time did you get up?" Edward asked. He sat down next to Melissa.

"Around 5:30 A.M.," Trevor responded. He pulled off his running shoes.

"Nah! Now that's crazy, and on a Saturday morning," Edward said, looking at Trevor on the floor. "The only place I want to be at 5:30 A.M. on a Saturday morning is curled up under the covers."

"I know that's right," Thomas Wayne said, as he cracked open a couple of eggs, "even though I've been up all night."

"How many miles did you run?" Melissa asked.

"Six," Trevor told her.

"Six miles?" Edward asked.

"He has to maintain his waistline," Melissa explained.

"Hmm," Edward said.

"Guess I'll get a carton of yogurt," Erin commented, opening the refrigerator door. She looked over at Trevor. "Ever since our last meeting, I've been trying to do things differently."

She sat at the counter with Melissa and Edward, grabbed a spoon off the countertop, and told them, "Trevor has given me a lot of good information and examples of eating healthier and exercising."

"Sounds boring," Edward commented.

"It's only boring to those not ready to change unhealthy habits," Erin teased.

"How is what we're doing, and were raised to do, unhealthy?" Edward questioned. He looked over at Trevor.

Trevor emphasized, "Our parents and ancestors did not have the knowledge we have today about what really constitutes healthier eating. That's why many of them have encountered long-suffering illnesses and have consequently died in their early forties, fifties, and sixties."

He walked out of the room to take a shower.

"My wife tries to get me to eat better, but—," Thomas Wayne interjected.

Dillard walked in, heard the chatting, and said, "Good morning."

He stood at the counter near Thomas Wayne.

"Hey, Dillard, fix us a cup of coffee while you're standing there watching," Edward said, arrogantly.

Dillard opened the cabinet to get some mugs and started to pour cups of coffee.

"One of the things I'd like for us to do is research the various diseases and illnesses in our family," Erin stated, spooning yogurt out of her container.

"Speaking of illness, one thing we know for sure is that Dillard and Erin had a crazy momma," Edward shouted, laughing and tapping his head with his index finger.

Dillard lunged at Edward to hit him, but Erin hopped out of her seat to get between the two. Dillard gasped as he stood erratically on his feet.

"Forget him," Erin said. "He's stupid. Has always been stupid. And he will continue to be stupid."

"Come on, guys. This weekend is about us. Restoration! At least that's what Trevor says," Melissa commented, as she looked at Edward with displeasure.

"That'll never happen with Edward's mean and hateful spirit. You're still the same bitter kid," Dillard accused Edward.

"You better get your boy," Edward said, standing in a defensive posture.

"Come on; let's eat," Melissa said. "Sit down, Edward."

"My coffee is cold," Edward said as he took a sip.

Edward walked over to the sink and emptied his cup. Before sitting down at the dining table, he poured another cup.

"Erin, don't forget that we have oatmeal. I can cook you an egg white, and there's some wheat sandwich thins in the pantry," Trevor said, walking into the kitchen area freshened up.

He had heard the commotion from the back room, but he decided to overlook it.

"Trevor, have you heard from Claire?" Erin asked.

"There's a bowl filled with bananas, oranges, and apples," Thomas Wayne pointed to a bowl on the dining table.

Erin walked over to the group and said, "All of you should have attended Trevor's fitness session at his church on Thursday night. Maybe you'd be inclined to eat healthier."

"No one is trying to hear about that healthy scrap, Erin," Edward said. "Now you just eat your yogurt, oatmeal, fruit, and some carrots, lettuce, and whatever other boring stuff you and Trevor eat. Don't expect us to follow in your footsteps."

Erin left the room to go and call her kids.

Trevor sat down at the bar and said, "Let me call Claire and check on her status. I forgot to tell her that I have gluten-free cereals."

As Trevor pulled his cellular out of his pocket, there was a knock at the front door.

"Someone is at the door," Melissa shouted.

"You think," Edward said sarcastically.

Melissa walked toward the door and opened it. It was Claire with a garment bag on her shoulder.

"Hi, Claire," Melissa said, as she moved to embrace Claire. "Trevor was just getting ready to call you. Give me your bag."

Claire handed her bag to Melissa and walked into the house. Trevor greeted her with a warm embrace. The others followed behind him.

"I was getting ready to call you," Trevor said, as he motioned for Claire to have a seat at the kitchen table.

"Me and Mark started out early this morning, so I thought I'd come on up here," Claire commented.

"Where is Mark?" Erin asked.

"He just dropped me off," Claire responded.

Claire was noticeably more frail than the last time they had seen her.

"We were just getting ready to eat breakfast," Trevor said to Claire. "I purchased some gluten-free cereals for you."

"Actually, I ate before I left home," Claire said. "I'll eat something a little later on. Where is the bathroom?"

"It's down the hall to your left," Dillard told her.

Claire left the room.

"Looks like she should have stayed at home," Edward muttered.

"The food is ready," Thomas Wayne announced.

Erin, Melissa, and Dillard set up the island in the kitchen with silverware, plates, glasses, and napkins. They arranged the food in chafing dishes in a buffet style so everyone could serve themselves. One by one, the cousins made their breakfast selections—bacon, pan sausage, links, biscuits, cinnamon rolls, and eggs. Erin, Melissa, and Dillard sat at the dining table with Trevor. Edward and Thomas Wayne sat at the counter.

Claire entered the room.

Melissa looked up and asked, "Are you alright, Claire?"

"I'm okay. I just have to make many bathroom runs," Claire responded.

Melissa resumed eating her pancakes, hash browns, sausage and cheese omelet, and bacon and sausage.

"Do you want something to drink?" Trevor asked.

Claire walked toward the refrigerator, "If there's some juice, I'll have some. Better yet, I'll get some water."

"Both are in the refrigerator," Thomas Wayne said as he pointed.

"Yeah, guys! Don't forget to drink your water," Edward said. "How much today, Trevor?"

"I typically drink 12 to 16 ounces of fluid two hours before I run. This allows my kidneys enough time to process the liquid. If my run is first thing in the morning, then I drink 8 ounces at least 15 minutes beforehand. That's why it's critical for me to have sufficient water intake the day before," Trevor said.

"Well, I'm drinking my water," Erin said.

"Claire, last night we all engaged in an exercise where everyone described their fondest memory of one another," Trevor said, as he stood up to get a stack of cards for Claire. "Look at the name on the top of the card, and then write down your fondest memory of that cousin and your age at the time."

Claire took the stack of cards and sat down on the sofa.

In the midst of Trevor's conversation with Claire, Edward turned to Thomas Wayne and asked about his blueberry scone, "Is that good? I'm thinking about getting one."

"It's yummy," Thomas Wayne replied as he laughed, "and I know blueberries are healthy, right, Trevor?"

The arrival of Claire seemingly brought about an air of awkwardness. Claire was real gaunt in the face and body.

It was apparent that conversation was necessary, so Trevor started to talk about their activities for the day.

"When everyone finishes breakfast, we're going to drive up to Lone Star Walking Trail," Trevor announced.

"For what?" Edward asked.

Trevor frowned and stated, "To trail walk."

"Haven't you already run this morning?" Melissa asked.

"Yes."

"What! You're trying to act like some superman or something?" Edward exclaimed.

"I thought you took a shower already?" Erin asked.

"I did," he responded. "I just didn't want dirt on top of dirt."

"Show-off," Edward muttered.

"If the man wants to waste water, that's his business. It's Uncle Bert's water bill," Thomas Wayne said.

"Thank you, Thomas Wayne," Trevor said, laughing.

The activity was Trevor's way of exposing his cousins to something fun and different to generate an interest in exercising. It would provide them with an option for not only cardio and strength conditioning, but also for balance and coordination. It would also serve as another activity for releasing negative energy, and it was a great way to further reconnect and renew their relationships.

"I thought we'd be going to that cool indoor fitness facility on the property," Thomas Wayne stated.

"Were not going to be able to do the outdoors, cuz," Edward said. "It's July! Probably already 90 degrees."

"Okay, guys, it's an all-or-none deal," Trevor stated. "Let's not forget why Uncle Bert set up this whole initiative."

"But... it's hot out there, man!" Edward shouted. "Uncle Bert didn't say anything about having a heat stroke."

"Start drinking some water," Trevor said. "Wear something light colored and comfortable. We won't be out there too long."

Thomas Wayne whispered to Edward, "Get with the program, man."

"All I know is, I'm not trying to walk in any woods where I'm subject to snakes and skunks," Edward said loudly. "And I'm not trying to have a heat stroke."

"The likelihood of us seeing snakes and skunks is slim," Trevor responded. "And by the way, the only person exempt from this excursion is Claire."

They finished eating and washing the dishes, so they left to change clothes. A short while later, they reappeared in the living room wearing their T-shirts, shorts, and tennis shoes. Trevor provided further instruction on what they needed to bring along for the walking trip. He had given them water belts to strap to their waists so they could stay hydrated.

The weather was beautiful, with an eighty-five degrees temperature. Trevor was excited about their walking a portion of the ten-mile narrow trail that looped around a combination of semi-steep and rolling forests of pine, oak, and mixed hardwood, and around cypress swamps and bayous.

Trevor started out leading the way with a backpack strapped to his back.

"Okay, guys, we're going to start out eastward. The trail is very well marked, but just stay close to one another. Watch out for downed trees, and walk gently across the bridges," he instructed.

The path was undeniably scenic. However, its terrain required them to focus their attention downward. Storm-uprooted trees were an expected sight on the path.

"Just take your time. We're out here to enjoy birds chirping, leaves rustling, and the smells and sounds of nature," Trevor said, as he carefully walked on a bouncy, wooden plank over a swamp.

Within five minutes, Erin, Melissa, and Dillard became extremely winded. They started gasping for breath, and sweat was pouring down their faces.

"Breathe," Trevor emphasized. He talked loudly as they followed behind him in a single file. "We won't be out here too long, since you don't have on the right footwear. Plus, I don't want to leave Claire at the van too long by herself. Let's talk about something, so I'll know you are okay."

"So, Erin, how is Brian doing?" Melissa asked.

"He's doing better," she responded.

As they walked along the trail, Erin talked about how the doctors informed her that Brian had juvenile type I diabetes. The doctor explained to them that Brian's pancreas had stopped working and that he would be insulin dependent.

"All I remember asking is, 'What do we do? What is onset juvenile diabetes? How do we get rid of it? How long will it last? Can it be cured?' Almost all the answer to the questions I asked were, no, no, no, no, and no. The doctor said that there was no cure, but that it could be treated," Erin said. "I sat there in the doctor's office thinking, *What has happen to my little boy? What did I do wrong? Is it something I did or did not do during my pregnancy?*"

Listening intently to Erin, Thomas Wayne missed seeing a stump protruding from the trail and fell on his knees.

They all stopped to make sure he was okay. He stood up and continued walking.

Dillard continued the conversation, "We found out that it's all in the genes—genetics. No one in the family has type I, but on all sides of the family, there are genes of type II diabetes."

"Brian was admitted to the hospital, and they began to work to lower his blood glucose level. The doctors educated me and Nick about the disease."

As they maneuvered the rugged trails with rocky, rooty, and slippery surfaces and water crossings, Trevor directed them to stop as they approached an open area. It was time for a water break.

"My feet hurt!" Melissa shouted. "I hope we're heading back soon."

"I know that's right, and I need to use the restroom," Edward said.

"My knees hurt," Erin said quietly.

"Mine too, after that fall," Thomas Wayne complained.

After a few minutes, they headed back to their vehicle. Melissa and Dillard talked about their dislike of feeling the rocks under their feet and the stress on their ankles. Except for her hurting knees, Erin found the rocks and roots fun and challenging.

Back at the lake house, Erin, Melissa, Dillard, and Thomas Wayne talked more about their experience on the trail.

"If we ever do that again, I hope to be in better shape," Erin admitted.

"Me too," Dillard echoed. "*If* I ever do it again."

Thomas Wayne stared blankly and then gave a slow nod.

"I assure you that's an easy fix," Trevor said. "All you need to do is get into a routine of doing some sort of activity like walking every day."

"I don't think trails are the best activity for fat folks," Edward said laughing. "How about a bowl of Blue Bell Ice Cream, Dillard?"

"Edward, it's for anyone who wants to do it," Trevor said sharply.

"I'm glad Trevor took us. I'm going to start walking more, outside, so I can connect with nature. It just may be what I need to dissolve the stresses in my life," Dillard commented.

"I know I need to do better," Erin admitted, looking worriedly at Trevor. "I'm even noticing where Chanitah has gained weight. She's too large for a twelve year old. I thought her being on the drill team would help."

"It only helps with healthy eating."

"It's just hot! It's too hot to be outside," Dillard said. "I didn't like exercising in the heat in high school, and I definitely don't like it now."

"Hopefully, the two of you will figure out how to make exercise a part of your life, for life. For you, Dillard, consider waking up thirty minutes earlier to exercise to an aerobic video or to exercise with one of the fitness gurus on TV. Erin, you can consider walking around the stadium/practice field instead of sitting in the bleachers during Chanitah's drill team practice. For someone else, it might mean walking around your office building with a group of co-workers during your lunch break."

"I really do prefer the outdoors," Dillard said, "just not in the heat. If you can get me past the heat, I'll see…"

"Plan your day so you can exercise during the coolest part of the day, like early morning (before seven o'clock) or evening (after seven o'clock). When exercising outdoors during the summer, you must be aware of heat and humidity. Our bodies are typically warmer than the environment. The body regulates heat by releasing sweat, which allows the body to cool itself," Trevor explained.

Later on that evening, the weather had cooled down. Trevor had allowed his cousins to have some downtime, and now it was time for them to reconvene in the living room.

"What are we eating tonight?" Dillard asked.

"I know I'm not eating that rabbit food Trevor has," Edward insisted.

Thomas Wayne looked at everyone and said, "I'll cook again. I can fire up the grill on the deck and grill some of that meat I brought. Sirloin steaks? Pork chops? Pork spareribs?"

"Sounds good to me," Melissa responded.

Trevor was outnumbered. But, he was okay with accommodating them, because he knew things could change over time.

"Claire, did you finish your cards?" Trevor asked.

"Yes, I did," Claire responded.

Thomas Wayne got up and walked into the kitchen.

"What's your fondest memory of me?" Melissa asked. She followed behind Thomas Wayne to assist him.

"I remember us being inseparable when we were kids," Claire said loudly. She wanted to make sure Melissa heard her response. "Most of our firsts were experienced together—our first trip to Astro World, our first job at Joske's, our first alcoholic drink, our first pool party, and you were there when I cried over my first heartbreak."

Melissa nodded and smiled as she selected meat from the refrigerator. She paused, looked over at Claire, and said, "John-John."

"You cried over John-John," Edward laughed. "Every girl in middle school thought she was his girlfriend."

"What about everyone else?" Trevor asked.

"I mainly remember being the one to keep everyone in order since I was the oldest."

Thomas Wayne shouted from the kitchen, "You all want to eat the cornbread dressing and broccoli-rice casserole."

"Sounds good to me, li'l brother," Edward commented. "Is that okay with you, massa Trevor?"

It was clear that everyone was becoming increasingly agitated by Edward's ugly statements.

Trevor got up and walked into the kitchen.

"Erin and Claire, I'll add some fresh chicken parts to the grill," Trevor said. "I have a fresh zucchini and squash medley made up that I can put on the grill also."

"Trevor, does our evening activity include partaking in the game room—a game of pool?" Dillard asked.

"No, there is another activity we're going to do after we eat."

Chapter 8

❖

A Haunting Past

The last meal of the day had been cooked and eaten. Trevor introduced the next activity while they all sat on the deck looking out at the lake.

"Is this some tear-jerker emotional exercise?" Melissa asked.

Claire interjected and said, "Grandma Saddie always said 'Change requires you to make an adjustment.'"

"She also said, 'We're reluctant to change what's comfortable,'" Trevor stated.

"Yada, yada, yada," Edward sighed. "Heard it last night, bro."

Ignoring Edward, Trevor continued, "Once I got to the root of my pain—the pain I was desperately trying to suppress—then my life changed. I know for certain that you all are dealing with similar hurt, pain, guilt, shame, embarrassment, and anger. The longer you choose not to face it, the longer it will continue to eat away at you. You'll look up one day and your life will be one big blob of waste."

"What did you do, Trevor?" Erin asked, softly.

"There came a point in my life where I stopped fighting the emotions and just allowed myself to feel. I started by writing down what I didn't want to face. For so long, I had focused on blocking my emotions, and although I appeared caring and thoughtful, I was actually cold and heartless. I had to accept what had happened to me and come to an understanding that God allowed it to happen. It was a part of his plan and purpose for my life. The hardest thing I had to do was forgive the person who hurt me. I couldn't be free to be happy if I didn't. And the one thing I deserved in life was to be happy deep down inside. Neither things nor people could do that for me."

"Aside from forgiving, it's hard to accept why something had to happen to you," Dillard added.

"What is the exercise, Trevor?" Thomas Wayne impatiently asked.

Trevor stood up to hand each one of his cousins a pencil and notepad filled with sheets of paper.

The top of the first sheet of paper read, 'Share a traumatic event or experience from your past which *you* believe has had a significant negative impact on your adulthood to include the way you think, feel, act, and perceive.'

Edward stared at Trevor and said, "I'm curious to know. What traumatic event or experience happened to you?"

Trevor looked surprised.

Edward paused a moment and asked the question again with greater intensity, "What traumatic event or experience happened to you? You're taking us through all of this psycho-babble stuff like you're some sort of expert. So, share your pain. You've talked around and around in circles about how you know what it's like being trapped in your childhood still holding on—that you've been in the valley and you know how easy it is to gravitate to the wrong things for comfort."

Trevor had shared his personal story with only two family members, his mother and Uncle Bert. He knew that if God was going to use him to help his cousins overcome, then he would need to open up and tell them how God had delivered him.

"I was around twelve at the time when someone I trusted did something so horrible to me that I placed the memory of it in a box, sealed it, and tucked it away in a closet. For years, I kept that box in the closet and went about trying to live a life of normalcy. I fulfilled my parents' expectations—went to high school and earned decent grades, went off to college and received a degree in electrical engineering, and I dated a lot of beautiful women along the way. I was the face of someone who did everything right and had accomplished," Trevor said calmly.

"Come on, man; get to the point!" Edward said, pleading rudely.

"Let him talk," Erin shushed him.

"All the while, I was silently walking around, going about my daily business, and appearing like the man who had it all. I was trying everything but the right thing to distract and detach myself from the emotional pain of what had happened to me as a child. For nearly twenty years, I tried to suppress the sporadic reminders. I did this by engaging in risky, unhealthy activities that included excessive drinking, having unprotected sex, to thoughts of suicide."

As Trevor continued to speak, his cousins looked stunned. They were now paying attention to what he was saying.

"My life was nearly destroyed," Trevor said, anxious to get through his story.

"When is he going to finish?" Edward mumbled to Thomas Wayne. "He's just saying all of this stuff to get us to share our innermost secrets. He just wants to have something to tell Uncle Bert. I'm not buying what he's trying to sell."

"When you know, that you know, that you know you're tired, then you're tired. I was tired of clubbing; I was tired of eating and drinking my life away; I was tired of women using me; I was tired of being fat," Trevor admitted.

"Just what I thought. Making excuses for being fat," Edward whispered to Thomas Wayne.

"Is that the story you shared during the fitness talk at your church? Is that the point when you decided to start exercising and you hooked up with your supervisor who introduced you to running?" Erin asked.

"Yes," Trevor responded. "Then, one thing led to another. Running helped to bring clarity to my life. It is the one thing that has made me a stronger, wiser, and better person, and consequently running has helped me settle down and appreciate my past and life's difficult moments."

"How did you end up in fitness?" Dillard asked.

"Although I was making a lot of money, I really wasn't happy as an electrical engineer. I prayed to God for direction. He showed me that I hadn't experienced the horror that had haunted me for years just by chance, and He showed me the mistakes I had made along the way by remaining silent. He allowed those things to happen so His name would be glorified and others would be blessed."

"More preaching," Edward whispered to Thomas Wayne. "Tired of it!"

"I was led to further my education in fitness and eventually started my own fitness business."

Trevor glanced at each one of his cousins. "Years later, I received an invitation to speak at a conference, the 'Life Beyond Trauma' conference. It was focused on helping survivors overcome traumatic experiences that were keeping them from doing the things they needed to do or from making the right choices they needed to make."

As Trevor spoke, Erin, Melissa, Claire, and Dillard sat at the patio table on the deck, listening intently. Thomas Wayne and Edward stood along the deck's railing.

"I remember the weeks of preparing my message. I contemplated over and over what I would say to individuals who had experience some sort of sexual trauma," Trevor paused, and then continued, "I started to think more and more about that horrible thing that had happened to me as a boy. I realized that it was time to share my personal story."

Amid his cousins' visible facial expressions were widened eyelids and raised eyebrows, following by a cascaded of frowns.

Trevor exhaled heavily as if reluctant to continue, "In the weeks leading up to the event, I had written what I believed would be an inspiring message detailing something I thought I had come to terms with in my life. But, when that day actually arrived, I told myself that I just wasn't ready to talk about it publically."

"So... what did you do?" Erin asked.

"There were several speakers ahead of me, some of whom were therapists and support providers talking about dissociative identity disorder and post traumatic stress disorder (PTSD), topics that I knew absolutely nothing about," Trevor said, as he reached for a bottle of water on the table. "As I sat, listening to individuals telling their stories of survival from the trauma of experiences such as incest, sexual abuse, and rape, I was the one who was inspired to be openly honest about what had happened to me. Their strength and courage to talk about things that had happened to them, their constant struggles, and the toll of those things on their lives and relationships, was a relief for me. I didn't have to fear judgment."

"Relief from what?" Melissa asked.

"For the first time, I didn't feel shame. I didn't feel isolated and alone. I was among people who had experienced my same horror, had found their support for recovery, and were leading extraordinary lives. When my turn to speak came, I couldn't help but share my horror."

"What did you say?" Erin asked.

Trevor felt that it was the right time to be transparent with his cousins. He knew that sharing his story would be a catalyst for helping them to let go of the personal pain they had been carrying inside for so long.

Trevor didn't want to reveal the name of the relative who had violated him. As he spoke to his cousins, he visualized images of laying asleep on a sofa and awakening to a man kneeling beside him, the man unzipping his pants, and then quickly placing his hand on Trevor's private parts. On that particular day, his mother had left him with one of her sisters while she had gone to the grocery store. He had been sick, and his aunt was supposed to care for him, but she had left him in the house alone while she was outside watching her kids play. Trevor remembered how he had abruptly jumped off the sofa and had run toward the front door to get outside the house. He never told anyone what the man, his uncle, did to him. Trevor was careful not to reveal the graphic details he had shared at the conference.

"I remember that message as though I said it yesterday", Trevor said softly. "For twenty years of my life revolved around eating everything that comforted me, drinking alcohol to the point I would black out, and having sex with every woman I met. Then, a few years ago, I reached a point in my life where it was time to face reality—and that was the fact that I was relying on food, alcohol, and sex as a cover-up, a cover-up of something that happened in my life that I didn't want to face or accept. Food provided me with a sense of power to help overcome my emotions, thoughts, and feelings of shame, blame, fear, resentment, and anger. It was that something I could control: I could eat what I wanted, when I wanted, and how much I wanted. Alcohol helped me to forget, and an active sex life was supposed to remind me that I was normal."

Trevor admitted to his cousins that he knew that if he was going to have a chance at emerging from a state of emotional dependency on food, alcohol, and sex, then he had to make some changes in his life, but first he had to address and reconcile the reasons for his behavior.

"What about the thoughts of suicide?" Melissa asked.

"At that point in my life, I was tired. Like I said earlier, I was tired of being fat and being subjected to a revolving door of unhealthy relationships with women who just wanted to use me for financial reasons. They didn't see me for anything but a cash machine. And I thought that was all I was worthy of. I needed them to validate my manhood, and I knew I had to pay in some way for that validation," Trevor paused. "I was so tired of always being in financial distress. I was tired of the thing that happened to me as a child that still haunted me. I was simply tired of being tired. Periodically, my thoughts would wander to the possibility of ending it all to be free."

"So, let me get this straight," Edward said. "You've been with a man?"

Erin became angered by Edward's question, "Your problem is that you don't know how to slam on the brakes."

"I know that's right," Dillard agreed.

"I knew he was one of those faggots, down low brothers —" Edward whispered to Thomas Wayne. He stood up and said, "I need a drink. Anyone else need a beer?"

"Mix me some Patron and orange juice," Thomas Wayne responded.

Edward walked into the kitchen.

Trevor stood up and said, "I only shared my story with you to help you face your reality and be released from your inner demons. I realized that I could not escape and live oblivious to what had happened to me. It was better for me to look beyond the horror and to see the blessings of growth, helpfulness, and maturity that inevitably evolved in myself and has blessed others. I now know that God permits the most hideous acts to come into our lives for His purpose."

Edward walked back into the room with his beer and Thomas Wayne's drink.

Trevor refocused his cousins on the exercise. He encouraged them to use their weekend together for a time to remember, forgive, and free themselves from their haunting pasts.

Chapter 9

Confessions from the Heart

An hour had passed. It was now time for the cousins to share. Trevor started searching for their whereabouts. He walked around the outside perimeter of the lake house. He saw Dillard sitting on the deck, writing. He went around to the side of the house to enter from the front door. He started to look around for the others. Erin and Melissa had retreated to the bedrooms where they had slept the night before. Thomas Wayne sat at the bar in the kitchen staring at his drink. Claire was reclined in the lazy boy chair in the living room area, and Edward was in the entertainment room playing pool.

Trevor gathered everyone together. He asked who wanted to be the first to share with the group.

Edward interrupted and said, "Y'all, in the entertainment room, there is a huge safe in the back of a closest. I'm thinking Uncle Bert has a lot of money and drugs in it. Let's break it open and find out."

"What are you doing all in his closet?" Erin asked.

Thomas Wayne's eyes widened thinking about the possibility that Edward's prediction may be true.

"Man, you are CRAZY!" Dillard shouted.

"That has to be the dumbest thing you've said this whole trip," Erin yelled.

"I'm curious to know what's inside it," Edward said while laughing.

"Whatever is inside, it's none of our business," Trevor said. "Now who wants to go first?"

Melissa volunteered to go first. She sat on the floor, looking down at her paper, and said, "When I was around fifteen, I told my mother about something horrible that had happened to me. She never believed me and accused me of inventing the story to get attention. She thought I was mad at her for not coming to my track meet."

Trevor looked at her and asked, "What did you tell her?"

"Earlier that day I was in a track meet, and I won two trophies. Although I was upset that she didn't come to my school, I was very excited and wanted to share my excitement with her. When I got home, she said she was going to Perry's Liquor Store on Wayside to buy some liquor. That meant she would be gone for a while. She didn't even have time to look at my trophies."

Dillard looked at her and said, "That was their spot for buying liquor."

Melissa continued, "She left me and Jason at home alone. He was asleep in our mom's room, and I was in my room next to the bathroom that separated my bedroom and my mom's bedroom. I remember being so tired from the excitement that I got in bed and must have fallen fast asleep. While I was asleep, someone jumped on my back, then a hand went over my mouth just as I was about to scream."

Claire, Trevor, and Edward vaguely remembered hearing their parents discussing the incident. Dillard, Erin, and Thomas Wayne were younger and not aware of what had happened. Everyone listened intently to Melissa.

"I remember the guy trying to pull my pants down as I fought. Then he hit me with his fist in my face. He told me that if I didn't cooperate he would kill my li'l brother," Melissa said, as she wiped tears from her eyes. "At that moment, all I could think about was Jason so I gave in. I can't remember the actual act, because I blocked that part out. But I remember him throwing me in the closet and saying that if I told anyone he would kill Jason."

"How long were you in the closet," Claire asked.

"I can't remember how long I was in the closet. I just remember hearing the door slam and running to check on Jason. He was sound asleep."

"Who did you tell?" Dillard asked.

"I called Aunt Helen. She came to get me and Jason," Melissa answered. She turned to look at Claire and said, "I don't know if you remember."

"I knew something had happened when my mom called me at work and told me to come home to stay with Jason while she took you to the hospital."

"It was daylight when my mom came to get me," Melissa said, ashamed.

"Who raped you?" Erin asked.

"It was Tammy's ex-boyfriend that lived across the street," she said.

Tammy was Melissa's older sister. She was in high school and four years older than Melissa.

"The football star at Kashmere Heights High School?" Thomas Wayne questioned.

"Yes, he had been over our house many times when my mom was there, but that day he broke into the house through the back door."

Claire sat quietly listening to Melissa share her story. She remembered her mother calling her at work to tell her what had happened to Melissa.

"What happened at the hospital?" Erin asked.

"The hospital is a blur," Melissa responded quickly. "I just remember being questioned by the police and going to court to relive the moment all over again."

"There was a lot of animosity toward you and your family because of the accusations," Trevor pointed out.

"I know. It was one of the most humiliating things I have ever endured," Melissa said. "It was as if his attorney accused me of asking to be raped. All I could think of was how do you ask your sister's ex-boyfriend to break into your house, beat you up, and rape you."

"What happened to him?" Dillard asked.

"He received four years in jail," Melissa said. "After that, my life went down and I didn't care about anything, not even running track. I made up in my mind that I would not depend on anyone. When I turned sixteen, I got a job at Pizza Hut just to be away from home."

Edward thought about how Melissa had started selling drugs to make more money. She would save her money and place it under her mattress. The all A student started doing poorly in school, and he had to help her pass her classes.

"I hated my mother for more reasons than me getting raped. I knew I couldn't depend on her because she stayed drunk and high most of the time."

"Is that why you moved to California?" Erin asked.

"Absolutely! Me and mother got into an altercation the summer before my junior year," Melissa admitted. "I took the money I had saved and bought a plane ticket to Los Angeles. I stayed with my dad's sister."

Melissa mentioned asking Claire's mom, Helen, to let her live with them, but she was told no.

"How has your life been impacted," Trevor asked.

"I have spent most of my life secluded inside myself with very little expectation and my guard up," Melissa shared. "I didn't want to let anyone in and ran anyone off who got too close. Needless to say, healthy relationships for me have been non-existent. I've been married and divorced twice, first at eighteen and again at twenty-four. The last marriage resulted in me having to live in a homeless shelter with my kids."

Melissa talked about how she reluctantly returned to Houston after she graduated from high school in Los Angeles. He knew her sister's ex-boyfriend would be getting out of jail.

"Plus, I had blocked out so much of my life. Sometimes it feels like I have three lives: The good times at Grandma Saddie's house, the bad time being raped, and the ugliness that leaves me scarred."

"I still can't get over the fact that you were homeless," Dillard said.

Everyone frowned with disturbed looks on their faces.

"Do you ever think about getting therapy?" Trevor asked.

"No, I just settled it in my mind that back then I didn't ask for that to happen to me, but it did, so oh, well; that's part of my life, and I can be a victim or I can just move on. Shit happens."

"I don't know if it's that shits happens or if it's that life happens. I'll have more to say about that later," Trevor paused and asked, "Okay, who's willing to go next?"

"I will."

They turned and looked at Thomas Wayne.

He picked up his glass and took a sip.

"Need a refresher li'l brother?" Edward asked. "Don't be airing our dirty laundry."

Thomas Wayne ignored Edward and started to talk.

"Whenever me and my five sisters and brothers came home from school, our mother would greet us at the front door with a kiss on the cheek. Then, one day we came home and she wasn't there," Thomas Wayne said sadly.

Thomas Wayne talked about how for weeks they would ask their father about the whereabouts of their mother and when she was coming back home. At the time, Thomas Wayne was eight, Edward was ten, and their other four siblings ranged in age from 6 months to six years old.

"I could never understand how such a loving, compassionate, and funny person could just up and leave her kids," Thomas Wayne said.

Trevor and his cousins vividly remembered their Aunt Lucille. She was a stay-at-home mom who occasionally worked for temporary agencies performing odd jobs. During the holiday get-togethers, they remembered how she picked them up from school in her station wagon when it rained.

Unknown to their cousins was the routine beatings Edward and Thomas Wayne's mother suffered. The ongoing physical abuse by her husband caused their mother, Lucille, to flee to Manchester, New Hampshire to live with her father.

"How has not growing up with your mom impacted your life?" Trevor asked.

"Dad married about four different times, trying to find the right woman to care for his six kids. What we really missed out on was love and affection. Dad was always gone, working excessive hours in the steel mill to support us. I imagine six young kids for any woman was too overwhelming," Thomas Wayne reasoned. "Especially if they weren't her own kids."

"We didn't have someone to hug us and tuck us in nightly like you did, Trevor," Edward commented.

"The only person I remember hugging me was my first girlfriend Margaret," Thomas Wayne said. "Most of my girlfriends would leave me because I was too clingy and needy. The first person who really taught me about love is my wife, Joanna. That's why I'll do whatever is necessary to keep her happy."

Edward remained silent. He was old enough to remember how his dad had accused their mom of cheating on him and threatened her if she left him. He witnessed the fights in their bedroom that left their mom visibly bruised the next day.

Edward blamed his mother for leaving them and not being able to stand up to their father.

Thomas Wayne shared, "I feel like we were denied the healthy home life most kids get to experience; the attention, affection, and support of a mom, a mother who got us ready for church and helps us with our Christmas and Easter speeches. Every time there was a knock at the door, I'd run to see if it was her. I look at my wife and how she has loved our kids through the years, how she made a big deal over something they drew in school, As and Bs on their report cards, their first crush, their disappointments, their scrapes and scratches, making sure they have on the right outfit for some outing, how she encourages them when they get Cs, our dinners together, the way she interacts with our children at the dinner table, things I never experienced. I love my wife for showing me those things I missed as a child. I was robbed of all of that!"

Trevor could see that Thomas Wayne was in a lot of pain, so much pain that Thomas Wayne didn't see it.

"What about your siblings? How are they?" Trevor asked.

"Our other sisters and brothers are seemingly okay. They were pretty young when Mom left. They didn't have a bond with her like me and Edward," Thomas Wayne said. "They are productive citizens with fairly stable relationships and normal lives."

Edward was in denial about how their mother's absence had affected him. He had a history of unhealthy relationships because of his need to control, intimidate, and often belittle. He dismissed the tension he'd felt as a boy when their mom drove into their driveway and their father was waiting for her to come inside. Back then, he knew he was minutes away from witnessing another physical altercation.

"When's the last time you saw Aunt Lucille?" Trevor asked.

"Me and my family went to Manchester last year. Mom lives in an assisted living center and doesn't get around very well," Thomas Wayne said. "I try and go every couple of years. I want my kids to know their grandmother."

There was an extended silence.

"Okay, who is next?" Trevor asked.

"My childhood was great," Claire admitted, "but when I found out that the man who had raised me as his daughter was not my biological father, I was devastated."

"Didn't you find a letter in your father's lock box?" Trevor asked.

"Yes, I was looking for some additional insurance papers after my father's death, or the person who I thought was my father, and stumbled across a letter," Claire said.

"What did the letter say?" Erin inquired.

"The letter was partially sealed and addressed from my mom to an Alfred Masters. As I was looking at the letter, I thought *'I should give this to Mom,'* but something inside of me said it was okay for me to open it," Claire said. "When I opened the letter, it read something like 'Alfred, I can't see you anymore. Our relationship was a mistake from the start and I deeply regret it. Although I love you very much, I know Matthew loves me more than you ever could. Despite all, he still wants to spend the rest of his life with me. Matthew knows the child I'm carrying is not his child. He's willing to forgive me and raise the child as his own. I know you will never leave your wife for me and our child. This way, your wife and no one else will never know about our affair. But, if I'm wrong about you not leaving your wife, please let me know.' "

Tears started to stream down Claire's face.

Claire's mother told her about Alfred Masters, a guy she met while working as an executive assistant for a politician. She and Alfred Masters, a city councilman, started having an affair, and months later she became pregnant. At the time, Claire's mom was unaware that her husband couldn't have children due an accident in the military. When she announced that she was pregnant, he knew the child wasn't his child. Rather than leave her, Matthew forgave Helen and raised Claire as his own.

"How did your father find the letter?" Melissa asked.

"According to my mother, she wrote the letter and had planned to give it to Alfred Masters during a final meeting. One morning, she had the envelope that had the letter inside and some other mailings in her car. She was getting ready to drive off and remembered she had forgotten something in the house. She went inside. While in the house, Dad asked her about a bill, and she told him it was in the car. Well, he went to the car and saw the letter addressed to Alfred Masters in the midst of the mailings. He opened the envelope and read it."

Claire's mother told her how hurt her dad was after reading the letter. She pleaded with him not to leave her. He demanded that Claire's mom call Alfred Masters right then to end their relationship. Her dad told her mom that he was keeping the letter, and if she ever had anything to do with Alfred Masters, he would leave her. Her mom told her how her dad made her quit her job and never really trusted her again. And because the letter wasn't sent, Alfred Masters never knew she was carrying his daughter.

"How old were you when Uncle Matthew died?" Dillard asked.

"I was twenty and in my second year of college," Claire answered. "I remember going downstairs to show my mother the letter. She looked at me and cried and cried."

"Do you know anything about Alfred Masters? Have you ever tried to find him?" Dillard asked.

"I did Google him and found that he had died some years earlier from stomach cancer," Claire said sadly. "He was twenty years older than my mom."

"Wow!" Edward added. "You really don't know who you are."

Dismissing Edward's comment, Trevor asked, "So, what's your relationship with your mom?"

"It's strained. I just feel like they should have told me about my biological father."

"Okay, who's next?" Trevor asked.

Edward looked at everyone and rolled his eyes.

Claire looked around the room and continued, "Now I'm thinking that all of the medical problems I'm having are somehow associated with my biological dad. The researchers haven't directly pinpointed what causes Crohn's disease, but it's an inflammatory bowel disease, and about 20 percent of people with Crohn's disease have a blood relative with some form of inflammatory bowel disease, most often a brother or sister, and sometimes a parent or child. And I haven't found anyone on our mother's side of the family with an inflammatory bowel disease."

"How did you find out you had Crohn's disease," Melissa asked.

"I started getting sick in October 2008 with diarrhea, abdominal cramping, fever—I thought it was a bug of some sort so I didn't go to the doctor right away. Within a few weeks, I was going to the bathroom more than twenty times a day, was losing weight, had joint aches, and I was very weak from dehydration. I went to see my primary care physician in late November of 2008. She put me in the hospital. I was under the care of a hospitalist, and he just gave me high-powered drugs and IV fluids."

"Sounds like a bad case of diarrhea to me," Edward mumbled. He yawned while looking over at Thomas Wayne, and placed his right hand over his mouth to signal boredom.

Thomas Wayne frowned at Edward with irritation.

"What is a hospitalist?" Erin asked.

"It's my understanding that physicians use hospitalists to care for their patients when they visit emergency rooms or are admitted to the hospital. My hospitalist communicated back and forth with my primary care physician and mainly handled my care during my time spent in the hospital."

"What were those medicines for?" Thomas Wayne asked.

"They were antibiotics used to treat bacteria in my body," Claire responded. "I stayed in the hospital for a week, but never saw a gastrointestinal (GI) doctor. I developed a rash that came back positive for Sweet's Syndrome."

"What is that?" Erin asked.

"Sweet's Syndrome is associated with Leukemia and Crohn's. I'm sorry, I know this is not a part of Trevor's exercise. But, it's weighing on my heart to finally talk about it all."

"No, go ahead," Trevor said. "I'm sure everyone is as curious as I am."

Claire went on to explain the progression of her ailments and her doctor's attempts for resolution.

"What is pancreatitis?" Melissa asked.

"Who cares?" Edward shouted.

"Shut up, Edward!" Dillard said loudly.

"I will shut up, stupid, when all this nonsense is over."

"Come on guys, enough is enough. Listen," Trevor said. He was visibly having a hard time staying calm. "Please continue, Claire."

"Pancreatitis is an inflammation in the pancreas," she responded.

Trevor talked about how the pancreas is a long, flat gland that is located behind the stomach in the upper abdomen. "It produces enzymes that help digestion and hormones that help regulate the way our bodies processes sugar (glucose)."

Claire explained that Remicade was a treatment process that helped to control the symptoms and flares of Crohn's disease.

"I've seen TV commercials for Remicade," Erin said. "What is it for?"

"After a few infusions of Remicade, I finally started getting back to normal. Unfortunately, five weeks later I was back to having twenty bowel movements a day. Remicade is normally given every eight weeks. So, for the last year, I've been going through this with being fairly normal for four weeks after the infusions and then sick for four weeks. I've averaged a week-long hospital stay about every three months. They upped the dose of Remicade and started giving it to me for six weeks along with other medicines."

Trevor could tell that Claire was becoming emotional. He interjected, "I know Claire has had a rough two years, but her condition is somewhat stabilized on medicines. I don't want her to focus on the past. She has a long future ahead of her, and that's what we're going to focus on," Trevor paused and asked, "Dillard? Erin? Are you going to share with the group?"

They bowed their heads.

Trevor stood up, sat on top of the patio table, and said, "I just want to thank you all who have opened up and were honest about those devastating and traumatic events in your lives. It's important for all of us to understand that what God has permitted to happen in our lives is not without purpose. I know that my horrifying experience left me devastated, frightened, and feeling alone, but it was for a purpose, a purpose I had to come to understand. Now, when I conduct talks about living healthy, I can relate to the ugliness people may have encountered in their personal lives. I have a testimony of what God permitted to happen to me, how it changed my life, and how God is using me and the ugliness of my experience to make a difference in the lives of others."

Erin looked up and said, "I don't think any of you have experienced the sort of trauma, devastation, and ugliness of me and my brother."

Dillard nodded his head in agreement.

Erin told them, "From what I remember, for a brief moment in our early childhood, we had a wonderful time. We lived in Kashmere Heights with two loving parents. They took us to church and on family outings. On the weekends, we would pile into the back of Dad's pickup truck and they would take us to the drive-in movies. Mom would take us to the zoo and Hermann Park for picnics. I have vivid images of her laying down a blanket on a grassy area near Miller Outdoor Theater and us eating fried chicken, potato salad, and drinking red Kool-Aid. After school, we would play kickball with the other neighborhood kids well into the evening. Then, one day, something happened, and our lives have never been the same."

Dillard added, "Trevor, I admit that what happened to you was horrible, as well as with Melissa. And Claire, I know you would have wanted to know the truth about your life. But you had two people who loved you immensely for twenty years. And you still have your mother."

"My brother is right," Erin said. "I wouldn't wish the life we had on my worse enemy."

"I definitely can't imagine what purpose God had in mind for me and my sister," Dillard pointed out.

Trevor thought back to the day Erin and Dillard were talking about. He was in the car with his mother and Grandma Saddie going to the grocery store. His mother and grandmother saw what appeared to be police cars and ambulances responding to an emergency in their neighborhood. They decided to follow them. Minutes later, they were traveling on a familiar street, Manor Drive. It was the street where Trevor's Aunt Ruby lived with her husband Milton and their children, Milton Jr., Dillard, and Erin. From a distance, they saw the police and medical personnel exiting their vehicles in front of Aunt Ruby's home. Trevor remembered the panic he witness from his mother and grandmother. His mother told him to stay in the car. Before they could make it to the house, a police officer stopped them. He informed them of the tragedy that had occurred inside minutes earlier.

The day before, a newly-hired social worker had visited Aunt Ruby's home to conduct a mental health assessment. Trevor's mother and grandmother had known that Aunt Ruby's behavioral patterns were questionable. She had suffered mental health problems since her childhood and was familiar with social services. But, after a recent treatment as a hospital in-patient, the psychiatrists had decided that Aunt Ruby was well enough to be discharged and could fall back into her role as a wife and stay-at-home mother.

"That day will forever be seared into my mind," Erin stated. "It was like any other day. It was a summer day, and we were outside playing. I remember our mother calling us into the house. But when we got inside, we didn't see her. She yelled out from Milton Jr.'s bedroom. Me and Dillard both went eagerly looking for her. When we got to Milton's bedroom door, we saw him lying on the bed, covered in blood. My mother had a knife in her hand, and both the knife and her hands were covered with blood. Dillard and I screamed. Next thing we knew, our mother started chasing us through the house. Even though we were seven and five, we had enough sense to know something wasn't right and that our mother intended to harm us too. We managed to get out of the screen door and ran next door to the neighbor's house."

The cousins were already familiar with the story of what had happened nearly four decades earlier, but no one ever talked about it.

"Of course, Mother spent years institutionalized in a mental hospital for killing our brother. And because Dad worked around the clock, we went to live with his parents, Grandma and Grandpa Mason. When Mother was released from the mental hospital, we couldn't see her. I guess Dad and his family was afraid she would hurt us. Then, when I was around sixteen, Dad had a heart attack and died. Then our grandparents died, and we had to go live with Dad's sister, Aunt Mildred. All I remember is how badly she and her husband treated us. We hid the bruises. We hid the scars."

Dillard interrupted, "Our mother died of a broken heart because she could not see us."

Trevor remembered the ongoing battle between the families to allow Erin and Dillard visitation with their mother.

"A few years ago, I obtained the police report of what had happened on that life-changing day," Erin said. "It revealed that our mother stabbed Milton Jr. thirty-six times with ten stab wounds to his chest. It talked about an eight-year-old boy lying in a pool of blood on a bed. It acknowledged our mother's confession of stabbing him and her reason why."

As Erin became increasingly emotional, Dillard continued, "Milton Jr. was asleep. He had been sick. He woke up with Mother standing over him. She admitted telling him to go back to sleep. Then he awoke to her stabbing him."

"What was her reason?" Melissa asked.

"She told the police officers that our father was going to sexually abuse us and that she had to kill her children to prevent it from happening," Erin said sadly.

A surprised and confused look consumed Trevor. He remembered lying asleep on the sofa at Erin's and Dillard's house and awakening to his uncle, their father, kneeling beside him unzipping his pants. The only person that noticed him after he ran outside was his Aunt Ruby. When she saw her husband peeking out the front door of their home, she knew something horrible had just happened to Trevor. But, she never asked Trevor nor did he say anything. From that day forward, Trevor made a point of avoiding his uncle.

"Did you ever confront your mother?" Melissa asked.

"No, it's not really something you talk about at the dinner table," Dillard chimed in. "She died when I was around sixteen. From the time she was released from the mental institution until the time she died, we were never really granted an opportunity to be with her, especially alone."

"No," Erin responded, "I was around fourteen when she was released from the mental hospital. We were only permitted to see her on special holidays for Thanksgiving and Christmas at Grandma Saddie's house. We never talked about it. I was well in my twenties when I obtained the police report. I just needed to know why that day happened."

Reconstructing the events in their lives, Erin and Dillard, on all accounts, had suffered a horrific and traumatic childhood that had left them bitter and numb of feelings. They had the memories of their brother's brutal stabbing, fear for their own lives, the confinement of their mother in a mental institution, and the harshness of family members who took them in, not because of love, but because of circumstances.

Trevor praised his cousins for sharing their stories and their secret feelings. He told them that their openness was the first step of healing. He told them that it now time for them to position themselves to move forward.

"Unfortunately, life doesn't guarantee us a childhood filled with great memories," Trevor stated. "I don't know if you all have heard the phrase that life is a journey, not a destination, well, that life begins with our birth. If all falls in line with what has been deemed normal; a two-parent household where the parents fulfill their role to protect, provide, love, and nurture their children, where parents raise their children to be productive, to be emotionally and mentally healthy, and to be self-assured adults with personal strength and values. Then, we should follow the normal steps of progression in life; getting a good education, a good job, marriage, and a family. Clearly, that didn't happen in our family. Our journeys have included the dismantled roads called devastation, trauma, fear, and pain. If you assess your actions, reactions, and choices in real time like I did, you'll admit that it's time to extricate yourself."

"Extricate? What!?" Edward shouted.

"Basically, it's time to free yourself and chart a new path," Trevor said. "Just think for a moment. If you died today, what would you want most to be remembered for? The fact that you never got over being raped as a young girl? The fact that you never got over your mother leaving you? The fact that the man who raised you was not your biological father? The fact that you never got over knowing that your mother killed your brother?"

Trevor looked intensely at each one of his cousins and continued, "Don't you want your life to count for something? Don't you want to leave your family with a legacy to follow? There is meaning and purpose behind what happened to all of us." Trevor paused. "There is some young girl right now being raped. There is some child whose mother has abandoned him or her. There is some child who has witnessed the murder of a loved one. They need to hear your story of healing and deliverance. But, if you continue to hold on to the past, you'll never be able to share your story and help someone move beyond their pain."

His cousins stared intensely back at him.

"I had to jump off that 'Road to nowhere'. I was tired of being in pain. I had to focus on moving my life in a different direction. Life is about choices. You have the power to choose good, bad, happy, or sad. It's you who gets to choose for yourself whether you're going to pursue happiness, fulfillment, and purpose, despite what has happened to you."

Edward said loudly, "I'm sure your little exercise was supposed to have some purpose. Unfortunately, I haven't figured out what it is, yet. Look at y'all. Trevor has all of you looking crazy as usual."

Everyone sat silent staring in deep thought.

Trevor left his cousins in the living room after giving them an idea of the final exercise on Sunday, their last day together. His next exercise would be focused on adding meaning to their life.

❖

Chapter 10

❖

The Gift of Tragedy

Trevor was the first to enter the kitchen area. He had decided to cook a breakfast item that he had heard of from one of his chef friends, the "Easy Egg White and Salmon Breakfast Frittata." After he turned on the oven to preheat it to 375 degrees, he took eight eggs out of the refrigerator. He then took a small bowl out of the cabinet to use to separate out the egg yolks. He carefully cracked and opened the egg over the small bowl. He was focused on keeping the contents of the egg yolk inside one half of the shell. He remembered how Grandma Saddie taught him how to transfer the yolk back and forth between the two shell halves, while the egg white dripped into the bowl. Then, he took a cutting board and chopped up one-fourth cup of green onion and one-fourth teaspoon of fresh, minced garlic. He opened the can of salmon and drained the juice over the kitchen sink. In the bowl with the egg whites, he added the drained salmon, chopped onions, and garlic. He added the mixture to a non-stick sauté pan and placed it in the oven.

His cousins entered the kitchen area and inquired about what he was cooking, as he was preparing to sauté some fresh spinach.

"What's in the oven, cousin?" Thomas Wayne asked.

"It's a dish I got from a chef friend. An Easy Egg White and Salmon Breakfast Frittata," Trevor responded.

"Egg whites?" Edward shouted. "Boy, you better pull out that pan of sausage and cook 'em with some eggs with the yolks intact."

Edward's comment generated laughter throughout the kitchen.

"On our last day together, I was hoping that you all would try something different."

Trevor began to explain the importance of food for helping them to live well and live longer. By making better choices, they could prevent, eliminate, or reduce their risk of the inevitable penalties for unhealthy lifestyle choices.

"Grandma Saddie died from the complications of diabetes. She battled the disease for most of her adult life, and her refusal to change unhealthy lifestyle habits led to the removal of her right toe and eventually the amputation her right leg. Among a variety of health ailments, you all know that cataracts led to her blindness. She died of a heart attack, which was a consequence of the diabetes. She just couldn't commit to making the necessary adjustments because of her love for food, especially sweets and carbs."

"Aren't you the voice of early morning gloom," Melissa said.

"Just stating the facts. And I want you all to be clear about where you'll eventually end up if some things don't change," Trevor stressed. "And then there was Uncle Buster who had a massive heart attack. But long before the heart attack, he had high blood pressure and high cholesterol. He loved his hard salami, premium pork sausage, and smoked turkey legs."

Thomas Wayne thought about his high blood pressure and the effect of the medication on his sex drive. He had been working with his doctor on switching medications because of his inability to get an erection.

Trevor continued, "Our family has a predisposition for heart disease and diabetes. But, we can offset their entry into our lives or minimize the impact with better eating habits."

"You're beginning to sound like an old, scratched record, repeating the same things over and over and over," Edward said. "Frankly, I'm not giving up my whole milk, my white bread, my honey buns, my fried chicken, my French fries, my Blue Bell ice cream, my liquor, or anything else I like to eat. Despite what Erin says, I know 'Thunder Thighs' isn't either."

Erin rolled her eyes at Edward's comment.

"Edward, I care about all of you. My only intent is to share information with you that will, number one, help you to fulfill Uncle Bert's stipulations, and, number two, will help you to live a life of meaning and purpose."

"Now that I know my biological father died from stomach cancer, I just may be predisposed for the same," Claire said, "especially with my diagnosis of Crohn's Disease."

All of Trevor's cousin ate the breakfast he had prepared, except for Edward. Edward pulled out a honey bun and ate it with a pint of whole milk.

For the final exercise, Trevor simply asked the question, "What do you dream about?"

They looked at Trevor, puzzled.

"You do not have to publicly share your dream. But I want you to ask yourself the question 'What do I dream about.' Regardless of how impossible you think it is, what do you dream about. That is, what is your ultimate desire—something you think about with much passion, much emotion? Those ideas, hopes, and aspirations that sparked much enthusiasm."

They were sitting around the coffee table in the living room, with their heads bowed in deep thought.

"Man, what sort of stupid game are we playing now?" Edward asked.

Trevor ignored Edward and said, "I know that God has given each and every one of you something that you dream about. Maybe you haven't recognized what He has shown you. Or, maybe you think it's too outrageous for you to consider, so you've never attempted to pursue it. Or, you did pursue it, but nothing ever resulted from your pursuits."

"You know what I dream about?" Edward asked.

"What Edward?" Melissa asked.

"Getting with Halle Berry!" He laughed with great amusement. "Now that's something to dream about."

They all shook their heads with annoyance.

Trevor talked to his cousins about having the courage to act upon their dreams. He wanted to lead them to the mindset of Uncle Bert. He explained the next exercise. It would require them to write down their dream.

"I know when I was a kid, I dreamed about owning a business," Trevor said.

"Yeah, and you tried owning a janitorial service and a desktop publishing service. Then, you went to school for real estate," Melissa recounted. "I think you even talked about having a funeral home."

Trevor's cousins started laughing.

"You're right, all while working as an engineer. I tried a number of things, because I knew early on that I wanted to be in business," Trevor stressed. "And my dream for that continuously inspired me to keep working toward my ultimate desire. Even when others made fun of my numerous attempts, I didn't let them distract me."

"Well, I dream of owning a Maserati GranTurismo Convertible," Thomas Wayne said.

"Yeah, right! You can't afford that Caddy you're driving," Edward said with sarcasm. "Borrowing from everybody in town."

"Come on, guys. I want you all to think about your dreams, whether it's to own a business, to drive a fancy car, to get your house fixed up, to share a message. Today's exercise will be focused on making your dreams a reality and adding meaning to your life. If you die a month from now, what would you want most to be remembered for?"

They all talked about the dreams they'd had as children—to be a doctor, a lawyer, and to have a family and live in a big home and drive nice cars. They admitted how they had stopped thinking about and believing in their dreams. The reality of the twists and turns in their lives made their dreams become something unreal. Although they had achieved certain things in their lives, those were viewed as attainable and hadn't provided much difficulty or discomfort. They were safe.

"Aside from the days of sketching out my funeral home business or trying to drum up business for the desktop publishing business or janitorial service, I knew I wanted to help people. I basically pursued those ventures with the intent of making money, and lots of it. But, my mind was always clear on helping people."

Trevor wanted his cousins to focus on the dreams their minds had explored and why they were reluctant to pursue them in real life. He reinforced over and over that they needed to find out and realize why they did not believe in their dream. Was it because too much effort was involved? Did they doubt their ability to accomplish it? He knew that Uncle Bert was looking for his cousins to exhibit belief, to possess the power to take action, to develop a state of conviction, and to work hard on making something a success.

"You don't need to share your particular dream with the group, but in an hour or so, I do want you to share how you want your life to be different after this weekend. The ultimate goal: to create your plan for pursuing the life of your dreams," Trevor said.

Trevor dismissed his cousins, and they all retreated to their favorite areas at the lake house.

At the appointment time, everyone reported back to the living room area.

Melissa told them, "For so long, I've settled with having low-paying clerical jobs, and doing so has left me frustrated with what I've achieved in life, which is virtually nothing! Now that I finally have an opportunity to be an accounting clerk, I know I want to be an accountant."

"Then there's the bipolar boss," Edward said, smiling.

"I've always liked working with numbers, and I've wanted to be an accountant since I can remember, but I never thought I was smart enough. So, at the age of forty-six, I've gotten up the nerve to go back to school. I've enrolled in the community college this fall," Melissa shared. "And I'm hoping that my decision to go back to school will influence my kids to do so. I must admit that I wasn't a good example for them to follow. They saw me switching jobs left and right for a few extra pennies and never exhibiting any stability. Now *they* are pretty much doing the same."

Dillard and Erin praised Melissa for her decision.

Trevor reiterated, "Melissa has reached that turning point in her life, where her frustration has finally provoked her to assess her life and make a decision to do something different. And that is my desire for all of you. She doesn't want to play it safe anymore."

"I don't have any dreams," Dillard announced.

"I share the same sentiments as my brother," Erin said.

Trevor paused and commented, "Well, if you don't have any dreams, then it's time to make some. You can't make a difference in your life and in the life of others without purpose. And purpose is often generated through your dreams, your desires, your passion."

It was Trevor's thought that the best way they could add meaning to their lives was to view their past memories and experiences, bad and good, as assets.

It was five o'clock on a Sunday afternoon, and their time together was officially over. Trevor told his cousins to be on the lookout for his emails. For the next six months, they would be spending an enormous amount of time with one another. He further reiterated Uncle Bert's stipulations. They would have to demonstrate a commitment to change and demonstrate a noticeably tangible decision to direct their lives along a path that was motivated by purpose.

❖

Chapter 11

❖

Personal Effects

For nearly two weeks after their retreat, Trevor sent daily health and fitness tips to keep their minds focused on living healthier and with purpose. The lack of response to his follow-up emails prompted him to send a certified letter to each of their homes.

He was wondering if the messages were having any sort of impact.

"I thought we were going to spend quality time together this evening," Jenny said, as she sat next to Trevor. "What are you doing now?"

He was deep in thought, writing an email on his tablet computer.

"Don't you think you've bombarded them with enough?" Jenny asked.

"You have to keep the goal in front of people," Trevor responded. "Come on now; you're distracting me."

She threw her arm around his neck and said, "Give them a break, Trevor. I know what you're trying to do. Inspiration is great. Motivation is great. But timing is everything."

"Shhh! I'm trying to write."

She let go of Trevor and turned on the TV.

He looked at her and said, "Okay, I guess the fact that I'm trying to concentrate on something doesn't mean anything to you?"

"Whatever!" she snapped and abruptly stood up. "I'm going to get a glass of wine."

He gently grabbed her arm.

"I'm sorry, Jenny."

He kissed her, passionately. She was miffed but eventually responded.

"Babe, let me read to you what I'm saying to them."

They both sat down.

In the letter, the message was the same, "In today's society, our ability to live a striving life and to experience God's best is often in competition with all of the choices and opportunities we are faced with daily."

"Stopped!" she looked over at Trevor. "Stop the preaching. Leave that to Pastor Gideon. They've got it. Send them some of those tips you tweeted the other day. That's want they need."

"Can I finish?"

"No!"

Trevor ignored Jenny and continued, "We are pulled in dozens of directions, and it's hard to focus our attention on what should matter most in our lives—God and our health! Most often it's because our lives are plagued with so much discord, conflict, and chaos (and that can be between others or ourselves) that we are unable to pursue the sort of life that God would like for us to experience with passion and enthusiasm. There are so many things that we allow to take the steering wheel from us and drive us in a direction contrary to what we really need and most often want. And, more than likely, we end up at a place where we're burdened and overwhelmed. This will impact the way we think, feel, and act."

Jenny got up and walked into the kitchen.

Trevor paused and continued, "Our Uncle Bert wants to throw you a life-line. All you need to do is exhibit to him that you're worthy of him handing over his business to you."

He decided to insert another version of his own personal testimony in the letter and said, "I realized many years ago that I have choices. I had a choice of whether I allowed shame, blame, anger, and pain to take over my life. I had a choice of whether I allowed bad spending habits to keep me buried in debt. I had a choice of whether I'd allow the pain of my pain to keep me from pursuing my purpose."

"Please stop," Jenny walked back in with a glass of wine.

Trevor looked up at her and said, "I have plenty more."

"I'm sure you do."

He smiled.

"Just send them that information you tweeted about portion sizes. A three-ounce serving of meat looks like a deck of cards; a three-ounce serving of fish looks like a checkbook; one serving of fruits or vegetables looks like a baseball; one-half cup of rice or pasta looks like half of a tennis ball. That's what they need along with everyone else. People simply do not have a grasp on accurate portion sizes. That's why they continue to overeat and gain more and more weight."

He pulled her close and kissed her insistently.

A few days later the telephone calls started coming in, but not for the reason Trevor had hoped.

The first telephone call was from Melissa, "Hi, Trevor. Have you seen the news?" she asked.

"No, I haven't. What's going on?" Trevor asked.

"Their talking about him on every TV station," she stated.

"Talking about who?" he inquired.

"Uncle Bert!" she shouted. "The FBI is searching Uncle Bert's home!"

Another call was coming through on his cellular phone. He looked, and it was Dillard.

"Hey, man, are you looking at the news?" he asked.

"No, but I have Melissa on the other line," Trevor said. "She's telling me something about Uncle Bert and the FBI searching his home."

"Yeah, the TV is showing men in black suit taking loads of boxes out of his house."

"Let me turn on the TV," Trevor said. "I'll call you back."

Trevor started getting more and more telephone calls from his cousins. He asked them to meet him at their Grandma Saddie's house at six o'clock that evening.

Dillard and Erin were the first to arrive, and then, Edward and Thomas Wayne. Finally Melissa and Claire.

Trevor had a twenty-inch, flat-screen television sitting on a table in the center of the living room. He had the television tuned to channel thirteen. The news reporter was in front of the camera, providing an account of the FBI's presence at their uncle's home.

'FBI agents searched the home and business of State Representative Bert Spencer, District 5, of Houston, Texas this morning in connection with a public corruption investigation that has already netted three guilty pleas by three associates, authorities said. Around seven o'clock in the morning, black-suited federal agents were spotted exiting Spencer's home and business with numerous boxes containing documents. The agents loaded the boxes into five SUVs parked across from the business at I-59 and Kelley after a morning-long search.'

As the reporter continued, Trevor and his cousins were visibly disturbed listening and watching the parade of federal agents that had descended on their uncle's home and business earlier that day.

"Have you tried to call him, Trevor?" Melissa asked.

"Yes, but I received his voice mail," Trevor responded. "I believe the federal agents confiscated his cellular phone, and no one is answering his business lines."

"I wonder if they've searched his lake house," Edward commented. "I told you all there was something strange about having that huge safe in that closet."

"You all think we need to go and get the safe out of there?" Thomas Wayne questioned.

"I ain't getting nothing out of nowhere," Edward jumped up. "I got my own set of problems. I definitely ain't trying to go to jail."

"What about the business he wants us to run?" Erin asked.

"Looks like that's going to be a wash," Edward stated.

"Yeah, all that stuff he fed us about living healthy and getting our lives right was just a bunch of bologna," Erin said.

"Okay, guys, it's too soon for us to jump to any conclusions," Trevor said. "We need to try and get in touch with Uncle Bert."

"All I know is that I'm not going to fulfill some phantom stipulations for nothing," Edward said. "I was only going along with all of this for my brother."

"I'm with Edward," Erin said.

Dillard, Melissa, and Claire sat quietly.

"Did you all receive the letter I sent to you?" Trevor asked sharply.

No one responded.

"Regardless of what happens with Uncle Bert, it's time for you all to dispel the demons preventing you from living your life to the fullest. During our time together, each one of you revealed deep hurts. I was hoping that the exercises had sparked thoughts of change in your present predicaments and sparked the pursuit of better choices."

❖

Chapter 12

❖

Proactive Steps

Acouple of weeks later, Melissa called Trevor to share the lifestyle changes she had made to become healthier. She credited Trevor for planting the seed that got her to thinking about living well and longer. Now she wanted him to come and speak to her co-workers.

"Trevor, thank you so much for sending us the healthy tips. I started keeping a food journal and was amazed once I started analyzing my food consumption."

"You are so welcome."

"My daily caloric intake was averaging 4,110 between the cheeseburgers, fries, sodas, mocha grande, blueberry muffins, spaghetti dinners, candy bars, and a pint of ice cream."

"Wow!"

"I'm trying to get my co-workers motivated about implementing healthier lifestyle habits," Melissa stressed. "I am so excited about losing ten pounds, and that was just by making simple changes. For starters, I've gone from three cans of soda to one can a day. Plus, I'm walking at the park in my neighborhood."

She wanted her co-workers to explore their options for and focus their attention on eating healthier and exercising. After sharing how small lifestyle changes had improved her blood pressure and blood cholesterol levels, she thanked Trevor.

Trevor came to her job on a Thursday during the lunch hour. Melissa introduced him to her co-workers: Valerie, the purchasing specialist, Melanie, a program manager, Carol, a courts manager, and Monica, an attorney.

"You did such an outstanding job sharing some insightful facts about living healthier at our family retreat last month that I wanted you to come and do the same for my co-workers."

"Thank you. I'm happy to be here today," Trevor acknowledged, sitting informally at a table in their training room.

"Linda, one of our co-workers in the IT department, was terminated last month. All throughout her tenure with the company, she was praised for her outstanding work and was considered one of the organization's most valuable employees," Melissa stated.

Interrupting abruptly, Carol said, "Linda has had multiple bouts with cancer over the past three years: breast, lung, and brain cancer." Carol was noticeably having a difficult time containing her emotions. "During her initial illness (breast cancer) in 2008 and her subsequent illness (lung cancer) in 2009, our organization provided the federally mandated twelve weeks of family and medical leave. Based on our leave policy, she was also provided an additional ninety days of medical leave beyond the family and medical leave. In 2010, she was diagnosed with brain cancer. Because Linda was unable to return to work after she exhausted all of her family and medical leave, she was terminated. Now, she's on COBRA, having to pay over $600 a month for her medical insurance, a cost she will not be able to continue much longer and she's still undergoing treatments."

"Linda's story is a sad and unfortunate situation, but it could happen to any one of us," Monica said, visibly worried.

"The impact of poor health on the workplace has become a major concern in organizations. That's why we're seeing more and more company-sponsored wellness programs," Trevor stated.

"Employees who are not practicing healthy lifestyle habits and who fail to meet the company halfway by taking advantage of its health programs may be risking their jobs. And I don't mean to imply that Linda's situation was the result of unhealthy lifestyle habits. We're all predisposed for disease and illness. In some cases, even when we're doing the right things, we end up facing a major illness."

"At our company, employees who are routinely sick, absent from work, or who are unable to perform their jobs at full capacity while at work are finding themselves in some precarious situations. Over the past year, I've noticed how our human resources department has revised policies that provide managers and supervisors with termination options once an employee's family and medical leave obligation has been fulfilled or when job performance is poor," Melissa commented.

"Linda was employed with our company for over fifteen years. She was a key factor in implementing and developing our IT department, and she took the agency to the next level in technology systems," Valerie stated.

"Employees are considered the backbone of the company. When an employee is unable to work, the company's ability to deliver quality programs, services, and/or products to its customers are impacted. As a consequence, the company's grant funding or profits can be at stake," Trevor stressed. "Your jobs require you to be at work every day and to operate at peak levels of mental capacity. Medical conditions such as diabetes, arthritis, hypertension, cancer, asthma, insomnia, or obesity can affect your ability to be at work every day or can severely reduce your effectiveness while at work, depending how well you manage your condition."

"That's why I'm ready to make some changes this year," Monica announced. "I know there's an increased chance I'll be in a similar situation like Linda if I don't, especially since cancer runs in my family. If there's any chance of offsetting its entrance into my life, I'm ready to do whatever is necessary."

Valerie started giggling and said, "That may mean giving up your mojitos and chocolate martinis."

Monica frowned.

"I've recently been diagnosed with diabetes," Melanie acknowledged. "I've learned that eating healthier will be paramount to the management of my condition."

"Absolutely," Trevor stated.

"My cousin had a stroke several months ago," Monica interjected. "Because she was unable to return to work after her family and medical ended, she was terminated. Unfortunately, her company didn't have short-term disability, and now she's waiting for her long-term disability to start. She is paralyzed on her left side. Meanwhile, the bill collectors are calling, and the medical bills are piling up."

"Did she have any symptoms prior to the stroke?" Melanie asked.

"I really don't know. I just know she didn't take care of herself. She had high blood pressure, high cholesterol, and diabetes. Like a lot of us, she is overweight. Plus, she smoked and suffered from severe migraines and severe depression."

Silence resonated through the room.

"It's time that people start to seriously consider their lifestyle habits and how their jobs are impacted by unhealthy habits. And it may not even be the employee with the medical condition, but a spouse, child, sibling, or parent, instead. The point is that unhealthy habits can affect your ability to be at work every day or severely reduce your effectiveness while at work, regardless of whether they are yours or those of your family members." Trevor paused, and then continued by saying, "Your best option for addressing unhealthy habits this year is to outline your strategies for developing and implementing healthier lifestyle habits, not only for yourself, but for those you're obligated to as well."

Before Trevor ended his talk, he shared some health facts with the group. "According to the Centers for Disease Control and Prevention, stroke is the third leading cause of death in the United States and the leading cause of serious, long-term disability. On average, every 40 seconds, someone in the United States has a stroke. A heart attack occurs about every 20 seconds with a heart attack death about every minute. Sudden death is more common among women having heart attacks. About 50% of deaths occur within one hour of the heart attack—outside a hospital. Lung cancer kills more men and women than any other form of cancer. We know that 8 out of 10 lung cancers are due to smoking tobacco. Breast cancer is the most common cancer in women and the second most common cause of cancer death in women in the U.S. Diabetes is the leading cause of new cases of blindness among adults aged 20–74 years. Diabetes is the leading cause of kidney failure, accounting for 44% of new cases in 2008. More than 60% of non traumatic lower-limb amputations occur in people with diabetes. Arthritis is one of the most prevalent chronic health problems and the nation's leading cause of disability among Americans over age 15. Arthritis is second only to heart disease as a cause of work disability."

"I've determined that living healthy is like driving a car. In today's society, we're trying to get to our destination as fast as we can. Have you ever seen the guy driving 80 mph down I-45 cutting everyone off to get ahead? He really can't wait to get to his destination. And, because of his urgency, he jeopardizes himself and everyone in his path. Well, there's really not much difference between him and someone who chooses the shortcut road instead of living healthy. Some will use a diet, a pill, skipping meals, or a gadget to finally get you where you want to go. Instant results, fast weight loss, and a temporary feeling of accomplishment can ultimately jeopardize your life and indirectly impact those around you," Melissa stated.

"Thank you so much, Trevor, for coming out to speak with my co-workers. I know the information you shared will motivate us to make some necessary lifestyle changes," Monica said.

Melissa walked Trevor to the entrance of their company lobby.

Trevor hugged her and said, "I'm glad I was able to share with your co-workers. Don't forget about Saturday afternoon."

Trevor had arranged for the cousins to start helping with the renovations of Grandma Saddie's house.

"I'll be there."

On a breezy Saturday morning, Claire was the first to arrive at Grandma Saddie's house. She had some information she wanted to share with Trevor before everyone else arrived.

Trevor was sweeping off the porch as Claire drove up.

"Hey, Claire, you're a little early," Trevor said, as he leaned the broom against the wall. He walked down the steps to meet her and proceeded to give Claire a hug.

"Hi, Trevor. I had something I wanted to run by you," she said, as they walked toward the steps. She sat down on the top step.

"What's up?" Trevor sat beside her.

"I am so tired, Trevor," Claire said with sadness. "I have developed another rash with red, painful nodules on my left leg, right arm, and right upper back. The stem cells program I enrolled in did nothing to help this. They did a skin biopsy, and it came back as Metastic Crohn's, so they placed me on another round of steroids. Metastatic Crohn's is very rare. I think less than 10% develop this condition. Needless to say, even though I'm tired, I know there's a purpose for it all. That's why, in a couple of months, in September, I'm going to join the Crohn's Team Challenge Program and train to walk a half-marathon. I'm so sick of being sick. I want to raise money to help find a cure for my disease."

"That's great, Claire," Trevor grabbed Claire and held her tightly. "Are you sure you're up to it?"

"I don't know, but I'm going to do it," she said. "All I can do is ask God to give me strength."

"Absolutely," Trevor said. "Maybe we can get some of the other cousins to train with you."

"That would be great."

Trevor and Claire were distracted by Erin's car. Erin and Dillard exited her car and walked up to the porch.

"Hey, guys," Dillard said, as he motioned to hug Claire.

"What are you guys talking about?" Erin asked. "Uncle Bert?"

"No, not Uncle Bert," Trevor responded.

"Have you spoken with him?" Dillard asked.

"I did speak with him the other day. He's doing fine. He's going about his business as usual. He has his attorneys lined up. The Feds are pursuing quite a bit of things. Namely, in 2004, when we had the Super Bowl game, they're saying he laid off a bunch of security officers and worked a deal where the security officers were hired by another company. Supposedly, Uncle Bert got a cut of the profits the company made from providing private security services."

"What's the big deal that he laid them off?" Dillard asked.

"Because his business couldn't provide security services. I guess it was a conflict of interest, since he was on several committees related to the Super Bowl. A smaller company was able to get the bid supposedly because of the owner's connection to Uncle Bert. They hired the workers Uncle Bert laid off to get the number of security officers needed for the bid. Then, the workers were laid off by the company and went back to work for Uncle Bert. All of that happened because of Uncle Bert, and he received a cut."

"Just crazy," Erin said, as she unfolded a chair and positioned it on the porch.

Dillard sat on the steps of the porch near Claire.

"Just a fishing expedition to bring him down," Trevor said. "Anyway, Claire just informed me that she's going to participate in a half-marathon. It's to raise money to find a cure for Crohn's Disease."

Claire smiled and said, "I'm wondering if I can get a couple of my cousins to train with me."

"Hey, look. Here comes Melissa, Thomas Wayne, and Edward," Dillard said, pointing and laughing.

"What's so funny," Edward asked, as he, Melissa, and Thomas Wayne approached them.

"Claire's talking about doing a half-marathon, and she wants a couple of us to do it with her," Erin said calmly.

"I can tell you right now what my response is—Hell no!" Edward said forcefully.

"I might consider it, but I've got too much going on at home. Having to get up at 3:00 A.M. to check Brian's blood glucose is wearing me out."

"When does the program start?" Dillard asked Claire.

"It starts in September. The half-marathon is in December here in Houston. I have to raise $2,500," Claire said.

"You don't have to say definitely today. You have a month or so to think about it," Trevor added. "Meanwhile, I'll be happy to give you some tips, Claire, and anyone else. I can get you started on a structured walk and run program that will guide you on how to build your endurance through progressively increased intensity. I know the Crohn's program will have coaches equipped to provide instructions on proper form and technique, injury prevention, resistance, and flexibility. Best of all, you will receive more valuable information on eating healthy, meal preparation, and sports nutrition."

Dillard wasn't ready to admit it to his cousins, but he needed to make some changes. His doctor had told him that he needed to lose weight, that his blood pressure wasn't improving, and that now he had prediabetes.

"First things first. You need to make sure to get fitted for the right footwear," Trevor said.

"What type will I need to get?" Claire asked.

"The type of footwear varies for everyone, depending on whether you're walking or running. If and when you get to the running stage, it's important to understand that you need a shoe specific to running. When inappropriate shoes are utilized for running, the results can be a plague of leg and foot problems. The best way to ensure that you get a running shoe that fits properly is to go to a specialty running store."

"Are running shoes very expensive?" Claire asked.

"Prices will vary. I see so many people walking and running in the wrong shoes—old tennis shoes, fashionable shoes, and recreational sports footwear. Women especially like to exercise in cute shoes that match their workout outfits. In the long run, they pay for it and have to take an extended break from exercising. If you're serious about getting started the right way, you have to go to a specialty running store. I typically go to a running store on Kirby Dr. Their shoe experts can guide you on selecting the correct walking and/or running shoe for your foot type—flat, high arched, or normal. The right shoe will offer the right motion control, cushion, flexibility, and stability for your foot type."

"What do you mean by motion control?" Dillard asked.

"Because I have flat feet, my feet tend to roll inward when I run. To control the inward motion, I need a motion-control running shoe. The motion-control shoe prevents my shoe from rolling inward. It's kind of like having a corrective shoe. The early years of running in the wrong footwear caused me to experience a series of common injuries, such as plantar fasciitis, shin splints, and knee pain."

"I didn't realize the importance of correct fitness shoes," Claire stated.

"For someone like Dillard, he'd need to concentrate on developing a structured walking program to help him lose weight. With running, each time your foot strikes the ground, you are applying a large percentage of your bodyweight in force to each leg and your spine. If you start out trying to run, your excessive body weight on the joints, tendons, and ligaments can make you more susceptible to injury."

"I'm not interested in running," Claire confirmed. "I plan on walking."

Trevor encouraged his cousins to focus on a daily walking program for at least one month. "That's good, Claire. For everyone else, one month of consistent walking coupled with sound eating habits will generate a weight loss of eight to ten pounds. Your body will be better conditioned. At that point, it will be safe to initiate a mixture of walking and running, for example: four minutes of walking with two minutes of running."

He recommended starting out on a treadmill, since it provided a soft surface. "You could workout at a gym where I train. Exercising on pavement can be extremely taxing on the body. The key is to start slowly."

He gave them some of the basic tips that helped him in beginning. His tips included exercising at least three to five days each week, why it was important to warm up for five to ten minutes before the main aerobic activity, and maintaining exercise intensity for thirty to forty-five minutes. He stressed the importance of gradually decreasing the intensity of his workout and stretching to cool down during the last five to ten minutes.

"Other than Claire, anyone interested in generating weight loss should progressively increase your minutes to sixty, striving for five days per week," he suggested. "First and foremost, visit your physician for a check-up before starting any exercise program."

"I did have a physical last month, and my doctor encouraged me to exercise," Dillard said. "I think I will join a gym downtown.

I received an advertisement on my door last week. The monthly cost of the gym is $19 per month. And, no contract! Is that a good rate?"

"That's good," Trevor acknowledged.

"I mainly want to start off on the treadmill. Are there any special considerations for the treadmill?"

"How much more are you going to talk about this? I've got things to do," Edward yawned, nodding. "I had a late night. Mr. Dreamer, I didn't get Halle Berry, but she was close enough."

"We'll get started shortly, Edward," Trevor continued, "Whether you walk outside or on a treadmill, you should walk at a pace that increases your heart rate. You can't walk at a casual pace and expect to burn calories. You have to walk at a quick pace or up an incline. Another thing—don't hold onto the rails. Holding onto the rails prevents you from maximizing your legs to do the work. Also, don't stand too close to the front of the treadmill. You will shorten your stride. Stand back and aim for a comfortable, normal stride."

While he was talking, Trevor noticed the neighbor, Mr. Whitehouse, walking up the driveway.

"I'm excited," Claire smiled, shaking her head.

"Looks like we have company," Trevor said, as he looked toward the driveway.

His cousins positioned themselves to look at what Trevor was referring to.

"Hi, Saddie's grandkids," Mr. Whitehouse was walking slowing with his oxygen tank.

Trevor stood up and started to walk toward him.

"Hi, Mr. Whitehouse," Trevor said.

"Hi, son. I saw all of the cars and thought I'd come down," he said.

"Yeah, we're here to start the renovations. Today, we're going to do some wall repair and painting."

"That's great!"

"We've got a lot to do, scraping the peeling paint, sanding, washing the walls with Trisodium phosplate (TSP) and water, spackling all of the holes, and priming," Trevor said.

"If you need any help, just let me know."

"Between the seven of us, I think we've got it, Mr. Whitehouse."

"Okay," he said. "I just get a little lonely being in the house. I get excited to see friendly faces. I never see my boys. They blame me for their mother's death, you know," he said.

"Why don't he just tell the old man to leave?" Edward muttered to Thomas Wayne. "I'll tell him if he won't."

"Just be cool, bro. Trevor will handle him."

"Don't be so insensitive, Edward," Claire said with irritation. "You need to think about someone other than yourself sometimes."

"I know that's right," Dillard chimed in.

"Shut up, fat boy," Edward lunged at Dillard.

Dillard took a deep breath, trying not to lose it, but he wanted to show Edward that he wasn't afraid of him anymore.

"What's going on?" Mr. Whitehouse shouted from the driveway. "Cut that out!"

There was dead silence on the porch.

"Mr. Whitehouse, let me go get my cousins," Trevor turned and hurried toward Edward and Dillard. He stood between the two, "Come on, guys. Let's get started."

Trevor turned away. He walked up the steps and stared at Edward with contempt.

"Dillard, go in the house," Trevor insisted.

"What you looking at me for?" Edward asked with a smile.

Trevor noticed that Mr. Whitehouse was still standing in the driveway. "We'll see you later Mr. Whitehouse." Trevor waved.

Erin walked behind Trevor, rubbing her eyes. Melissa followed behind her, shaking her head. Claire walked inside, looking at her watch.

"I need a drink," Thomas Wayne said. "I'm going to the car."

"I'm with you," Edward said. He walked down the steps and followed Thomas Wayne.

Thomas Wayne whispered to Edward, "I have my papers if you're interested."

"Not interested in the marijuana, but yes to the alcohol."

Trevor looked at them with heightened aggravation.

Trevor handed out assignments to his cousin and gave them each a dust mask to wear. They would attend to the walls and paint the living room, the kitchen, the dining room areas, and their grandmother's bedroom. After laying down plastic on the floors, Erin, Melissa, and Claire used paint scrapers to remove loose paint from the walls in various rooms. The guys were responsible for the ceilings.

Erin rushed around handing out supplies. She climbed up a ladder to wash down her side of a wall in the living room area and talked about her son, "Now that I'm more educated about eating healthier, I tell him that he should eat healthier, not just because he has diabetes but because it's the right thing for his body. I know it's hard for him sometime, but he copes with it. When he was first diagnosed, he was very upset and he'd ask, 'Why me?' on several occasions or, 'Why did it have to be me? Why not Chanitah?' Now I don't hear him complaining about it much at all. I often encouraged him to not worry about the whys, that he just has to know that he is diabetic and has to take a couple more steps in order to take care of himself."

"Now that I know I have prediabetes, I'll be following more in your footsteps and eating healthier," Dillard admitted while walking into the living room area.

"I'm so glad to hear that," Erin commented as she down next to Dillard. "Dillard favors quick and simple ready-to-eat foods, like a rotisserie chicken from Walmart, cinnamon rolls, honey buns, and ice cream bars."

"According to Trevor, as long as it's not fried, it's okay," Thomas Wayne said, walking into the living room. His speech was slurred and his gait was unsteady.

"It's chicken," Edward said rudely, following behind Thomas Wayne.

"Are you okay, Thomas Wayne?" Trevor asked.

"Yeah, man," he said, standing dazed in the living room.

"What's the deal, Trevor?" Dillard asked, while walking into the kitchen to fill a bucket with water.

"Well, there are a number of things to consider," Trevor said, as he removed his dust mask. "First things first, you don't want to eat chicken that has been under a heat lamp in its skin most of the day. Also, rotisserie chicken tends to have a high sodium content because of the seasonings used for flavoring. For someone who needs to monitor his or her sodium or salt intake, which is most of us, a rotisserie chicken may not be a favorable option. I advise my clients to buy fresh chicken parts, to bake or grill and season them with paprika, red pepper, rosemary, Mrs. Dash, and fresh lemon juice."

"Cooking takes too much time," Dillard added, walking into the living room with the filled bucket.

Melissa and Claire walked into the living area to listen to the conversation.

Edward interrupted, "I'm not going to be here all evening. You all need to focus on the assignments Mr. Trevor has handed out. Come on, Thomas Wayne; let's get to those bedrooms."

"Hold up, bro," Thomas Wayne said. "Trevor is talking."

"And?" Edward responded agitated.

"And, some of us want to hear what he has to say," Erin said.

"All I know is that you all can get with him on your own time," Edward stressed. "I thought we were here to paint this old house."

Trevor walked over to Edward and said, "Chill, man! Our time together is bigger than repairing this house. It's about us spending time together, engaging in conversation, learning more about one another, and discovering ways to make our lives better."

"Trevor, don't get in my face." Edward gave Trevor a slight shove to move him out of his path.

"Why are you so angry, Edward?" Erin asked with a frown. "Surely that's not healthy."

"I know that's right," Claire added.

"Come on, guys," Trevor said. "Edward is right. We don't want to be here all night. But, just a few more comments since we're talking about cooking."

"Thanks, Trevor," Dillard said.

"If your goal is to live a longer, healthier life, in order to prevent or eliminate disease and illness, or even place yourself in a position where you can better manage your current medical condition—you are going to have to do some things differently. Thomas Wayne, Edward, and Melissa have high blood pressure, and now you're on medication. Dillard has high cholesterol, and now you're on medication, plus, you have been diagnosed with prediabetes. If you don't get your blood sugar under control, you'll be on medication for that as well. Your doctors have told you that you need to lose weight, that you need to eat healthier, and that you need to exercise."

"I know mine has," Melissa confirmed.

"So, now the things to think about become; why it is hard for you to follow your doctor's orders or advice; what you are going to do differently, how you are going to do it, and when you are going to get started. Those things can be tough to figure out, because you're trying to figure out how to strike a balance between your perfect world (the world a lot of people live in every day) and the real world (the world we should be living in according to the health professionals)."

Edward walked into the living room, drinking a cola, and said, "I'll bite. So what's the perfect world and the real world?"

"In my perfect world, maybe not yours, but mine—I'd be able to eat what I want, from where I wanted it, and when I wanted it. There are no restrictions—there are no consequences," Trevor said.

"For example."

Trevor said, "On Monday, I'd be able to eat my favorite two-piece fried chicken dinner (spicy), red beans and rice, a biscuit, and a soft drink."

"From Popeye's," Dillard quickly interrupted as he sat on the floor.

"Yes, of course," Trevor answered and continued, "On Tuesday, I'd be able to eat my favorite combo—a burger, fries (super-sized), and a chocolate shake."

"McDonald's has the best chocolate shakes," Melissa commented. "Do you know how many calories it is?"

Trevor took his cell out of its holster on his waist. He started entered some information. His cousins continued the conversation, talking about their favorite foods.

Trevor looked up and said, "A 12 ounce chocolate shake at McDonald's is 580 calories. The 16 ounce is 720 calories."

"Wow! I usually get the 16 ounce with a burger and fries," Melissa said. "I dare not ask about the calories, fat, and sodium of the hamburger and fries."

Trevor started to scroll on his cell phone, "I don't know which burger you typically eat, but the Big Mac is 540 calories, 1040 milligrams of sodium, 29 grams of total fat, and 10 grams of saturated fat."

"I'm assuming that's a lot of calories, especially for a chocolate shake and burger. And you didn't even include the fries," Erin said. "How much fat should we be taking in?"

"Most recommendations you read suggests a total fat intake of no more than 30 percent of the calories. For example, at 2,000 calories per day, your suggested upper limit on fat intake would be about 67 grams. Your intake of saturated fat should be less than 10 percent of calories. At 2,000, that would be about 22 grams," Trevor stated.

"Just so I can inform my friend, how many calories is a medium order of fries?" Erin asked.

"Yeah, right! Friend, uh," Edward said, softly.

Trevor looked down and scrolled, "Okay, a medium order of fries is 380 calories, 270 milligrams of sodium, 19 grams of total fat, 2.5 grams of saturated fat," Trevor said. "And the 16 ounce chocolate shake has 300 milligrams of sodium, 20 grams of total fat, and 12 grams of saturated fat."

"So, a burger, fries, and shake is 1,640 calories, 1,610 milligrams of sodium, 68 grams of total fat, and 24.5 grams of saturated fat," Erin confirmed.

"If someone is using 2,000 calories per day as a guide, then they're in trouble," Melissa said, "especially if you include what they eat for breakfast, snacks, and dinner."

"Absolutely," Trevor responded.

A terrified look came over Melissa's face.

"Guess it's doesn't take much to understand your mounds of body fat," Edward said, laughing. "What I don't understand is why you insist on wearing those tight-fitting clothes."

"Shut up, Edward!" Trevor shouted loudly.

"Just stating a fact," Edward said as he retreated to the kitchen.

"I think we got a little off track," Trevor said, as he placed his cell phone back in its holster. "On Wednesday, I'd be able to eat at my favorite Mexican restaurant. I'd order the grande nachos with mounds of corn tortilla chips covered in refried beans, ground beef, shredded cheddar cheese, and jalapeno peppers. On Thursday, I'd eat one of the personal pan pizzas (the meat lovers with beef, sausage, pepperoni, ham) from my favorite pizza joint. On Friday, it'd be a fried seafood platter loaded with fried fish, shrimp and/or oysters, fries, and coleslaw."

Melissa thought about her meal at Deaux's Seafood Kitchen with a group of church members. She shared the Shrimp & Crawfish Fondeaux appetizer and garlic bread with one of her church sisters. For her main entrée, she ordered the seafood platter with fried shrimp, fried tilapia fillet, blue crab cake, and stuffed shrimp & stuffed crab. Because she was full after eating the appetizer and entrée with a glass of fresh-brewed mango iced tea, she ordered the Sweet Potato Pecan Pie with vanilla ice cream to go.

"On Saturday, it'd be Italian food like lasagna with layers of pasta, cheese, and ground beef," Trevor said, as he glanced over at Melissa who was deep in thought. "On Sunday, Soul Food Sunday, I'd eat brisket and/or ham with macaroni and cheese, corn bread dressing, collard greens seasoned with some sort of pork, and for dessert, pecan pie and ice cream."

Melissa quickly looked up.

"For breakfast, I'd eat any one of my favorites on any given day with my favorite breakfast foods like pancakes, an apple danish, a couple of Shipley's glazed donuts, a blueberry muffin, an egg and sausage biscuit, or an egg, cheese, and bacon taquito. And, when the boss gets on my last nerve, I'd seek comfort from a Dr. Pepper, Mrs. Baird's chocolate-covered donut holes, and/or a package of Peanut M&Ms."

"I don't know about anyone else, but that's the perfect world I'm living in here and now," Thomas Wayne said, laughing.

"If that's your perfect world, then it's filled with meals, snacks, and beverages high in calories, high in saturated fat, high in cholesterol, high in salt, high in sodium—all of the products your doctor has probably told you to reduce for health purposes," Trevor said.

"True," Melissa agreed.

"Now what's the real world—your real world, Trevor?" Dillard asked.

"The real world (the world we should be living in according to the health professionals) focuses your efforts on eating healthier foods," Trevor said. "For lunch, my selections would be much different. On Monday, I would eat one piece of baked chicken, a serving of brown rice or mashed sweet potatoes, steamed broccoli or some other fresh vegetable, and a sliced of whole wheat bread."

Dillard said quickly before Trevor could continue, "I don't like the texture of brown rice, Trevor."

"Aside from being more nutritious, and unlike white rice, brown rice doesn't cause blood glucose levels to rise as rapidly."

"Yes, that's what I've read. My doctor gave me a handout that suggested eating two or more servings of brown rice a week to reduce one's risk of developing Type 2 diabetes." Dillard added, "Lord knows I don't want to get Type 2 diabetes if I can help it."

"I switched over to brown rice many years ago. I add it to my stir fry dishes. I use it in my jambalaya dish, and when I prepare a black bean burrito. When you add it to a dish, that texture gets buried."

Edward walked in and said, "Looks like I'm going to be the only one working at painting today."

"Trevor is almost finished," Erin said. "You're on Tuesday."

"On Tuesday, I'll eat a burger made with ground chicken (oven cooked patty) on a whole wheat bun filled with mixed greens and sliced tomatoes with a serving of fresh fruit. On Wednesday, it'll be something like freshly prepared Spinach enchiladas (with fresh sautéed spinach) rolled in whole wheat tortillas with slow-cooked black or kidney beans and a serving of fresh fruit. On Thursday, my homemade tuna salad on a bread of mixed greens and diced tomatoes with a serving of fresh fruit. On Friday, baked white fish (cod) or grilled salmon (wild caught, not farm raised) with a fresh vegetable medley (squash and zucchini) and a serving of fresh fruit. Or, I would do something different like fish tacos (grilled fish rolled in a whole wheat tortilla with mixed greens and tomatoes)."

"Trevor, you'll need to send us these meal suggestions on email," Erin said.

Trevor continued, "On Saturday, I'd eat lasagna made with whole-wheat pasta, low-fat cheese, vegetables, maybe a little ground chicken, or a slice of homemade pizza topped with vegetables (spinach, zucchini, squash, and tomatoes) and a serving of fresh fruit. On Soul Food Sunday, I would eat a version of oven fried chicken (where the skin has been removed and whole-wheat bread crumbs or something comparable is used for coating); macaroni and cheese made with like low fat cheese, low-fat milk and buttermilk, and soft tub margarines, collard greens seasoned with herbs. For breakfast, I would eat oatmeal one day, a cold whole grain cereal the next, a carton of yogurt, slice of toast with fresh fruit on another day, or a breakfast taco with a whole wheat tortilla with spinach, tomatoes, and eggs inside."

"Erin's right. You have got to send those to us," Dillard said. "The real world is serious."

"Absolutely. In the real world, you've got to figure out how to cut calories, cholesterol, fat, salt, and sugar. In most instances that only happens by cooking more meals at home, and, simply creating healthy recipes."

"It's been hard for me with so much going on in my life," Erin said. "Between work and my new job responsibilities, the kids' school activities, Brian's medical condition, my separation from Nick, and growing medical problems, exercising is low on my priority list. It would probably be the same for eating, but Brian's condition has forced that issue. Now I have to think about the same for Chanitah because of her weight."

"Last week, she was given a written warning for coming to work too late," Dillard said.

"Excessive tardiness," Erin said.

"People don't realize how much is at stake when they fail to exercise good lifestyle habits," Trevor stressed. "One of my clients worked for a company for one year, just enough time for her to become eligible for family and medical leave. Her doctor informed her that she had gallstones, and she took time off for necessary medical treatment. A few months down the road, she fell at home and suffered a hip injury. She fractured her pelvis. After a period of time, her doctor released her to return to work. But, because she was in so much pain, she constantly arrived to work late or called in sick. Eventually, she had used up her family and medical leave so her job was no longer protected. They fired her."

"They fired her?" Erin said bewildered.

"Yes," Trevor said gently. "Another client told me about a friend he reconnected with after 40 years. The friend told him about a heart attack he'd had a few years ago that caused him to need a triple bypass. Due to complications with the triple bypass, he has to stay in the hospital for a year, having to learn how to walk again. While in the hospital, he developed a staff infection and lost his two kidneys. Because he was a veteran, all of his hospital stays and medical treatments have been through the VA Hospital. At the time of his heart attack, he was self-employed and had no medical insurance. Now, he lives on $1,200 a month from the VA disability, has 25% heart capacity, and goes to dialysis three times a week for four hours. My client's friend tells him that things may have turned out differently had he taken care of his body. That is, had he not spent the majority of his life drinking and smoking."

Thomas Wayne turned to look in the kitchen at Edward. He was visibly worried. Edward sat at the table unconcerned.

"I shared those stories with you all to illustrate the ultimate impact of unhealthy lifestyle habits and the impact it'll have in the long run. Whether you're young or old, employed, unemployed, or retired, you have to take care of yourself so you can better manage life's success and setbacks. And, that only happens through eating healthier and exercising."

"Well, I know I'm going to start to do better," Dillard said.

"Employers like Uncle Bert are looking for their employees to demonstrate good judgment in any given situation, solve problems, make good decisions, and render good customer service. Well, if you're always absent from work, or sick, or not feeling well when you're there, then those activities are compromised. Then, your job is at stake, your finances, your ability to support and provide for your family, your mental and emotional state, your physical well-being—"

"Can we finish our tasks now," Edward interrupted, clapping his hands.

Trevor looked at him, blatantly irritated.

"I know you all need to get home, so let's finish up the painting task for today," Trevor said as he stood up.

The cousins found out that painting the living room, kitchen and bedrooms were not easy home improvement projects. Edward complained about his neck hurting while painting the living room ceiling. Thomas Wayne gritted his teeth over the sloppy job Erin and Melissa had done with scraping the paint off the walls in the bedrooms. Dillard had paint on his head. They all had plaster and paint on their clothes.

Trevor was pleased with the energy they exhibited and the stirred emotions of humor and criticism the project ignited. It all worked together for producing dialogue and engaging camaraderie among the cousins.

"Tomorrow is family and friends day at my church," Trevor announced, as everyone was packing up. "I'd love for you all to attend."

"Is this one of those mandatory gatherings?" Edward asked.

"No, it's not, but I'd love for you all to come."

Edward headed toward the front door and said, "Huh? Not this time, cuz."

Thomas Wayne trailed behind, placing a couple of paint brushes in a box and said, "Maybe next time." He walked out the front door.

Erin came out of the kitchen. She was wiping her hands on a towel and said, "I'll pass this time."

"I'll have my kids on tomorrow," Dillard said while drinking a bottle of water.

"Sorry, Trevor. Tomorrow is the pastor's anniversary at my church," Melissa said. "I'm on the program to give the welcome."

Claire walked over to Trevor, "Me and Mark plan to stay in tomorrow. I don't want to overexert myself."

Except for Melissa, Trevor was disappointed in the lack of consideration and the array of excuses. But he couldn't get discouraged. He knew his efforts to deliver his cousins from lifestyle habits that were anti-God would need to be increased. Their homes were in turmoil, and they hadn't come to terms with the actions that would be necessary for fixing their situations. They were struggling with emotions and feelings that were stopping any progression of change.

After everyone had left, Trevor kneeled down in the center of the living room and began to pray, "Lord, I know it's because of You and all You've done in my life that I committed myself to helping Uncle Bert with his mission. When I consider their current state, I am more and more grateful and thankful that You delivered me from a life of fear, shame, blame, and pain that kept me captive for so long. I know my cousins are in bondage with the same sort of thoughts, feelings, and actions. Now that I have the wisdom and knowledge You've given me, I know I'm expected to help them overcome. But, my cousins are just not ready. And, I am afraid that I'm not ready for such an assignment. I am asking You, Lord, to show me now, how to wisely find a way to get through to them so they can experience your joy, peace, and love. I pray that they see in me the qualities of a spirit filled with love, peace, deliverance, and forgiveness that can only be credited to Your presence in my life. I know that it is because of You that Uncle Bert chose me. Now I'm praying that as Your vehicle for change, I pray my cousins are opened up to receive the great things You have in store for their lives. Lord, I pray that You will please turn their minds and hearts toward You and pleasing You, Lord. Because I am Your child and know firsthand Your power to deliver and change, I will not give up on my cousins nor my ability as Your vehicle for change. Please save and restore their lives. Thank You my Lord and Savior! Amen."

Chapter 13

❖

Unfinished Business

It was 10:30 A.M. on a Sunday morning at Golden Hill Missionary Baptist Church. Trevor sat in a pew among the 2,000 attendees. He was dressed in denim jeans, collared shirt, and a brown linen blazer. The church was filled to capacity with members and their family and friends. During the service, the congregation sung several old and new songs of praise and worship followed by scripture reading. Meanwhile, Trevor couldn't help but reflect on his cousins and their excuse for not attending the church service. Then came the time in the service where visitors were asked to stand for acknowledgement.

The assistant pastor stood in the pulpit and addressed the congregation.

Trevor looked over his shoulder to the right. Dillard was standing with his two children. Dillard saw him and smiled. He motioned with his eyes for Trevor to look to his left. To Trevor's amazement, Melissa was there with her oldest daughter Mandy. Sitting behind Melissa was Claire and her husband Mark. With tears welling up in his eyes, Trevor managed to smile at Melissa and Claire.

Pastor Gideon walked up to the pulpit.

"When you pray, some amazing things can happen in your life," he began. "Some sayings never die. We have always heard people say that prayer changes things. Now I'm going to say something that may cause you to shift in your seat, especially some of my older members. It is my belief that it is not prayer that changes things."

Pastor Gideon paused for a moment. He made eye contact with two older members who were looking somewhat perplexed by his comment. He continued with his sermon.

"The problem with thinking that prayer changes things is that if we believe prayer changes things, then we'll think it's us. I come to tell you today that it is through your prayer that God has the power to change your situation. Brokenness. Anger. Frustration. Abuse. Alcoholism. Sickness. Sexual Abuse. Money problems. If you want change, deliverance, and/or freedom from the things preventing you from leading a life pleasing to God, then I want you to understand that when talking about prayer, you need to practice prayer. The songwriter says, 'O what peace we often forfeit, O what needless pain we bear, All because we do not carry everything to God in prayer'."

The Pastor began to focus his message on a passage of scripture that talked about the time when Peter was in a jail cell awaiting execution. He talked about Peter's position and posture. How, when facing execution, Peter slept while connected to two guards. Peter knew he had a relationship with God and slept, worry free.

Dillard was sitting up straight in the pew, anxiously waiting for the next words to come out of the pastor's mouth.

"Prayer is important, because it is through prayer that we find ourselves having a little talk with Jesus," he continued, "Is there anybody here who knows God can change your situation?"

Amens and hallelujahs resonated throughout the church.

Pastor Gideon began to slowly walk along the pulpit.

"All during my childhood and in the midst of the trials of manhood, I know my mother has never ceased to pray for me." He gave a grateful smile and said intensely, "Intercessory prayer is good, but every now and then you've got to pray for yourself.

Because nobody knows like you know the situation you're dealing with. When you pray, the angel of the Lord will show up."

A big smile broadened Trevor's face. He knew this was a message his cousins needed to hear.

"Now, I know a lot of you all pray. But I also know you get frustrated because you believe God is not hearing you. You're still in waiting mode, waiting on the Lord to show up. And the fact of the matter is not that He didn't hear your prayer nor that He has not shown up, but you just don't know how to recognize when He shows up. To illustrate my point, let me have your full attention for a few more moments. I feel your eyes telling me to speed it up so you can get to the dinner the hospitality committee has prepared."

He chuckled and walked down the steps of the pulpit to stand in front of the congregation.

"There was a man who got trapped in a storm. The waters were rising, and he sat panicky in a little canoe. His canoe turned over. He managed to swim against the rising water to get on top of the roof of his house. A man came by in a boat and told him to get in. The man sitting on top of his roof said 'No.' He said, 'I'm waiting on the Lord'. The water kept rising. Another means of escape came when a man in a helicopter dropped a rope. He told the man on the roof to grab it and hold on. The man said, 'No I'm waiting on the Lord.' "

Pastor Gideon smiled, turned around, and walked up the steps to the pulpit.

He continued, "After a while, the man died. But even after death, he was saved. When he got to Heaven, he had an issue with the Lord. He said, 'Lord, You told me to wait on You and I waited, but You didn't show up.' The Lord said, 'I showed up. As a matter fact, I came two times. The first time I came by, I was in a speed boat, but you chose not to get in. The second time, I dropped a rope from a helicopter, and you chose not to grab hold.' It's important that you all here today understand that God just may not descend from

Heaven to answer your prayers. He will work through somebody around you to give you what He wants you to have."

In his closing, he said, "Get close and stay close to the Lord—Pray. Whatever situation you're in, you don't have to worry, because God will take care of you and your situation. Pray. As long as you have a relationship with God, He will bring you up and out. Don't be misguided. God will let you fall, so He can lift you up. Whatever you're going through, your personal communication with God will help you to overcome. You must believe in God's power to change. Pray."

Immediately after the church service, Trevor eagerly exited the main sanctuary and hurried to the visitor's reception room. He arrived before his cousins. Minutes later, Dillard arrived with his two children.

Trevor swung his arms around Dillard and held him tightly.

Tiffany and Walter stood hovering behind their father, arms crossed and watching.

Trevor scooted past Dillard, shaking his head at Tiffany and Walter. He said, "I am so happy to see the two of you. Tiffany, the last time I saw you, you were a baby. And Walter, you were probably around five."

Tiffany and Walter gave each other a quick glance.

Trevor opened his arms wide to hug Tiffany and gave her a big kiss on both cheeks.

She remained silent and smiled.

Trevor stepped over to Walter and said, "You look just like your father at fifteen." He hugged Walter.

Dillard was grinning immensely.

"Man, you're almost as tall as me," Trevor said. "Are you playing any sports? Football? Basketball?"

"I run track," Walter responded.

"That's great. Your dad ran track and was pretty fast. I remember one track meet where he won the 400 meters with a time of 49.48," Trevor said.

"My dad!?" Walter exclaimed.

"Yes, your dad," Trevor said with assurance.

Walter grinned proudly and said, "Uh huh."

Dillard was anxious to speak to Trevor alone. He pointed Tiffany and Walter in the direction of the refreshments.

"Man! I can't believe you came," Trevor said, smiling ecstatically.

Dillard looked serene and said, "Late yesterday, after we left you, I had to pick up Tiffany and Walter. Erin's car died, so I didn't have any means of transportation. I had to catch the city bus at 8:00 P.M. to go across town and get my kids. So, I got there. Veronica was ranting as usual. After dealing with her, my kids had to carry their overnight bags to a bus stop. We waited over an hour and got to the house around 11:30 P.M. I felt like such a failure to my kids. In the wee hours of the night, I found myself thinking about my life and meditating on what you've been trying to get us to address. I just know I'm tired of trying to make sense out of chaos."

Overjoyed by what he was hearing, Trevor noticed Melissa and her daughter quickly approaching them.

"Melissa and Mandy are coming," Trevor said quickly to Dillard. Dillard turned around.

"Hey, guys," Melissa said, as she and Mandy approached Trevor and Dillard.

"Hey, Lady," Dillard said, as he positioned himself to hug her.

"Mandy! Girl, you're all grown up," Trevor said with surprise, as he hugged her tightly.

"Hi, Cousin Trevor and Dillard," Mandy said, smiling as she and Trevor embraced one another.

Dillard waited his turn to hug Mandy. Then, he walked away to go and check on his kids.

"How old are you?" Trevor asked Mandy.

"Twenty-eight," she said.

"Twenty-eight! Where did the time go?"

Seconds later, Claire and Mark appeared.

They all greeted one another with great enthusiasm.

"I am so happy to see all of you!" Trevor exclaimed.

"Even though we may not act like it, you've been getting through to us," Melissa said.

Claire smiled, "Absolutely."

"Claire has been like a changed person since you all reconnected with one another," Mark said. "And, Trevor, I want to personally thank you for the support and encouragement you've shown her."

"That's what family is supposed to do," Trevor responded.

Dillard walked back with Tiffany and Walter. They were all excited about being in each other's company.

"I don't know if you have any plans for lunch, but I can prepare a scrumptious meal," Trevor said. "Halibut in white wine."

"Hey, cuz, your church is having dinner on the grounds," Dillard said laughing.

"I haven't heard that saying since I was a kid," Mark said, shaking his head and smiling.

"Corn on the cob, turnip greens, fried pork chops, fried chicken, fried fish, potato salad, peach cobbler, pecan pie, banana pudding, and homemade bread," Dillard said.

"Mmm-hmm. Now that sounds like some real food," Mandy said.

"Your cousin Trevor has us thinking healthy, sweetie," Melissa said.

"I hadn't planned on staying, since I had a healthier meal waiting on me at home," Trevor said. "I need to go and find Jenny."

Mandy exchanged a look with her mother.

Dillard nodded and placed his arm around Tiffany and said, "No greasy food for us today."

Jenny walked up as they were preparing to leave.

"Hey, babe, I was just coming to look for you," Trevor said. "My family is coming over to the house for dinner. Can you come?"

"I'll be there after we finish in the media room."

"Great!"

The cousins retrieved their visitor's gifts and headed for Trevor's house.

Trevor was thankful to God that Dillard, Melissa, and Claire were considering meaningful changes in their lives. They were on their way to confronting their demons and focusing on doing things differently.

The following weeks after the momentous church service, the cousins met at Grandma Saddie's house to complete the renovation project. They painted the interior, laid new flooring, and worked with Trevor to coordinate the repair of outdated wiring, the replacement of appliances, installation of a central air conditioning and heating system, rebuilding of the front and back porches, a new roof, and fencing around the yard. The old house had begun to look like it did in its glory days.

Trevor was proud of what his cousins had worked to accomplished. Despite Edward's combative demeanor and Thomas Wayne's jittery spirit, they managed to overcome a cycle of emotional setbacks.

Nearly three months had passed since their weekend retreat. Trevor sat in his office, planning the next excursion for his cousins. He knew that once Claire started her half-marathon training, her ability to attend any weekend outings would be limited.

In the middle of typing an email to his cousins, his cell phone rang.

"Hello," Trevor said.

"Hey, Trevor. It's Dillard."

"Hey, man, what's up?"

"We never got a chance to finish the conversation I started when me and my kids visited your church," Dillard said. "Mainly, I wanted to thank you."

Trevor interrupted, "No thanks necessary. I love you and want to do whatever I can to help you."

"I love you, too. Because of you, I was able to face and accept things I had been running from for so long," Dillard said. "For so long, life has been like driving around every day with a bunch of unwanted passengers. If I looked over to my right, sitting beside me was the anger I feel toward my parents for leaving me in the state they did where others mistreated me for so many years. If I looked behind me, there was worry about the financial problems my wife left me with. If I looked in my rear view mirror, there sat the resentment I feel toward my relatives for lack of support and years of hurtful comments and insults. If I looked back over my shoulder to the right, there sat the shame I feel because my kids see me as weak."

"First, please don't give me any credit. It is God's presence in your life that has led you to forgive and let go," Trevor said.

"I started to pray and ask for a change," Dillard admitted.

"So many people never get to the point in their life where they ask God to fix whatever their situation is," Trevor said. "I remember asking God to deliver me and restore me, because things weren't happening quick enough, that is, according to my timetable, and I almost gave up. But, God answered my prayers and my life changed. Even now when I get discouraged and disappointed, I pray."

"I know God used you to reach me," Dillard said.

"You keep on praying and praising the Lord. Nobody knows like you know what the Lord has done for you," Trevor said.

"I've finally saved up enough money to buy a car," Dillard said proudly. "Erin is getting ready to take me over to David McDavid to look for a used car."

"I'm happy for you," Trevor said. "I'll be praying that you get a good deal on a car that's safe and reliable."

"Thanks, Trevor. I'll talk to you soon."

"Look out for the information that I'll be sending about our next retreat."

"Will do. Love you."

"Love you, too, Dillard."

Chapter 14

❖

Stumbling Blocks

It was seven o'clock on a Friday evening. Trevor sat at his desk, staring bewildered at his computer screen. He was dreading opening the fifty unread email messages in his inbox. He started to open them; then he stopped. He logged out and placed his head in his hands. He sat like that for a moment. He reached for a box underneath his desk and looked through it. He pulled out a bottle of pills and a sheet of paper. He placed the pill bottle on top of his desk on the floor and started to read information on the sheet of paper. It was the lab results of recent blood work. It revealed that his low-density lipoproteins (LDL) cholesterol was out of the normal range. His doctor had prescribed him cholesterol medication and Trevor was having difficulty accepting the results.

Trevor's cell phone rang. He glanced at the cell that sat on his desk just inches away from his reach. He let out a sigh and answered it, "Hello."

"Hi, Trevor."

"Uncle Bert!" he perked up. "How's everything going? I haven't been able to connect with you. I've been worried about you. I didn't recognize the telephone number."

"No need to worry; all is well," he responded, "Just keeping a low profile and staying out of the public's eye. How are you and your cousins?"

"We're fine. I've scheduled another retreat for next weekend," Trevor said pleased.

"That's good," Uncle Bert hesitated and said, "You sound a little distracted. Did I catch you in the middle of something?"

"No, I was just going through some papers and was thinking about what sort of exercises we'll do next weekend."

He looked at the lab results lying in front of him.

"Have your cousins come around?" Uncle Bert asked.

"Progress is in the making," Trevor responded.

He got up from his desk and walked into the kitchen.

He opened the refrigerator door and took out a container of fresh cut cantaloupe and said, "Claire is planning to walk a half-marathon. Her training program will start in a couple of weeks."

Trevor sat down at the bar in his kitchen with the container of cantaloupe.

He continued, "Dillard and Melissa have been visiting my church regularly. I know Dillard is on the road to recovery. As far as the others, they are a work in progress."

"I know you'll give them that game day locker room talk," Uncle Bert said optimistically.

"What in the world is the game day locker room talk?" Trevor said stumped.

He started to eat his cantaloupe.

"Think about it," Uncle Bert said in high spirits. "At halftime, the coach enters the locker room with the players. That's where the real talk begins. In your scenario, you're the coach. You tell your players, your cousins, the truth. Something like, 'I want to change the concept of how you think. If you want to win, you've got to do some things different. It's halftime, and you're losing the game. Look at the scoreboard of life and check your score. You're experiencing setback, after setback, after setback. You continue to toddle back and forth with forgiveness, trust, vision, purpose, and faith. Your lifestyle habits have you on the verge of a serious health catastrophe. You have the power to unleash, but only you can make the choice to let go. If you change the way you think, you'll change the way you live. There's no reason why your life can't be different.' "

"Thanks, Uncle Bert. That all sounds good, but I think I have a little something different in mind," Trevor said with confidence.

"Okay, I trust your methods," Uncle Bert said. "I may need for you to use that locker room talk on me."

"How's the investigation going?" Trevor asked.

"For years, I've been zealous in my pursuit of justice. So much so, I've made some enemies, offended many, and now I'm a target of my political rivals. I'm sure you've heard much in the news—raids, subpoenas. With all that has happened, there are no indictments, yet. My business associates are having to explain and detail the degree of my relationship with them. My financial records and their financial records are being thoroughly examined. Meanwhile, my attorney is on the ground, relentlessly pursuing answers for this entire invasion, and my accountant as well. I can't say that I'm not concerned, but—"

Trevor heard worry in his uncle's tone and said, "Just know that I am praying for you."

"Thank you. I appreciate your prayers. But don't worry about me; just focus on your cousins," Uncle Bert said peacefully. "I know the Lord for myself. I know what He has done and can do in my life. My trust and faith is in Him. Fear will tarnish your perspective, and I can't allow that to happen."

"Glad we had a chance to talk, Uncle. I'll keep you posted."

"Great! I'll be in touch."

Trevor placed the container of half-eaten cantaloupe back into the refrigerator and retreated to his bedroom to call Jenny, "Hey, babe."

"Hey, you, where are you?" Jenny responded. "Are we still going to the movies later on?"

"Oh, no! I completely forgot about our date tonight. I am so sorry."

"This is becoming a habit. Last week you forgot about my awards ceremony. The week before that you forgot about my dad's birthday dinner."

"Babe, the situation with my uncle has me off track. Then, there's the commitment I've made to him to help my cousins."

"I'm trying to be understanding."

She was disappointed and mad.

"How about you come over here? We can play some basketball out back before it gets dark. I can make us some tuna sandwiches."

"I'll pass. Let's get together if you're on track tomorrow."

"That's fine. Just know that you are important to me, Jenny. I need for you to be patient with me."

"It's getting hard, but I'm still here."

She hung up.

Trevor laid across his bed, thinking about Jenny. They had been dating for eleven months, and he knew he really liked her. He didn't want to continue doing things that may jeopardize their relationship.

The following morning, Trevor was conducting a health and fitness symposium with one of his chef friends at St. John Missionary Church. He invited one of his friends, Chef Hardette, and his cousins to attend.

"Coach Trevor!" Samantha shouted from a distance while exiting her car in the parking lot. She was a member at the church.

Trevor was walking toward the church with Chef Hardette and his cousins.

"Hi, Samantha!" Trevor turned and loudly responded.

She quickly approached Trevor. Another lady was walking quickly alongside Samantha.

Samantha was visibly winded when she and her friend caught up to Trevor. "I'm so glad to see you, Coach."

"It's good to see you," Trevor said, stopping to hug her. He pointed toward each of his cousins and said, "By the way, these are my cousins, Erin, Melissa, Claire, Dillard, Edward, and Thomas Wayne, and a good friend of mine, Chef Hardette, who is, of course, a chef."

Out of breath, Samantha responded, "Hi, Chef Hardette and cousins. This is my friend, Charlotte. She's visiting from South Carolina. I invited her to the seminar."

Chef Hardette, Erin, and Melissa greeted the ladies.

"Hi, Charlotte, it's nice to meet you." Trevor smiled as she looked over at Charlotte.

Wearing an oversized T-shirt and denim skirt, Samantha quickly interjected, "My twentieth class reunion is coming up, and I need to lose at least sixty pounds by December. We're going on a winter cruise. I have less than three months to get it done. What's your recommendation? A lady at work told me about a weight loss product that can help me lose a lot of weight quickly. She lost fifty pounds in two months."

Edward leaned over and whispered to Thomas Wayne, "You can see every roll of her flesh through that T-shirt. Don't they have some sort of rules about what to wear at church?" He thrust his arm around Thomas Wayne and started laughing.

"Samantha, I thought you were going to join the walking program I recommended in January," Trevor looked puzzled and continued, "and my healthy living classes."

"Yes, it was the plan. Some things came up, though. I've been super busy since January."

"You've heard me say many times over and over," Trevor said looking disappointed, "that in order to achieve weight loss goals, you must outline some BOLD goals. That's why I asked Chef Hardette to come today. In terms of eating healthier, she's going to provide you with some good options for doing so."

"I know, but I don't have time for all of that," Samantha laughed.

"I know that's right," Edward mumbled.

"I can only help you if you're interested in making true lifestyle changes," Trevor emphasized. "Several months ago, I encouraged you to complete the self-examination exercise that I recommend to all of my clients. Until you identify the feelings, thoughts, interests, and activities preventing you from living healthier—you'll never be able to do so. The self-examination helps to focus your attention on addressing why you continue to harbor unhealthy habits, and, furthermore, why you fail to pursue activities like the walking program and my healthy living classes."

"This is déjà vu. Sounds like that mumbo jumbo he says to us. You'd think he'd get tired of repeating himself," Edward said quietly to Thomas Wayne. "If I slip out, you think he'll notice?"

"Man, be quiet before he hears you," Thomas Wayne said.

Charlotte nodded slowly and quickly interrupted, "What are bold goals."

"We will discuss them in the seminar," Trevor responded. "But first we're going to do some physical activity."

There was a one-half mile concrete park trail across the street from the church.

Trevor, his cousins, and fifteen attendees walked across the street to Friendship Park. Everyone was laughing and talking over each other, asking Trevor questions, except Dillard, whose expression was dark and strangely gloomy.

The attendees completed a series of assessment forms. Afterwards, Trevor conducted a comprehensive physical evaluation to assess each person's aerobic fitness, body composition, muscular strength and endurance, and flexibility. He explained to the participants that both the evaluation forms and physical assessments would more clearly identify any specific health concerns, facilitate setting personal goals, and establish benchmarks to help them measure their progress. He retrieved various items from his gym bag. He took their weight, blood pressure, and percentages of body fat and lean muscle mass.

Dillard, Thomas Wayne, and Melissa refused to complete the forms and participate in the physical evaluation.

Everyone else waited patiently until it was their turn.

An hour passed, and then the assessments were completed.

"Let's prepare to walk," Trevor said. "Let me put my bag and notebook in my car first."

Trevor walked across the street to his car to put up his bag.

He returned carrying a blue water cooler and placed it on the ground. Everyone in the group was sitting at picnic tables under the pavilion in the park.

He stood in front of everyone and said, "I do want you to be clear about my strategy for helping you to establish and achieve your fitness goals. Oftentimes, when people make a decision to start exercising, they go in with a preconceived notion to lose a lot of weight in a short period of time."

He looked over at Samantha.

"However, the real goal should be to discover ways to implement long-term healthier lifestyle habits, which include a gamut of activities, like eating healthier, eating less, drinking plenty of water, getting enough sleep, along with exercising. I'll develop a structured program to help you with all of those things."

"It's getting hot out here," Edward said, while sitting next to Claire and Thomas Wayne at a picnic table.

Claire interrupted to prevent Edward from embarrassing Trevor, "Actually today is a good day. It's only seventy-eight degrees."

Everyone started laughing.

"Today, I'm going to focus your attention on building your strength and endurance with consistency and intensity. For that to happen, each week you must add to what you are doing. Progression!" Trevor emphasized.

He continued by explaining how a good walking program with some simple strength training exercises would help them to build strength and endurance. He educated them on how lean muscle tissue helps increase metabolism and burns fat throughout the day.

"Sounds like a plan," Samantha said, anticipating the start.

"Let's get started. I have bottles of water in the blue container," Trevor said, pointed to the blue cooler filled with bottled water.

"It's too much trouble to carry water," Charolette said. "I usually wait until after I finish to drink my water."

"Never exercise without having your water with you or near you," Trevor stressed. "We're going to start walking westward toward the tennis courts. We will walk around the path four times."

"That's about two miles!" Leslie shouted. She was over the benevolence ministry at the church. "Isn't that a little aggressive for a beginner?"

The group started walking.

"You'll be okay, as long as you were okayed by your doctor as indicated on your form," Trevor assured her. "It's important to warm up five to ten minutes before your main aerobic activity. Then, you'll start to increase your pace. Okay, it's time to speed up our pace."

"Okay," Leslie said, picking up her pace. "I need to work off the breakfast I ate."

"What did you eat?" Trevor asked.

"A Jimmy Dean sausage, cheese, and an egg biscuit sandwich with coffee. Just heat it up and go."

Erin flinched, listening to Leslie talk about her breakfast. She thought to herself, *I know that's a lot of unhealthy fat and sodium.*

"And it doesn't get any better for lunch?" Leslie said.

"I'll bite," Erin said, walking alongside Leslie. "What did you eat for lunch yesterday?"

"Well, I treated myself to one of my favorite restaurants, and I had the cheesy bacon cheeseburger," Leslie admitted loudly, hesitating to continue.

She was several people behind Trevor.

Trevor turned around and said, raising his voice, "A cheesy bacon cheeseburger!"

He stepped off the main path and waited to walk alongside Leslie.

"That has to be one of the unhealthiest burgers. I'm talking about an artery-clogging menu of beef, pork, and cheese. That kind of food leads to obesity, diabetes, and heart disease."

"I guess adding the fries and a strawberry shake were a really poor choice," Leslie said, avoiding Trevor's eyes as he started to walk alongside her and Erin.

Trevor looked up ahead and backward to make sure everyone was doing okay. Chef Hardette was among the group and enjoying the conversation. Everyone else walked quietly, listening to Trevor and Leslie.

Melissa thought about the chipotle chicken sandwich she'd eaten with large fries and a drink the day before.

Samantha thought about the Cinco Combo she'd eaten that included a crispy beef taco, a soft chicken taco, plus three enchiladas—cheese and onion, beef, and chicken.

"Now I don't know about the rest of you, but if you're serious about living healthier, you've got to be committed to making better eating choices. Depending on your day's activities, you're going to be faced with good and bad food choices. The key is to avoid the selections high in calories, fat, cholesterol, and sodium—like the cheesy bacon cheeseburger and fries," Trevor said loudly to make sure everyone could hear him.

"Sometimes it's just the mere fact that eating what you like makes you feel better about what's going on in your life," Melissa said.

"Most people traditionally eat more and make poor food choices in response to their feelings, feelings of depression, loneliness, anger, stress, problems at work and/or home, and issues with kids." Trevor paused to look at the sports watch on his wrist. "It's been fifteen minutes—time to take a drink. This should be a good spot to stop."

They stepped off the path onto a grassy area.

Trevor retrieved his water bottle and instructed the group on how often and how much to drink.

He continued, "You can't allow food to be your reaction to life's trials and discomforts. There will always be things you don't have control over, like the actions of a boss, husband, or kids. But your health is a different story. You do have control over the choices you make every day."

"You're right," Leslie agreed. "My doctor told me that I need to lose weight, follow a healthier diet, and exercise. He says doing those things will increase my chances of getting off my high blood pressure and cholesterol medications."

"Sounds like you have some decisions to make, Leslie. You've got to discover creative ways of making your favorite foods healthier, which involves preparing the majority of your meals at home."

Chef Hardette interjected, "For instance, the primary goal is to eat more fruits and vegetables. In order to boost your veggie intake, add vegetables every chance you get. Start with breakfast: you can prepare a Frittata using superior eggs, fresh spinach, tomatoes, mushrooms, and a low-fat cheese. When making your favorite pasta dish, like spaghetti, add vegetables like broccoli, zucchini, and squash to the meat sauce. Use half as much pasta and twice as many vegetables. When ordering out, instead of fries, get the restaurant's veggie ensemble; most will have steamed vegetables. Or, you can substitute with a fruit medley."

"Those are some good suggestions. I've never thought about making my own Frittata," Stephanie said.

"Let's start walking back," Trevor said.

Chef Hardette walked over to Stephanie so she could provide her with additional tips.

"How much water should we be drinking," Samantha asked.

"You should drink at least the recommended standard of eight to ten glasses of water a day. For those of you with health issues, you need to consult your physician. Your intake could be significantly less. For instance, if you have an underlying kidney, liver, or other disease, it may be difficult for your body to handle fluids."

Chef Hardette looked back at Trevor and said, "Also, keep in mind that if you're active, the amount of water needed increases."

"Absolutely, plus, if you apply a more recent rule of thumb, you can drink half your body weight in water," Trevor said, loudly to make sure everyone could hear him.

"Half my body weight? I weigh 230 pounds!" Leslie shouted.

"So for you, that is approximately 115 ounces," Trevor stated. "It's important to understand that your body is comprised mostly of water, and, as a consequence, if you're not getting what your body needs to function properly, you could be placing your health in jeopardy."

"That's entirely too much water," Edward said.

"It's well documented that drinking sufficient amounts of water helps the body to digest and absorb vitamins and nutrients. It also detoxifies the liver and kidneys and carries waste away from the body. The consequences of not drinking enough water every day can be tremendous. You can become dehydrated, incur a buildup of toxins and waste in your body, develop bladder infections, kidney stones, and a series of other health problems. With all of that said, water is critical to our health. But, like I said, your intake will depend on any health issues you may have."

"How do you know if you have enough water in your body?" Leslie asked.

"Look at your urine. If it's clear or pale yellow, you're doing a good job of staying hydrated. But if it's intense yellow or gold, you probably need to drink more water," Trevor stated. "But, if you are taking vitamins, your urine may be a neon yellow or bright yellow."

Edward mumbled to Thomas Wayne, "I'm thinking this is our third time around."

"I'm tired of the colored urine discussion," Thomas Wayne said, smiling.

"I'm tired of it all. The talks, family gatherings, psycho mumbo jumbo, and hanging around a bunch of fat folks whining and making excuses about being fat," Edward said to Thomas Wayne.

"Just focus on the money," Thomas Wayne said quietly.

"We're coming upon our last loop around. We've walked for nearly twenty-five minutes. That's the goal for today. Let's cool down the last five to ten minutes. I'll show you some stretching exercises. Stretching helps to improve your flexibility, your range of motion, and to reduce your risk of injury," Trevor said loudly.

"Trevor, I read an article recently that said that many foods are also good sources of water," Stephanie said.

"Water in juicy fruits like oranges, grapefruit, grapes, watermelon, and apples can help keep you healthy and hydrated. Carrots, tomatoes, and cucumbers also contain plenty of water," Trevor said. "Leslie, there's the fitness center."

"Great!" Leslie said, sounding relieved. "What about drinking soft drinks, fruit juices, sports drinks, and coffee? They contain water."

"Don't slow down. We still need to keep walking, but walk slower for our cool down phase," Trevor said, monitoring their pace. "Be careful about drinking soft drinks, fruit juices, coffee, and other drinks. All these drinks can help quench your body's thirst for fluids, but they typically contain a lot of calories. They may quench your thirst, but their true effects are deceiving, and because you're not dehydrated, you think everything's okay. The typical 12-ounce soda contains about 39 grams of sugar, not to mention the bargain saver sizes, such as 20, 24, and 32 ounces. Take note of how much sugar is in your beverage of choice. Sugar decreases the rate at which fluid is absorbed into the body. Plus, caffeinated drinks, such as coffee, tea, and sodas will prompt the body to lose water."

"There's a lot to living healthier. Still, though, I'm thankful I have time to get on the right track," Stephanie said.

"It does that, with effort," Trevor confirmed. "After our discussion, Chef Hardette is going to provide you with some strategies for cooking healthier meals."

❖

Chapter 15

❖

Decision Time

Once everyone was assembled in the meeting room, Trevor handed them a bottle of water and began the discussion about bold goals.

"Bold goals are goals that are balanced, open, labor intense, and deliberate," he said, standing in front of the group.

"What does that mean—bold?" Samantha asked. "I've heard of smart goals, but not bold goals. That sounds like something homemade."

The group started to laugh.

"Probably so, homemade," Trevor confirmed, with laughter, "balanced in that you consider the impact the goal will have on every aspect of your life. For example, let's think about a goal to walk four times a week for 30 minutes. First, what impact will doing so have on you personally, professionally, spiritually, mentally, and emotionally?"

"Right," Stephanie said. "For seven days a week, I'm busy from sunup to sundown. I have two kids who are very active in extracurricular activities. Most days I work nine or ten hours and then may have to bring home some work to finish. My husband is not very supportive with the kids or maintaining the house, so I have to make sure the house is cleaned, clothes are washed, and meals are provided. On Tuesdays, it's mission meeting. On Wednesdays, it's Bible study. On Thursdays, it's choir rehearsal."

"Just think. None of that you've mentioned will happen if you get sick," Trevor said candidly.

Everyone stared at Trevor.

Goals are open when you have publicized the changes you are pursuing. You'll inherit a support system that will routinely ask you about what you're doing—sort of an accountability factor. Then, your goals are labor intense in that you understand you must move beyond your comfort zone for change to occur, and deliberate, in that each step you take each and every day must include a relentless pursuit."

"Did I miss the purpose of your bold goals?" Dillard asked.

"Looking at goals from a different perspective, that is, bold goals, can help you to implement your plan of action and achieve desired results for minimizing the risk for disease and illness."

Samantha let out a long sigh, "Okay, you've got my attention, Coach."

Edward nearly choked while drinking his water. He cleared his throat and whispered to Thomas Wayne, "As fat as she is, someone should have gotten her attention a long time ago."

"Samantha, I've heard you talk about your intake of soda—you admitted drinking four to six cans every day. For a 12-ounce can, that's at least one thousand empty calories consumed every day. Eliminating soda can be a great step to achieving weight loss and a healthy diet."

Charlotte muttered, "All that sugar. I've told her that over and over."

Good sugar, Erin smiled and thought to herself.

Trevor continued, "First, you must make a commitment to stop! Then, outline your bold goal for stopping. If you want to just go cold turkey—no sodas at all—keep in mind that you'll go through the caffeine withdrawal that will include headaches. Just get some over-the-counter headache medication. If you don't want to go cold turkey, set a bold goal to stop a little bit at a time. For example, if you're drinking four sodas per day, cut back to three tomorrow, then only drink two the next day, and so forth. Remove all sodas from home and work. Look for alternatives to drinking soda, but not some other sugary drink. Switching to water is a great way to cut down your calorie intake and lose weight."

Samantha frowned. "I love my sodas. Between working full-time and running my part-time graphic design business—deadlines, unproductive employees, and demanding clients, keep me in stress mode. My coping mechanism is a soda every few hours."

"Once you have really addressed the problems at work and have learned how to manage your business operations more efficiently, you'll see your way clear to implement your bold goals. You'll be able to focus your attention," Trevor said calmly.

"He's right, Samantha," Charlotte agreed.

Trevor responded, "Each waking day for all of us is filled with obligations, demands, pursuits, and circumstances surrounding work, family, church, relationships, and an array of personal decisions. But, the reality is that all of those things are a part of life and will be revolving and evolving as long as you're on this Earth. That's why, in the midst of it all, you have to pause and determine how you're going to live healthier."

"Amen," Charlotte said.

"Samantha, I know you want to lose sixty pounds, say in six months, and that's achievable. Just focus your attention on setting bold goals to reduce soda intake, eat healthier, and exercise. The weight loss will happen because of lifestyle changes," Trevor stated.

"Coach! At the beginning of year, I established my bold goals. I had my own sixty pounds to lose," Charlotte admitted. "Number one on my list was to get a physical examination. To my surprise, the results of my blood work revealed high blood pressure and high blood sugar levels. Once I faced my reality, I set goals to exercise, cook healthier meals at home, and get more sleep. Now I'm twenty pounds lighter."

"Now that's a great testimony, Charlotte," Trevor said, sounding pleased with Charlotte's achievement. "A physical examination is a great way to find out what you need to focus on." Trevor paused. "Samantha, with the right bold goals, this time next year you can look back and congratulate yourself on a job well done to achieve your goal of losing sixty pounds and living healthier. What a testimony you'll have to tell."

❖

Chapter 16

❖

Raucous Moments

On Friday evening, the cousins started to arrive at Grandma Saddie's house. Trevor had received chastising texts and email messages from Edward, Melissa, and Thomas Wayne about the location change for their weekend retreat.

Trevor drove slowly down the narrow street. All was quiet in the neighborhood. He was proud of the changes to the bylaws the neighborhood association club had made to preserve and improve Kashmere Heights. He pulled up in front of Grandma Saddie's house. He exited his car with his overnight bag.

He walked up the steps, pulled out a key, and opened the door. He walked from room to room, finally stopping at the blue room. He placed his bag on the floor and laid on the bed in his favorite cargo shorts. He reached to look in his bag and pulled out his *Runner's World* magazine. While he was flipping through the pages, there was a knock at the front door.

Dillard had arrived with traveling bags in his left and right hands.

"Hey, man," Trevor said, as he reached for one of Dillard's bags.

"Hey, cuz, what are you doing?"

"I was just laying on the bed, waiting on you guys," Trevor said. "Me and you will be sleeping in the blue room. Give me your bags and I'll put them up. Where's Erin? I guess y'all didn't come together."

"I forgot to tell you that I got a little car, a used Ford truck. I came from work, but Erin should be right behind me."

"Good for you. I am so happy for you."

Dillard handed Trevor his bags. He proceeded to sit down in a chair. He looked around and didn't see the television. He picked up a healthy living magazine lying on the coffee table and said, "I guess this is going to be another television free weekend."

"Absolutely," Trevor responded.

"The house has really shaped up," Dillard looked around at the furnishings Trevor had added.

Luxuriously furnished in attractive traditional furnishings, the house looked as if it was Trevor's permanent place for living. The living room included a beautiful camel-color sofa, two upholstered high-leg chairs, an antique walnut coffee table with two matching end tables, and a brown leather ottoman along a wall. On the colored walls were framed photographs of various family members.

Dillard stood up to look at photos of Trevor with Thomas Wayne, Claire, and Melissa as kids. They were dressed in beach shorts and T-shirts. In a photo of Trevor and Thomas Wayne, Thomas Wayne was laughing and holding a bucket filled with sand.

Trevor sat down on the sofa. "There's water and juice in the refrigerator and fruit on the table."

"I'm okay for now," Dillard said. He sat in one of the high-leg chairs. "What's on the menu for tonight?"

"It's a surprise," Trevor said, laughing.

"No fried chicken, pizza, or Chinese takeout, I suppose," Dillard said with amusement.

"I suppose not," Trevor smiled. "How's work going?"

"Been trying to get a promotion, but nothing has come through yet."

"You'll get a break."

"I need one, trying to keep up with these child support payments," Dillard said.

Suddenly, they heard loud voice emerging from outdoors.

Trevor and Dillard stood up to go outside.

Edward and Thomas Wayne stood in the driveway arguing.

"All I want is my money," Edward said, enraged. "You now owe me over $9,750."

"You'll get your money," Thomas Wayne said casually.

Dillard and Trevor looked at one another, unsure about what to do.

"Guess I'd better get out there before things get out of hand," Trevor said, as he walked down the steps. Dillard remained on the porch.

"You need to get rid of that expensive-ass car," Edward said intensely. With growing anger, he started to pace along the sides of the cars in the driveway.

Thomas Wayne leaned on his car, laughing uncontrollably.

"Hey, guys," Trevor said, as he approached them quickly.

"My brother is tripping as usual," Thomas Wayne said.

Suddenly, Edward lunged at this brother, grabbing his shirt by the collar and pushing him up against his car. He placed his right arm around his neck and bent him over backwards, stating, "You think I'm playing with you. I want my money, dopehead."

Thomas Wayne tried to get away from Edward.

Edward said forcefully, "I need my money."

"Man, get off me," Thomas Wayne said.

Edward grabbed his neck with greater force and shoved him against the car while yelling and cursing at him.

"Let him go, Edward," Trevor pleaded. He tried to position himself between the two.

Edward released his hold on Thomas Wayne who fell to the ground.

Trevor placed his hand on Edward's back to calm him.

Edward walked toward the house. He stopped and hesitated. He quickly turned back and punched Thomas Wayne in his stomach. Thomas Wayne doubled over in pain. His breathing intensified.

Trevor wrapped his arms around Edward's shoulders and led him away from Thomas Wayne to the house.

Edward turned and looked back at Thomas Wayne, doubled over, and said, "I ain't playing with you. I want my fucking money."

Dillard went and stood beside Thomas Wayne and asked, "Are you okay?"

"He's an ass," Thomas Wayne said. "I told him I'd get him his money."

Thomas Wayne straightened up, took a couple of breaths, and rubbed his stomach.

Trevor walked back to check on Thomas Wayne.

"Come on, Thomas Wayne," Trevor said. He placed his arm around Thomas Wayne's shoulder. "What's up with the money, man? Edward is going to hurt you bad if you don't get him his money. It sounds like you're terribly overextended. If so, we need to figure out how to get you out from under."

"Edward is pretty serious about getting his money," Dillard said.

"I'm okay," Thomas Wayne said while walking. "Just need to get some things straightened out. My brother can be impatient."

"Okay, but I don't know how someone can be impatient with wanting their money," Trevor shrugged his shoulders. "I'm here for you. I know how bad decisions can get you into trouble financially."

"I said I'm okay," Thomas Wayne said, agitated.

Edward was sitting on the sofa when Trevor, Dillard, and Thomas Wayne entered the house.

Heads were bowed in deep thought, and there was dead silence.

A knock at the door startled the guys.

Trevor raised his head and said, "It's open. Come in."

It was Erin, Melissa, and Claire.

Trevor got up to greet his cousins with a hug.

"Hi, cousins," Trevor said with a smile. "It's good to see you."

Erin, Melissa, and Claire entered the living room with bags in tow. Claire closed the door behind her.

Erin appeared exhausted. She collapsed on the ottoman. Claire and Melissa squeezed in and sat on the sofa with Edward.

"Anybody want something to drink?" Trevor stood in the middle of the living room.

"I'll take a water, Trevor," Erin responded.

Trevor walked into the kitchen.

Claire and Melissa felt the tension among the guys.

"Wow, Trevor, the house looks great," Melissa said as she looked around.

"You did an outstanding job decorating the place," Claire commented. "I need for you to come to our house."

"Thanks, ladies," Trevor said.

Claire stood up to look at the pictures on the wall.

"This is like some wall of family fame," Claire said laughing. "You've displayed a lot of our milestone occasions, graduations, weddings, and family get-togethers. Here's a picture of me and Melissa with new bikes for Christmas."

Melissa walked over to see the picture.

"That is too funny," Melissa commented.

"Hey, guys," Erin said, looking at everyone. "I don't know about you all, but I've had a rough day."

Edward gave her a stern look, then looked over at Thomas Wayne.

Melissa looked baffled as she sat down.

"I think it's supposed to rain tonight and all day tomorrow," Melissa said.

"That's what the forecast is," Trevor said. He handed Erin a bottle of water.

Trevor sat on the floor. His stretched out his legs and sat in front of the group.

"Guess that means we will not be exercising," Claire said, laughing. She sat down on the sofa.

"Don't worry; I have plenty of indoor fitness activities," Trevor smiled.

"I hope we won't be cooped up in this house all weekend," Edward said. "And what happened to the lake house? It has plenty of room to accommodate us. This house is too small for seven folks, with everybody taking turns to use that small bathroom."

"I remember a time when we had twenty or thirty folks in this house," Trevor boasted.

"That was when we were kids," Edward said coldly. "We didn't know any better."

"Well, this weekend we will be spending our time together here. The primary purpose of restoring Grandma's home was so we could come back to a place that made us all feel loved, happy, and safe."

"It really looks nice, Trevor," Claire commented.

"Absolutely," Erin said.

"Nothing like it was a few months ago," Dillard added.

"You all did a great job," Trevor smiled.

Edward and Thomas Wayne remained quiet, listening.

"So, what do you have planned for us?" Melissa inquired. "More activities, I'm sure."

"Definitely more activities," Trevor answered. "But tonight, it's about dinner."

"I don't smell anything. Did you cook?" Erin asked.

"Nope, I didn't cook," Trevor laughed. "But don't worry. We are *all* going to cook tonight."

"What!" Edward shouted. "Aw, hell naw!"

"Yes," Trevor said. "A friend of mine who is a fitness expert and nutritionist should be here soon."

"Is she cooking or are we cooking?" Erin asked.

"She is going to give us a course in cooking healthier meals," Trevor said.

Trevor talked in detail about the benefits of home cooked meals. First, he discussed its money saving aspect. His example of the higher cost of packaged and prepared meals drove home the fact that with raw ingredients, eating at home was cheaper.

"Over a two week period, I helped one of my clients and her husband understand how cooking at home was cheaper. The first week, they ate all of their meals out, breakfast, lunch, and dinner. They have three kids, ages 5, 10, and 15. Breakfast each day averaged $25; lunch averaged $20, and dinner did also. That's $455 a week for eating out."

"Wow! That's a lot of money," Erin said. She thought about how much she had been spending on restaurant eating. "Me and the kids typically stop by McDonald's for breakfast. I try and get my son something healthy because of his diabetes. Prior to his diagnosis, he would eat lunch at school for about $4 a day. Then, I'd stop off somewhere in the neighborhood and pick up something for dinner. Two large pizzas for $13.99."

"I know that was a way of life for me and Veronica. I know we spent a mint on eating out. And, I know she continues to do so," Dillard said.

"The second week, I went with my client and her husband to the grocery store and purchased food for them to eat for a week. But first the husband and wife had to outline what meals they would eat. For breakfast, they considered cold cereal, oatmeal, an egg and vegetable pita dish, or a fruit, oats, and yogurt. For lunch, a spinach chicken salad, tuna salad, or an easy turkey and spinach wrap. For dinner, ginger chicken stir fry that they could eat two or three days. Bottom line, I got them down to around $100 a week. And that was for a family of five."

"Wow!" Dillard said.

"They were probably eating stuff they didn't like," Edward muttered.

Trevor ignored Edward's comment and said, "If people took the time to put a pencil to the paper and do some price comparison and calculating, they would be surprise at how much they could save. You can bring your home-cooked leftovers to work for lunch. That's a significant savings in itself. I save myself around $100 each month. My client also saves by buying food in bulk from places like Sam's Club and Costco, using store coupons, and eating more meatless meals."

"I'm not going without meat," Thomas Wayne said. "That's the hallmark of my meals."

Edward stared at him in disgust.

"Also, you are now well aware that food manufacturers and restaurant chains use higher levels of salt and fat to make their products taste better to the consumer. Another benefit of preparing your meals at home is that you can control the amount of salt and the type of oils you use in your recipes," said Trevor.

"Do you think that's why we're gaining so much weight as a nation?" Melissa asked.

"Yes, I do. I am a firm believer that eating out increases the possibility of weight gain as well as heart disease, diabetes, cancer, and, consequently, digestive disorders, autoimmune disorders, arthritis, and so many other illnesses and diseases."

"What about sandwiches at the deli shops?" Melissa asked.

"They are using processed meats. For example, processed chicken breast for that chicken breast sandwich. And, it contains more sodium than you'd imagine."

"That's all I eat, and I still have high blood pressure," Melissa said. "I guess my weight probably has something to do with it also." She sucked in her stomach discreetly.

"When you carve out the time to plan your weekly meals, you save time and money. Angela is coming over tonight to help you create meals that provide a balance of protein, carbohydrates, and fat to provide essential vitamins and minerals. Balanced meals contribute to helping you to feel satisfied."

"What about eating ice cream late at night," Erin asked while laughing.

Before Trevor could answer, there was a knock on the door. He raised up off the floor.

"It's probably Angela."

He opened the door.

A slender lady in her early forties stood in the entranceway, dressed in a dark-brown jogging outfit.

"Hi, Angela," Trevor said. He gave her a big hug.

Angela was grinning. "Hi Trevor."

She walked inside.

Trevor started to introduce her to everyone.

Trevor shared some background information about Angela who was a personal trainer and nutritionist.

"She is praised by many for total body workouts and her ability to incorporate new routines to keep her client's body and mind engaged. Her nutritional counseling is very valuable, as she provides strategies for becoming creative in the kitchen."

"Thank you, Trevor, for your kind words." She looked at his cousins and said, "Trevor often invites me to his healthy living symposiums to conduct cooking demonstrations. I'm so happy to be here with you all this evening."

"Well, let's get started," Trevor said. "I'd like for us to eat before eight o'clock."

They all walked into the kitchen.

"Did you get the ingredients for the ginger chicken stir fry?" Angela asked Trevor.

"Yes, I did."

He opened up the refrigerator to get the frozen mixed vegetables and diced chicken breast. He placed them on the countertop near the diced garlic clove and diced ginger root. He opened a cabinet and took out a bottle of extra virgin olive oil and Chinese rice wine vinegar. He opened another cabinet and took out a box of Quinoa.

His cousins and Angela waited to the side for him to retrieve everything she needed for the meal.

Thomas Wayne quietly turned and walked away. He sat at the kitchen table to watch.

"I believe that's everything," Trevor said, as he looked at Angela.

"Great," she responded and walked over to the countertop. "Tonight, I'm going to prepare ginger chicken stir fry."

Melissa shrugged her shoulders. She exchanged a puzzled look with Erin.

"Okay, who's going to assist me?" Angela asked, as she looked around for pots and utensils.

"I will," Dillard responded.

"Okay, we begin with boiling eight cups of water in a large pot."

Trevor handed Dillard a clean measuring cup and a large pot. Dillard walked over the sink and turned on the water. He filled the measuring cup with water and poured it into the pot. Then he repeated doing so until he had poured eight cups of water into the pot.

"Okay, place it on the stove," Angela instructed. "Once it's at a boil, we'll add the quinoa."

Melissa interrupted quickly and said, "What is quinoa?"

"It is a seed."

"Why me," Edward whispered, as he shook his head and rolled his eyes.

"We'll boil it for about 10 minutes and then reduce the heat and cover. Then, we'll cook it for an additional 15 minutes or until the quinoa has absorbed the water."

Angela turned and asked, "Edward, can you add two tablespoons of extra virgin olive oil to this skillet?" She handed Edward a large skillet. "We're going to heat olive oil over medium-high heat."

Trevor pointed to the extra virgin olive oil.

"We're going to sauté the garlic and ginger, then add the diced chicken breast."

"I'll add the garlic and ginger, and then the diced chicken breast," Claire said.

"Dillard, watch the quinoa."

"Will do."

"Then, we'll add the frozen vegetables to the sautéed mixture and Chinese rice wine vinegar," Angela said.

"Hey, Thomas Wayne, you'd better come over and help out," Dillard said.

Melissa looked over at Thomas Wayne and whispered to Erin, "What's wrong with Thomas Wayne. He's sitting over there looking worked up about something."

"I don't know," Erin said. "Something must have happened before we got here. Edward is looking a little more hateful than usual."

They both smiled quietly.

Trevor moved to add the frozen vegetables and Chinese rice wine vinegar.

"Okay, place the lid on the skillet to allow the vegetables to steam for about five to eight minutes."

"The chicken and vegetable mixture will be served on top of one-half cup of quinoa," Angela stressed to emphasize portion control.

Dillard took the quinoa off the stove. It had a fluffy, creamy, and slightly crunchy texture. He took a spoon, tasted some of the quinoa, and commented, "It has somewhat of a nutty flavor."

Angela removed the skillet from the burner.

"Wow! That didn't take any time to prepare," Erin said.

Trevor stated, "By the time you drive to a restaurant, place your order, wait for your order, return home, and serve the meal, you could have made a healthy meal from scratch with time to interact with your family." Trevor paused. "My weekdays are typically hectic, so I prepare half the week's meals on Sunday and the other half on say Wednesday. For people struggling with fitting in exercise, then, something like my routine can allow time for exercise."

Angela started to explain the nutritional benefits of the ginger chicken stir fry dish, "This meal is gluten free, low-cholesterol, heart healthy, and diabetic friendly."

"What's the caloric intake?" Trevor asked.

Edward grumbled, "Who cares?"

"With a serving size of one-half cup of quinoa and one cup of stir fry, it's estimated to be 445 calories. I'll leave you all a copy of the recipe which includes all of the nutritional information."

"Also, ginger is great for the digestive system. It heats the body, boosting circulation and metabolism. You can use ground ginger root, but fresh ginger root that you chop yourself is best," Trevor said.

"Right," Angela agreed.

"So, let's eat this stuff," Edward said meanly.

They grabbed plates and eating utensils. Angela helped them with measuring for the preferred portion size.

Once seated at the table, they gave thanks and ate. They chatted about the meal and their weekend together. Edward and Thomas Wayne sat silently at the table.

After an hour, Angela departed. Before doing so, Trevor asked her to come back in the morning for breakfast.

Chapter 17

Beyond Payback

It was a rainy Saturday morning, and Trevor was in the kitchen unloading groceries.

Thomas Wayne came in, opened the refrigerator, and started moving food items around. "What's up, cuz? You been out already?"

"Good morning," Trevor responded. "Needed to get some items for breakfast."

"Looks like it's drizzling," Thomas Wayne said, as he closed the refrigerator door. He could see spattering against the kitchen window.

Thomas Wayne set a container of orange juice on the counter.

"Need a glass?" Trevor asked.

"Yeah."

"Upper right cabinet."

Thomas Wayne retrieved a glass and poured some orange juice.

Trevor turned on the Mr. Coffee. "I better get some coffee brewing."

"Right," Thomas Wayne responded, as he sat at the table.

Trevor spoke quietly, "So, what's up with all that money you owe Edward."

"Everything is okay. We're doing some renovations around our home that I didn't plan for. Plus, the AC unit went out and we had to replace it. It cost us $15,000," Thomas Wayne said.

"I try and follow the rule of having six months of savings for those unexpected and unplanned events."

"I know," Thomas Wayne said. "We just have a lot going on right now. The kids are in private school. That's $3,000 a month for the two kids."

"Wow! That's a lot of money," Trevor said, looking surprised. "Must be one of the high-end schools."

"Yes, it is."

"I see why you have to work all those extra jobs," Trevor commented. He placed a newspaper on the table and sat across from Thomas Wayne.

Thomas Wayne looked weary. "And that don't even include the fees for books, class trips, and lunch."

Claire, Melissa, and Erin entered the kitchen.

"Hi, guys," Claire said in high spirits. "What's with the serious looks?"

"Hi, Ladies," Trevor said as he stood up. "I've got some coffee brewing."

He walked over to the coffee machine. He opened a cabinet door and grabbed several mugs one by one.

"I'll take one of those," Melissa said, as she reached for one of the mugs. He handed one to Claire and Erin.

"No coffee for me," Claire responded. "I'll get some juice."

Once they all had their beverage of choice, everyone sat at the kitchen table. Claire opened the newspaper and took out the section with the crossword puzzle.

"So, do we need to get started on the eggs, bacon, and pancakes?" Erin asked with a smile.

Trevor laughed and said, "No, cuz, Angela is coming back this morning to demonstrate some creative meals for breakfast."

"Great," Melissa said sarcastically, as she took a sip of coffee.

"Then comes the games," Claire said laughing.

"Don't forget exercise," Erin chimed in.

Everyone started laughing.

"Where's Dillard and Edward?" Claire asked.

"I'd better go and check on them," Trevor started walking away. "I'll make sure Edward didn't kill Dillard in the middle of the night."

"Or, vice versa," Erin said. She looked at Trevor with a smirk.

Trevor knocked on the door. After getting no response, he opened it and walked inside. Dillard was sound asleep on one twin bed, and Edward was talking to someone on his cellular phone.

Trevor looked over at Edward, "Hey, man, good morning to you." He waited for Edward to acknowledge him.

Dillard turned over and looked up at Trevor. Rubbing his head, eyes half-closed, he said, "Hey, Trevor."

"Hey."

"Guess I was exhausted from the week. I never get to sleep this late."

Edward concluded his call and placed his cellular phone on the night table. He got out of the bed, brushed pass Trevor, and walked out of the room.

Trevor dismissed Edward's action and said, "Angela will be here soon for a breakfast demonstration."

"More healthy stuff," Dillard commented. "But, I do admit that the ginger chicken stir fry was tasty."

"I'm sure whatever she comes up with for breakfast will be tasty as well."

"Okay, let me get cleaned up."

"I'll see you in the kitchen."

Trevor walked down the short hallway. He could hear Edward in the bathroom brushing his teeth.

"Looks like it's going to rain all day," Melissa said while reading the local news section of the newspaper.

"It's okay. If we had to be cooped up together, I'd rather it be on a rainy day than on a sunny day," Thomas Wayne said.

"Now that's a matter of preference. I'd rather a sunny day so I could walk outside when you all start acting crazy," Melissa said laughing.

"I know that's right," Claire said.

Trevor walked in.

"Hey, guys, here's an article talking about one of Uncle Bert's business associates," Melissa said. "Says Tyler Jackson is under investigation by the FBI for his real estate transactions to State Representative Bert Spencer. 'In 2008, Jackson purchased foreclosed land throughout Houston and sold a combined 200 acres to Bert Spencer, earning a profit of over $5 million. Court documents unsealed earlier this month show that federal agents are reviewing e-mails, contact lists, appointments, pictures and file attachments routed through e-mail accounts used by Jackson.' "

Edward walked in as Melissa was reading excerpts of the article.

"Y'all know all this stuff Trevor is putting us through is meaningless. Once the Feds get finished with our Uncle, Trevor, there will not be a business to inherit or a fortune to pass on to the next generation. I don't know why we're still here," Edward said as he poured a cup of coffee.

The room was silent.

Melissa sighed and stared at the newspaper.

Erin shook her head in disgust at Edward.

Trevor reacted by getting pots and pans ready for Angela.

Thomas Wayne whispered to Claire, "Just ignore him and maybe he'll go away."

"I doubt it," Claire said softly. "He's saying it to get a rise out of us."

Dillard walked into the room and noticed the tension.

"Hey, guys," he greeted.

There was a knock at the front door before they could answer Dillard.

Trevor hurried across the room to the front door. He opened it and saw Angela standing on the porch in her rain gear.

"Hi, Angela," Trevor said, as he motioned for her to come in. "I'll take your rain jacket."

"Hi, Trevor," she said. "It's pretty nasty out there. Supposed to rain all day."

"Thank you so much for coming out in this weather."

She walked into the kitchen area with Trevor.

"Hi, everyone," Angela said with a big smile.

They all spoke, except Edward.

"What's on the menu?" Claire asked.

Angela stood in the center of the kitchen and said, "An egg and vegetable pita for your cousins and fruit with oats and yogurt for you."

Trevor urged everyone to gather around to watch Angela prepare the egg and vegetable pita.

Erin assisted by cutting whole pita breads into halves. Melissa diced mushrooms and tomatoes. Thomas Wayne and Dillard separated out egg whites from the yolk. Trevor, Claire, and Edward stood to the side watching.

Angela began to heat one teaspoon of olive oil in a skillet on medium-high heat. In a medium bowl, Thomas Wayne and Dillard scrambled egg whites and placed them to the side. Angela took the diced mushrooms and tomatoes from Melissa and added them to the skillet. She cooked them for two minutes, and then she added the egg whites and scrambled the mixture.

"Okay, everyone, get a plate and a half pita. You can add the egg and vegetable inside the pita. Be gentle with opening the pita because they tear easily."

Edward walked into the living room and sat on the sofa.

While they fixed up their pitas, Angela asked Trevor about the oats, yogurt, and blueberries. He walked over to refrigerator and opened it to get a container of oats, a carton of plain yogurt, and a bowl of fresh blueberries.

"Great," Angela said, as he placed the items on the counter. He looked over at Claire and said, "Mixing the blueberries (one-half cup), oats (one-half cup), and plain yogurt (one-half cup) is real simple."

Erin interrupted Angela and said, "What is the nutritional content for the stuffed pita?"

Angela motioned for Claire to mix the ingredients and responded, "One serving is estimated to be: calories 244, total fat, nine grams (saturated fat, three grams, monounsaturated fat, four grams, polyunsaturated fat, one gram), cholesterol, 18 mg, sodium 481 mg, total carbohydrate 16 grams (dietary fiber, four grams, sugar, six grams), and protein 22 grams."

"What about mine?" Claire asked.

"A serving size which is approximately one one-half cup: calories 264, total fat, three grams (saturated fat, one gram, monounsaturated fat, one gram, polyunsaturated fat, one gram), cholesterol, two milligrams, sodium, 97 milligrams, total carbohydrate, 47 grams (dietary fiber, six grams, sugar, ten grams), and protein 13 grams."

They were all enjoying the food when Edward said, "You're all giving up what y'all want to eat for a promise. I keep telling you; when the Feds get finished with Uncle Bert, he will not have a business or money after paying his attorneys. He may even go to jail."

Angela nearly choked on her food as she listened to Edward's ranting.

"Edward, you're such an asshole," Erin said, sounding exhausted from his negative comments.

"Y'all don't want to face the truth."

Angela interrupted, trying to get the conversation focused on a positive topic, "Most of us have heard the old saying, 'Breakfast is the most important meal of the day.' I have read a variety of medical sources that have tied eating a healthy breakfast with less chronic diseases, a longer lifespan, and enhanced health. They also suggest that starting your day with a good breakfast increases your energy level and may help with controlling one's body weight."

Edward growled loudly and slouched down on the sofa.

Breakfast was over, dishes were clean, and Angela had departed. Trevor asked his cousins to meet him in the living room for their first group activity.

He looked around the room, waiting, as Erin, Dillard, and Claire sat on the sofa, and Thomas Wayne, Edward, and Melissa took their seats on the wing-back chairs. They were looking around as if for something in particular.

Trevor started to speak to them. "All of us in our lives have experienced pain, hurt, and unfairness at the hand of someone close to us. It's no secret that among the seven of us, we have been mistreated, betrayed, discounted, and abuse. But, the fact of the matter is that we can't change the past, no matter how bad we want to. Since we reconnected, I've seen in all of you a frustration I let reside in myself for years, while constantly trying to figure out why and always asking myself why. 'Why did this happen to me? Why did he hurt me? Why did she betray me?' "

Dillard, Erin, and Melissa became noticeably moved by Trevor's comments. Trevor looked around at all of their faces. "And I know that for years you've been struggling, trying to figure out why, asking yourself, 'Why me? Why my family? Why did my mother kill my brother? Why did my mother leave her children? Why did my mother hide the paternity of my father?

Why did he rape me? Why do I hurt?' I had to get past my own past, so I let go."

Edward stared blankly at Trevor, unmoved and unimpressed.

"You can't continue to allow your past to affect your future. You will never be able to live healthy, mind, body, and soul, and with purpose, until you dissolve and resolve. You will never be able to live the life that God has outlined for you until you get past your past and let go," Trevor paused, then continued by saying, "Our next activity is called 'The Rocks of Life'."

Trevor picked up a backpack that was filled with rocks.

"This backpack is filled with rocks and represents all of the thoughts and feelings weighing you down, preventing you from achieving."

Trevor began to walk around the room with the backpack of rocks hanging off his right shoulder.

"I want everything to take a rock out of the bag and read what it says," Trevor instructed.

He walked over to Melissa and bent over for her to get a rock.

Melissa took a rock out of the bag and said, "It says 'Bitterness'."

Trevor looked around at everyone and said, "I'm not here to judge any of you, but I know someone in this room has a heart that is consumed with bitterness. You're bitter because of things that have happened to you in your past, and the bitterness that consumes you, that you continue to carry around with you, will forever weigh you down and will prevent you from moving forward."

He walked over to Dillard and motioned for him to get a rock.

Dillard took a rock out of the bag and said, "Anger."

Trevor looked around at everyone and said, "I know someone in this room has a spirit rooted in anger, and that anger has made you critical, negative, antagonistic, vengeful, and unpleasant to be around."

Edward rolled his eyes as though he couldn't wait for the end.

Dillard stood up and walked into the kitchen. He opened the refrigerator and grabbed an energy bar Angela made before she left. He turned around and noticed Erin nodding her head. She leaned back and motioned for him to bring her a bar. He placed a bar on a paper plate for her.

Trevor walked over to Erin and bent over for her to get a rock.

Erin took a rock out of the bag and said, "Resentment."

"Just like bitterness and anger, resentment will contaminate our spirits and keep us from experiencing God's best for our lives. As in the case of bitterness and anger, your attitude will be so unpleasant and difficult to deal with that others will avoid being around you."

Dillard tiptoed back into the room. He glanced over at Edward as he sat down beside Erin and handed Erin the paper plate.

"What are you looking at me for," Edward demanded.

Erin took the paper plate from Dillard and immediately started to eat the energy bar.

Trevor continued, "Yes, bitterness, anger, and resentment will affect your relationships with others, such as your spouse, your kids, your co-workers, and the person at the grocery store. It will affect your relationship with Jesus Christ. You can't pray effectively."

Trevor walked over to Claire and bent over for her to get a rock.

Claire took a rock out of the bag and said, "Financial problems."

"I often look at people I know and wonder why that person is still stuck in the mindset they were in ten, twenty, or thirty years ago. Why is that person not growing? He's smart and talented, or she has a great ability. What is really holding that person back from making a difference in his or her life and in the lives of others? Most often, at the core is some hurt, pain, resentment, anger, or bitterness, the rocks in his or her life, or that something from their past that is keeping him or her from living their full potential."

Trevor walked over to Thomas Wayne and motioned for him to get a rock.

Thomas Wayne took a rock out of the bag and said, "Shame."

"Shame is what I felt for years, and I don't know about you, but I knew I didn't want to live a life filled with shame, pain, blame, and resentment. I came to the realization that I first had to become transparent with God. I had to recognize and admit so that I would know what to ask God to take away from me." Trevor hesitated, then continued, "By no means am I taking you all through all of this to dredge up the past or have you relive something that happened to you that has cause years of intolerable hurt and pain. I don't want you all to continue life as is. I want God to heal your heart and restore your spirit."

Trevor walked over to Edward and motioned for him to get a rock.

"Don't even think about it," Edward said coldly. "I refused to play your little rocks game."

Trevor stared at Edward, and then said, "Fine, I'll pull a rock out on your behalf."

He placed the backpack on the floor and reached for a rock. He looked at what was written on the rock and smiled, "It says forgiveness."

Trevor looked at his cousins intensely.

"Bitterness, anger, resentment, and shame are like strongholds in our lives, and the only way those strongholds can be dissipated is through the power of God. Many years ago, I asked God to help me to forgive those who had hurt me."

"Now that's hard," Erin said. She took the empty plate from her lap and placed it on the coffee table. She raised up and sat on the edge of the sofa.

"I know that's right," Melissa echoed.

"I'll admit that it is hard to forgive those who have hurt us mentally, emotionally, and physically," Trevor said.

"And treated us badly, abused us, talked about us, and belittled us," Dillard said.

"Especially if they hurt you over and over and over again," Erin said. She looked at Trevor, on the verge of tears.

Dillard looked to Erin, who shook her head.

"It's good you got over your hurt and pain, Trevor," Claire said. "And, frankly you're not telling me something I haven't heard over and over from my pastor. It's easy for someone to tell you about forgiveness, but we all have to get there on our own timetable. Sure, I'd love to forgive my mother for keeping the identity of my biological father a secret, but it's easier said than done."

Trevor looked at Claire and said, "The longer you let something fester, the more diseased the area will become. Hurt and pain is a part of life. What doesn't kill you will make you stronger. Even today, when someone hurts, mistreats, lies about, slanders, or offends me, it's okay. I pray to God for me to not have an unforgiving spirit. I never want to let negative thoughts and feelings rule over my life again."

Trevor closed out the activity by detailing how God had used adversity in his life to advance him. Trevor pleaded with his cousins to not let the past determine their futures. They could not let what happened to them so long ago control their destiny. He reiterated how abundant their life could be once they let go of the past, that a relationship with God would change their life from bitter to pleasant, brokenhearted to happy, and fractured to whole. It was time for them to ask God to clear their minds and their hearts, not to let something that happened years ago destroy what God wanted to do in their lives.

Chapter 18

❖

A Twist of Fate

After their morning activity, it was time for fitness. Trevor had identified three exercises they would perform together.

"Since it's raining outside, we'll exercise indoors," Trevor said to Erin, Dillard, and Melissa.

Thomas Wayne and Edward had retreated to the back rooms, and Claire was in the restroom.

"What can we possibly do in the house?" Dillard asked.

"First, we're going to walk in place for twenty minutes. We are going to start out slow, then build our intensity."

"Surely one can't lose weight by doing this," Erin said, as she started to move her legs up and down.

"You'd be surprised," Trevor responded. "We're going to warm up for at least five minutes."

Before they started, Trevor gave each one of them a pedometer that tracked heart rate, steps, distance, and calories burned.

"I saw a lady at work with one of these, but this one looks fancier than hers," Erin said, as she clipped the gadget to her shorts.

Trevor took a few minutes to show them how to measure their stride and where to properly wear it.

"This is nice," Erin said, admiring the stylish device with its platinum-colored faceplate.

Melissa yelled out, "Thomas Wayne and Edward, get in here! Trevor has a cute toy for us."

There was no response from either man.

"It's a little more than a toy," Trevor said laughing. "This is a great device to use as a barometer for how active you are every day. The goal is 10,000 steps, which is equivalent to about 5 miles."

"That's a lot of steps," Melissa said.

"That's the goal," Trevor emphasized. "Okay, let's warm up."

"What's the purpose of warming up?" Dillard inquired. "Let's just get to it."

"Warming up gets your body ready for the real exercise activity. It's the stage you use to raise your body's core temperature. By doing so, you improved your ability to move your joints and muscle tissues with ease, and it also gets your respiratory and cardiovascular systems ready to build your exercise intensity progressively."

"I see," Dillard responded. "I joined the gym and have been walking on the treadmill. I think I start out too fast."

They walked in place for twenty minutes, while Trevor discussed things to consider when exercising, "It's important to make sure you're exercising at the right intensity level."

Their devices tracked heart rate. Trevor explained the connection between their maximum heart rate and target heart rate range. They needed to exercise at an intensity of 60 to 85 percent of their maximum heart rate for cardiovascular benefit.

"Exercising below your target zone may prevent you from burning sufficient calories or improving your cardiovascular fitness. But, on the other hand, exercising above your target zone may be too intense and can lead to injury."

"Melissa, did you get your physical exam?" Trevor asked as they continued to walk.

"Not yet," she responded. "My insurance doesn't kick in for 90 days. I'll be able to get insurance next month."

"When is the last time you had a physical?" Trevor asked.

"It's been years."

"What about you, Erin?" Trevor asked.

"I'm going to get one," she responded. "With so much going on, I just haven't had the time. But I know I'm fine, just fat."

"Even if you think all is well with your body, it is still important to see your health care provider regularly to check for potential problems. Most people who have high blood pressure don't even know it," Trevor stressed. "The only way to find out is to have your blood pressure checked regularly. Likewise, high blood sugar and high cholesterol levels often do not produce any symptoms until the disease becomes advanced."

"Right! I didn't know about my prediabetes until after my physical examination," Dillard said. "Other than my high cholesterol, I was walking around thinking everything else with me was okay."

"Plus, keep in mind that you may have exercise restrictions due to a health condition or medication and are not even aware of them, and these restrictions will affect your intensity level. But, if you don't visit your doctor, you'll never know," Trevor said.

Trevor raised five of his fingers. "Okay, let's cool down for five minutes," Trevor said. "The cool-down phrase is to return you heart rate gradually to its pre-exercise level."

After the cool down, Trevor was ready to show his cousins some light calisthenics and simple stretching exercises.

"Now what, Trevor?" Erin asked. "I'm ready to sit down."

Trevor went to a bag on the floor and pulled out a jump rope. He handed the jump rope to Dillard. Then he retrieved a foam exercise mat that was securely rolled up.

"I know you don't think I'm getting ready to bounce all of this up and down," Melissa said, as she looked sternly at Trevor.

Trevor motioned for Dillard to come near him.

"Although it's not for everybody, jumping rope is a great workout for your entire body. Your legs, arms, wrists, shoulders, and even your core get a tremendous workout in just a few minutes."

Claire walked into the room and sat on the sofa.

Trevor unrolled the exercise mat and motioned for Dillard to stand on it. He adjusted the jump rope so it was the right length for Dillard.

"Okay, Dillard, start with the rope behind you," Trevor said as he watched Dillard. "When we were kids, we'd swing the rope over our heads, moving our hands and rope forward."

Dillard tripped and fell while trying to jump over the rope.

Erin, Melissa, and Claire started to laugh.

Trevor went over to help Dillard up off the floor.

"I'm glad I was on the mat, or else that might have been really painful."

"Come on; try it again."

Trevor stressed the importance of technique.

"Jump over the rope with your feet together," Trevor instructed.

He made sure Dillard's shoulders were down and relaxed and that his elbows were inward and close to his body. He made sure his wrists remained slightly below his elbows while jumping the rope.

"I'm tired."

"Just jump a few inches off the ground. If you jump too high, you will tire yourself out very quickly."

Erin and Melissa sat watching Dillard, hoping they wouldn't have to participate.

Trevor noticed that Dillard was using too much of his arms and shoulders and said, "Make sure you use only the wrists to turn the rope, not your arms and shoulders. Keep your knees bent and your back straight. The goal is to land on the ball of your feet."

Erin and Melissa frowned as Dillard continued.

"When you get really good, you can try the familiar reverse jump, crisscross jump, and twisting jump," Trevor said to Dillard with amusement.

Dillard was clearly exhausted after three minutes. "It wasn't that hard when we were kids," Dillard said, breathing heavily.

Trevor looked at his cousins and said, "I just want you to understand your options for getting fit. Jumping rope is a great activity that provides an effective workout in only 15 to 20 minutes and can be done almost anywhere."

"I'll try it, but not today," Claire said while sitting on the sofa.

"What are some other exercises one can do at home?" Erin asked. "I don't have money for a gym, and even if I did, I'm not interested in exercising around others."

"There are all sorts of calisthenic exercises you can do, like sit-ups, crunches, pushups, leg lifts, squats, and lunges to strengthen and tone muscles throughout your body," Trevor responded.

"Sit on the floor," Trevor asked Erin.

"Nope, not me," she said, shaking her head.

"Melissa?" Trevor asked.

"Nope," she responded, laughing.

"I'll sit," Dillard said as he sat on the mat. He took a deep breath. Claire started laughing.

"Leg lifts are simple and help to reduce excess belly fat," Trevor said. "Place your hands at the sides of the body with the palm facing the ground. Keep both of your legs straight with your toes pointing at the ceiling."

Dillard did as he was asked.

"Now, bend both your knees so they are pointing toward the ceiling."

Dillard continued to follow his instructions.

"Extend your legs so the heels are directed toward the ceiling."

Dillard tried, but he couldn't.

"Your goal is to raise them up to form an L-shape with your body."

"You're kidding, right?" Dillard rolled over on his side, trying to form the L-shape.

"Come on," Trevor said, as he helped Dillard to situate his body. "Your lower stomach muscles will be contracted so you can raise your tailbone off the floor."

He instructed Dillard on raising his tailbone and lowering his legs.

Dillard completed three sets of twenty repetitions.

"Calisthenic exercises help build lean muscle and strengthen your core. They enable you to better perform cardio exercises and burn fat more efficiently," Trevor stated.

Trevor continued by having Dillard to do sit-ups. "With your knees slightly bent, feet on the ground, place your arms behind your head. Do not pull your head or neck. Now, go all the way up."

Dillard's feet kept rising up off the ground.

"Hold my feet down," Dillard insisted.

"That's how we did it back in the day in gym class," Melissa smiled.

"Just focus on keeping your feet pinned to the ground while sitting up," Trevor said.

"That makes it harder," Dillard commented while trying to follow Trevor's instructions.

"Your goal will be to work your way up to three sets of twenty or more repetitions, Dillard."

"Well, today I'll just shoot for ten."

Dillard struggled and achieved ten sit-ups.

"Okay, now, everyone, let's sit on the floor," Trevor instructed.

"Walking is fine," Melissa said laughing, "but, trying to sit on the floor is a different story."

"I know that's right," Erin chimed in.

Everyone sat on the floor, and Trevor handed each one a towel.

"We're going to do a hamstring and calf stretch," he said. "Sit with one leg stretched out in front of you. Then bend the other leg at the knee to where your foot meets the inner thigh of your extended leg. Place the towel around the foot of your extended leg.

Keep your leg straight and toes pulled in. Pull your upper body straight down over the extended leg and into it."

Trevor walked around the room.

"Keep your back straight, Melissa."

"Okay," Melissa said.

Erin watched Trevor assisting Melissa to make sure she was doing the exercise properly.

"Hold for 20 seconds, then repeat on the other leg."

He continued to walk around.

"Okay, now we're going to do a quad stretch."

He instructed them to lay face down. They placed the towel around their right ankle and pulled the foot upright behind their body.

"Hold for twenty seconds and repeat on the other side," Trevor further instructed.

Next was a tricep and shoulder stretch where they took the towel over one shoulder and grabbed from the bottom with the other hand.

"Stretch the right tricep by pulling down with the bottom arm. Then, stretch the front of the shoulder by pulling up with the top hand."

They repeated on the other side.

Trevor had them complete a variety of other stretching exercises for their shoulders, chest, lower back, and legs.

"I didn't do so bad for my size," Melissa commented.

"All of you did well," Trevor said proudly. "Stretching is good for relieving tension, maintaining range of motion in your joints, and increasing flexibility. You can do it regardless of your size."

"Hey, cuz, are we going to get a break anytime soon?" Dillard asked.

Trevor laughed and said, "We'll get back together in a couple of hours for dinner and our final exercise."

Dillard headed to the kitchen in search of a snack. Erin, Melissa, and Claire remained in the living room. They chatted about their families and the other happenings in their lives. Since Edward and Thomas Wayne never joined them for the exercise session, Trevor went to the back rooms to check on them.

All of the cousins were seated in the living room when Trevor introduced the last exercise of their retreat.

He retrieved an orange tin pail and said, "Although we can't predict the future, we all wonder about the future. That is, 'What will I be doing in say five years?' And, even better, we often set goals to achieve some desired outcome for some point in time, the future."

Edward groaned as Trevor talked.

"This exercise is titled, 'Your life in two years.' All we have talked about are things and actions that'll help you to live healthier so that you can increase the likelihood of having a better future."

"Get to the point, man," Edward said.

Trevor ignored Edward's outburst and continued, "The time is now, and the choice is yours. Your actions and choices will determine how you end up. Today, we're going to play a hypothetical. What if your actions today could influence how you end up in two years?"

Trevor asked each one of his cousins to take a card out of the pail. He instructed them not to read it until everyone had a card.

"Okay, Melissa, read what's on your card," Trevor instructed.

She turned over her card and said, "Using a combination of better eating habits and consistent exercising, I am no longer taking medication for high blood pressure."

"Wow! That was a good card for you," Trevor said happily. "I'll pray that's your reality in two years or before."

"Dillard?" Trevor asked.

"I went on a diet and lost 50 pounds. Within a year, I have gained the 50 pounds back plus an additional 20 pounds."

Dillard frowned.

"I pray that's not your story in two years," Trevor said. "But, it's a fact today for so many. They lose interest and commitment, slack off with exercising, revert back to the same eating habits as before, or they simply stop the weight program that was filled with tricks and techniques."

"I'll go," Thomas Wayne said, looking at Trevor.

"Okay," Trevor said.

He turned over his card and read, "While I was in the hospital trying to get my diabetes under control, I lost a major client because I couldn't fulfill my contractual obligations."

"Now that may not be Thomas Wayne's story in two years, but it will be for someone," Trevor stressed. "Earlier this year, I had the opportunity to speak to a group of small business owners, mainly sole proprietors. Of course, my message to them focused on living healthier. I explained to them that when they become sick or stricken with some disease or illness, so does their CEO, CFO, sales and marketing team, because they are all of those positions at the same time. Their business operations are impaired until they're up and running again. That impairment, whether it's a day or two or indefinitely, depending on their situation, can cause them to lose a client or potential clients."

"A friend of mine should have been at that talk?" Claire said. "She owns her own catering business. She suffered some medical condition a few months ago and hasn't been able to work."

Trevor shook his head. "When a business owner becomes critically ill, it stifles their ability to manage a project or secure that major business venture that was going to take their business to the next level. The stakes are even higher, because many of them may or may not have medical insurance. So, then they may have to take out a second mortgage on their home to try to keep the business going. They may have to build collaborations with others to borrow money. And, they haven't even factored in the impact on their personal lives (family and relationships)."

Trevor motioned for Erin to read.

Erin read her card that said, "I was fired after 20 years. My husband was on my insurance and now he has been diagnosed with cancer. I don't have the $600 a month to continue the medical insurance."

Thomas Wayne sat in his chair, looking worried.

Trevor looked around and said, "Now that's a tough one."

Claire raised her hand and read what her card said, "My kids' eating habits are better because of the changes I have made in our household."

"Now that's a good one," Trevor said. "Parents and guardians should take a proactive approach to lead their kids toward healthy lifestyle habits. Preventing kids from becoming overweight means parents and guardians must change the way their family eat, exercise, and spend time together."

The only person left to share what was on his card was Edward.

"Edward, what does your card say?" Trevor asked.

"It says I'm tired of listening to this nonsense," Edward said sarcastically.

Melissa was sitting next to Edward. She grabbed the card out of Edward's hand.

She silently read the card, then said aloud, "My ministry is flourishing because of the lifestyle changes I made. Because I'm not focused on being sick daily, I'm able to pursue and implement the vision God has given me."

"Glad I didn't read it," Edward said angrily.

Trevor pulled out a couple more cards and read, "My employment was terminated for excessive absences. My manager said I was sick and out of the office too many days. I couldn't get my stomach problems under control."

Trevor paused and read the other one, "Initially, I was looking for instant gratification. But, I realized that if I wanted to lose weight and keep it off that it would take work. No one loses weight and keeps it off without trying. Now I walk for 60 minutes at least 4 days a week."

Trevor handed Melissa a card to read.

She read the card that said, "Having been obese all of my adult life, I always looked for a quick fix to weight loss. After this exercise, I realized that if I wanted to lose weight and keep it off, I had to work at it. Now I walk for 60 minutes at least 4 days a week and have lost 70 pounds in two years."

Trevor looked around the room. He handed a card to Erin to read.

She read, "My husband and only child died last year, and now I'm alone at the age of 75, trying to recover from a stroke that has paralyzed my right side."

The room was silent.

Trevor handed a card to Thomas Wayne to read.

He read, "I am a single parent who has been diagnosed with thyroid cancer. My kids are five and nine. I can't take care of them, and I have to rely on others."

Trevor said, "What you all have read this evening is someone's life in two years, good or not so good. So, you all have some decisions to make," Trevor hesitated, then continued, "When the pastor at church extends the invitation to join the church, he often says, 'Don't leave here the same way you came.' My hope for you all is that you don't leave here the same way you came."

Chapter 19

Transitional Moments

One month after their retreat, Trevor was feeling both pleased and concerned about the state of his cousins. While Claire was puzzled about the medical prognosis of her condition, she was excited about how well she was performing in her half-marathon training program. Dillard had even decided to join the program to support her and to also get focused on living healthier. Melissa had enrolled in Houston Community College to pursue an accounting degree and had started taking classes. Trevor had made several attempts to talk with Edward, Thomas Wayne, and Erin, but he had been unsuccessful in doing so.

On his way back from speaking at a conference in Galveston, Texas on a Saturday evening, Trevor reflected more and more on his cousins. Traveling through the heavy rain, he was consumed in thought.

As he approached the 610 loop, his cellular phone rang. The Bluetooth came on. The voice on the other end said, "May I speak with Mr. McElroy?"

Trevor answered, "This is he."

"This is Nancy Sampson from Ben Taub Hospital. Your name was given as a contact for Edward Cartwright."

"That's my cousin," he quickly interrupted. "What's happened?"

"Your cousin had a stroke," she responded. "He's on the fourth floor."

Trevor was only minutes from Ben Taub Hospital.

When he arrived, he immediately went to the fourth floor. The nurse introduced Trevor to Dr. Welby, the ER doctor. Dr. Welby began to explain that they had been running tests on Edward for the past twelve hours.

"He had a major stroke, and we're not sure if he'll survive or not," Dr. Welby stated.

Trevor asked to see Edward.

He walked into Edward's room and immediately discerned that his vital signs were as serious as the doctor had stated. He was covered with many devices that were connected to his body; a tracheostomy and ventilator to assist him with breathing. Trevor began to pray that God would allow his cousin another chance.

"It's amazing that he's still alive," Dr. Welby said, as he walked up behind Trevor. "Is there someone else you can call? A wife? Mother? Father?"

Trevor thought about Thomas Wayne and his cousins.

"Yes, his brother," Trevor said. He walked outside the hospital room and down the hallway to a waiting area. He unclipped his cellular phone off his jeans and began to search for Thomas Wayne's telephone number. He called and did not receive an answer. Then he thought about Melissa.

Trevor called Melissa's telephone number and she answered.

"Hi, Melissa. It's Trevor," he said.

"Hi, Trevor. You sound strange. What's going on?"

"I'm here at Ben Taub Hospital. Edward has had a stroke, and it doesn't look good."

"Wow! I'm so sorry to hear that," Melissa said, trying to act concerned. "I'll be praying for him. Let me know if you need anything."

"Can you come up to the hospital?" Trevor asked.

"I would, but it's raining too bad out there. I don't drive in the rain."

Trevor was stunned by Melissa's comment.

"Come on, Melissa; I'm talking about your cousin. He may die," Trevor stressed.

"I hear you, but I can't come. Keep me posted," Melissa said. She hung up the telephone.

Trevor stood in the waiting area, shocked, looking at his cellular. He decided to call Claire.

Claire answered, "Hey, Trevor. It's good to hear from you."

"I was calling to let you know that Edward is in the hospital and that he may not make it. He had a stroke," Trevor said sadly.

"Oh, my goodness!" Claire exclaimed.

"Can you come to the hospital?" Trevor asked.

There was a moment of silence.

Claire responded and said, "I had a Remicade infusion on Thursday, and I'm having multiple bowel movements. I simply can't come. But he's in the best hospital for stroke victims. Keep me posted."

"That's fine. I'll call and check on you later," Trevor said.

He tried to reached Erin and Dillard but was unable to do so.

He walked back into Edward's hospital room. Edward's nurse walked in and informed Trevor that the first 72 hours were the most critical.

In the following days, Trevor visited Edward and his doctors to get status updates on his recovery. On the third day, they inserted a feeding tube in his stomach, but the prognosis continued to be dire. He had contracted a sinus infection and pneumonia. Trevor had notified his cousins of Edward's condition, but they refused to come and see him.

Trevor stood near the window of the waiting room. He took a deep breath and started to scroll through his cellular telephone. He pressed the button to call Melissa.

"Hi, Melissa."

"Hey, Trevor."

"Edward is still in the hospital. I wanted to know when you might be able to stop by."

"You know, I just got in school and the classes are already kicking my butt. I really wish I could stop by there, but between work, school, and my women's ministry, my days are filled to capacity," Melissa said.

Trevor could hear a lot of talking in the background and the sounds of people ordering food.

"Where are you?" he asked.

"Um… I'm at Red Lobster with some of the ladies from my women's ministry. We're discussing the volunteer program at the homeless shelter. Have you had the cheddar bay biscuits? They are simply delicious."

Trevor thought of the nutritional content of Red Lobster's cheddar bay biscuits; 150 calories each and 350 milligrams of sodium.

She hung up.

Trevor called Dillard.

Dillard listened to Trevor's status report about Edward and said, "Man, that used car I purchased is acting up. Think I've gotten a jalopy, one of the flood cars. Right now it's not working."

"I can come by and pick you up."

There was a pause.

Dillard responded and said, "I've been keeping my kids. I don't want to leave them here by themselves. Also, my presence probably wouldn't be good for Edward."

Dillard hung up.

Trevor called Erin.

"Surely you must be kidding, Trevor, mean as Edward has been to all of us," Erin said.

Trevor was disappointed with his cousins and their lack of compassion. He turned and started to walk back to Edward's hospital room.

Jenny walked up to him from a different hallway and tapped him on the shoulder.

Trevor looked at her helplessly, at a loss. He leaned down and gave her a big tight hug.

Jenny kissed Trevor tenderly on the cheek and said, "It's going to be okay."

He took her by the hand, and they walked down the hallway toward Edward's room.

By the ninth day, Edward's pneumonia was gone and he had become conscious and aware of his surroundings. Recovery was slow. The doctors had discovered that he was paralyzed on his right side and had lost his ability to speak.

Trevor was exhausted. He called a mandatory meeting at their grandma's house.

Dillard drove up just as Trevor finished mowing the yard.

He walked up to Trevor and said, "Hey, you should have called me. I would have helped you."

Trevor snarled at him and said, "Mowing the yard is not what I need assistance with. I need for you and the others to go to the hospital and visit your cousin."

Dillard snapped back, saying, "How on Earth do you expect any of us to go to that hospital? The way Edward has treated all of us! I can't believe you! Just know that you're the only saint in this family."

"I'm no saint, but I don't walk around holding a grudge against people for the way they treat me. If someone is in need, like our cousin, I discard my feelings and do what's right. And that's what I expect from you, Erin, Melissa, Claire, and Thomas Wayne."

"Sorry to disappoint you," Dillard said. He walked up the steps and went inside the house.

Trevor rolled the lawn mower around to the back of the house to put it in the garage.

Erin, Melissa, and Claire arrived at the same time.

"Hey, ladies," Claire said to Erin and Melissa as they exited their cars and walked toward the house.

"So, what's this meeting about?" Erin asked.

"I'm sure it's about Edward," Melissa stated, "and going to the hospital."

"Well, we better be careful about not going," Claire said. "Trevor may try and use not going against us. He may tell Uncle Bert that we're not complying with his stipulations."

Claire threw her arms around Erin and they all started laughing.

"I'm about to say the hell with the money," Erin said, cynically.

Melissa nodded in agreement, as she knocked on the front door. Dillard let them in.

"Hey, Cuz," Claire said to Dillard after walking inside.

They sat on the sofa.

"Where's Trevor?" Erin asked.

"He's in the back yard," Dillard responded. "He just finished mowing the yard. I think he's mad at us."

"We figured as much," Claire said. "By the way, did you get our training schedule for the week?"

"I did," Dillard said.

"How's the marathon training going?" Melissa asked.

"Actually, it's going okay," Claire said, "I'm up to seven miles of walking. Plus, I've raised $1,500 of my $2,500 and Dillard is running."

"You've lost a lot of weight," Melissa said, admiring Dillard's physique.

"I've lost 30 pounds, and it feels great," Dillard said with excitement. "I never, in a million years, thought about being a runner."

"You look great!"

"Thank you! I'm glad it's October. I can't imagine trying to run in the summer heat."

Erin sat in silence. She was depressed about her size.

A few minutes later, Trevor came through the back door.

"Hey, Cousin Trevor," Melissa said.

"Hey," he said.

"So, what's this meeting for?" Claire asked. "Where is Thomas Wayne?"

"I haven't been able to get in touch with Thomas Wayne," Trevor said. "I called you all together to discuss your lack of care and concern for Edward. I know firsthand that he is a difficult person to like and love, but he's blood, and he needs all of us. A part of this process that Uncle Bert has outlined for all of you involves more than eating healthy and exercising. It's about a total shift in thinking."

Claire whispered to Melissa, "I told you."

"For years, our family's foundation has been cracked. Those cracks represent anger, resentment, blame, hurt, pain—all of the emotions I thought you all were working to resolve."

Melissa quickly blurted out to Trevor, "Huh? We've made great strides with our emotional issues."

"I thought so, too," Trevor said. "I thought you were on your way to being a cohesive, unified unit, but that thought is out the window. What is even more disappointing and discouraging is people who walk in some church Sunday after Sunday and still act like you all when they leave—no change."

Dillard glanced helplessly at Trevor and said, "I just started going to church."

Melissa raised up from the sofa and walked into the kitchen, smiling.

"What do you want from us?" Dillard asked.

"I want you to act like someone whose heart has been changed, like someone who knows what it's like to be forgiven."

Melissa walked back into the room and handed everyone a bottle of water.

"What's the status on him," Melissa asked, sitting down.

Trevor explained that Edward was alert and that the doctors were trying to wean him off his feeding tube, IV, tracheostomy and ventilator. They hadn't been successful. While Trevor was talking, he received a telephone call.

He hung up and said, "That was the hospital. Edward has taken a turn for the worse. I need to get to the hospital. His brain has begun to swell. He's at Ben Taub in ICU."

Trevor stared at his cousins in defeat and walked out the door.

Chapter 20

❖

Revelations of Darkness

By the time Trevor arrived at the hospital, the doctors had gotten Edward's medical situation under control. He went into Edward's hospital room and prayed over him. After a few minutes, the nurses came in and motioned for him to leave.

Trevor walked down the hallway toward the waiting area. Claire, Melissa, Erin, and Melissa exited the elevator as he passed by.

An overwhelming joy overcame Trevor when he saw his cousins.

"How is he doing?" Claire asked.

"It's going to be a long road to recovery, but I know he's going to be okay." Trevor smiled.

They followed Trevor to the waiting area.

"We thought about everything you said, Trevor," Melissa said. "For years, our relationships with each other has been broken. To get us to see what we didn't see or didn't' want to see, you have poured out your heart and soul to help us, and we appreciate you for that. Just as you've been a positive example for us, we want to be a positive example for our kids and our siblings."

Melissa began to weep.

"She's right, Trevor," Dillard said. "We're truly grateful to you."

Trevor didn't know if his cousins' statements were sincere or if they didn't want to jeopardize getting Uncle Bert's wealth. He knew only time would reveal their sincerity or real motives.

Edward was eventually sent to a local rehabilitation center where he would stay for two months to receive intensive speech therapy. Trevor visited Edward nearly every day to track his progress. His cousins went two to three times a week.

Meanwhile, Trevor set out to find Thomas Wayne. He stopped by his home. To his surprise, Thomas Wayne's place was abandoned. The lawn, bushes, and weeds had not been trimmed. There were old newspapers, phone books, and coupons that littered the walkway of the home. Visible notices from Rivermount Home Owners Association covered the front door.

Trevor walked back to his car. He decided to call Thomas Wayne's job at the Sheriff's Department substation located on Clay Rd.

"Clay Road Substation, how may I route your call?" a lady asked.

"Hi, I'm trying to get in contact with Thomas Wayne Cartwright," Trevor stated.

"Thomas Wayne Cartwright no longer works here," the lady responded.

Trevor sat in his car looking puzzled.

"Are you sure, ma'am? He's a deputy sheriff there. Maybe he's been transferred to a different location?"

"Sir, he no longer works for the Harris County Sheriff's Department."

"Is there any way I can speak with whoever was his supervisor? I have an urgent family matter."

"Hold please."

Trevor waited patiently.

"Hi, this is Sergeant Turner," a man said. "I understand you've asked about Thomas Cartwright."

"Yes, sir," Trevor replied. "My name is Trevor McElroy and he's my cousin. I haven't been able to reach him. I remember that he was a deputy at this particular location. Has he been assigned to another location?"

"I'm sorry, Mr. McElroy, but Mr. Cartwright hasn't worked for the Harris County Sheriff's Department since earlier this year."

Trevor frowned at the comment Sergeant Turner made.

"Sergeant Turner, that's strange. I was under the impression that he was working at your office along with a bunch of extra jobs."

"Mr. McElroy, I'm sorry. I'm not at liberty to share any additional information." A moment of silence prompted Sergeant Turner to say, "Can I assist you with anything else, Mr. McElroy?"

"That's okay. Thank you, Sergeant Turner."

Trevor was surprised and frightened. He thought about others he could call who may be aware of Thomas Wayne's whereabouts, like his wife. He tried desperately to remember where she worked. He called Thomas Wayne's other siblings, but no one had heard from him.

While thinking about ways to find Thomas Wayne, Trevor decided to do two weeks of needed laundry on a Friday evening.

In the midst of sorting the colored from the white, his cellular telephone rang. He answered and a man asked, "May I speak with Trevor McElroy?"

"This is he."

"Mr. McElroy, this is Kyle from ADT Security. We're receiving an intruder alert at a residence on Kittridge Street."

"That's my property," Trevor said.

"Do you want us to send a police officer to the residence?"

"Please do. I'll be there in twenty minutes."

Trevor grabbed his keys. He opened the door and Jenny stood there with her right arm raised, getting ready to knock.

She had a bag in her left hand and asked, "Are you going somewhere?"

Trevor looked confused. "Did I forget a visit?"

"The spaghetti dinner at the church."

"What are you talking about?"

"We're having the fundraiser spaghetti dinner for the children's nursery at the church." Jenny frowned. "We agreed that I'd come over here and you'd drive."

"Oh! I completely forgot. I've just been so—"

Jenny quickly interrupted Trevor and asked, "Where on Earth are you going?"

"I got a telephone call from the security company that my alarm is going off at Kittridge. I am so sorry, but I've got to get over there right away. I'll call you later."

Trevor ran down his walkway past Jenny.

She looked exasperated and said, "I'm tired, Trevor."

Trevor didn't respond and continued on.

When he arrived, two police officers were in the driveway talking to his neighbor, Mr. Whitehouse. Trevor jumped out of his car and joined them.

"Are you Mr. McElroy?" one of the police officers asked.

Mr. Whitehouse said loudly, "Hi, Trevor. I came out to greet the officers for you. I've been sick all day, but it's the neighborly thing to do. I risked my safety to walk down here in the dark, nine-thirty, like a good neighbor should when he knows something to tell."

Trevor smiled at Mr. Whitehouse and said, "Thank you so much."

Looking at the officer, he asked, "Yes, sir, what's happened?"

"Hi, how are you doing?" the police officer said. He extended his arm to shake Trevor's hand. "I'm Officer Calhoun, and this is my partner, Officer Henson." Officer Calhoun looked over at his partner.

Trevor looked at the two, waiting for someone to let him know what had happened.

"Someone kicked in your back door," the officer said. "We need for you to go inside and see what was taken so we can file a report."

Mr. Whitehouse started to speak but then hesitated, shook his head, and then continued, "I was telling the officers that when I looked out my window, I saw your cousin, the one with that big black Cadillac, speeding away like a bat out of hell as the alarm was sounding off. The way he drove out the driveway, he had backed in. I'm sure he backed in to make it easy to get things out of the house and into his car. Looks like someone was in the passenger seat. I can't be sure, though. My eyes are starting to fail me. I just know my heart skipped a beat or two."

It was dark and only the street lights provided visibility for the officers, Trevor, and Mr. Whitehouse.

Officer Calhoun thanked Mr. Whitehouse for the information he'd shared. He asked Trevor, "Who is your cousin with the black Cadillac?"

"Thomas Wayne Cartwright," Trevor replied. "He has a black Escalade."

"Do you have an address for him?"

"I do, Timblewood Estates, 112 Langdon Terrace, but I just found out that he is no longer there. He was a sheriff deputy for Harris County, but I just found out he no longer works there."

"We'll check that out," Officer Henson said as he wrote something on a pad. "We need a list of people who may know his whereabouts so we can question him."

Trevor explained to the officers that he had been looking for his cousin but hadn't been able to find him.

Trevor led the officers around to the back of the house in the dark. The officers used their flashlights to provide light. Turning the corner to enter through the back door, Trevor noticed that the garage door was partially opened. The garage was detached from the house.

"Have you all looked in the garage?" Trevor asked.

"No," Officer Henson replied.

"The lock on the garage door is off," Trevor said.

He and the officers walked closer. They saw the padlock lying on the ground. Trevor felt along a wall to turn on the garage light, and then they walked inside.

Officer Henson knelt down to pick up the padlock and said, "We could dust the lock for fingerprints, but it probably wouldn't matter. I'm sure a number of people have touched this lock."

Upon walking inside, Trevor quickly noticed that a toolbox and all of the lawn equipment he had recently purchased were missing. He also noticed that electrical tools and equipment that he had been storing there for Edward was gone.

One of the officers asked, "Is your cousin on drugs?"

Trevor turned around suddenly and said, "Not to my knowledge."

Mr. Whitehouse walked slowly through the entrance of the garage door and said, "All of the burglaries in this neighborhood are because of drug addicts."

Officer Henson wrote down something on his pad.

Mr. Whitehouse said, "An empty house is a target every time for thieves and addicts."

Trevor closed the garage door as they all walked out. He and the officers walked toward the back door. Mr. Whitehouse followed behind slowly with his oxygen tank. There was fresh broken glass on the ground around the back door. The officers informed Trevor that they had already dusted pieces of the broken glass for fingerprints.

Inside the house, Trevor noticed muddy tracks. It had been raining in Houston for several days. He walked around. The officers and Mr. Whitehouse remained behind in the kitchen.

Trevor walked back into the kitchen area and said, "Looks like the flat screen is gone, along with the telephones, a digital scale, and the iron."

He walked around in the kitchen, looking in the upper and lower cabinets.

"And my Krups combo espresso and coffee maker, blender, and George Foreman's grill are gone," he stated.

The officers finished taking information for their report. Trevor closed the back door and informed them that he would be staying at the house for the night.

"Is there some database you can check to see if my cousin, Thomas Wayne, is in the hospital? I'm thinking he may be hurt and unable to notify us," Trevor said.

An hour earlier, Thomas Wayne had been involved in a car incident near Humble, Texas. Officers had responded to the area of 777 Brady Landing. The call indicated that a black Escalade and a Ford truck, one black and the other dark blue, had deliberately rammed each other.

The officers arrived at Big Country's Auto Parts. The owner was pacing frantically up and down the sidewalk.

"Officers, what took you so long?"

"What's the problem," one of the officers responded rudely.

The other officer interjected, "Sir, I'm Officer Wesson and this Officer Milburn. We received a complaint of disorderly conduct."

"Yes, Officer Wesson, behind my building!"

The owner motioned for the officers to follow him.

"I'm afraid they are going to pull out guns and start shooting."

The officers quickly followed the owner behind the building. They could hear loud yelling and screaming, "You hit my Escalade!" Thomas Wayne shouted.

"You stole my fucking money!" the other man shouted.

"I got something for you," Thomas Wayne commented.

The officers quickly approached Thomas Wayne and the other gentleman who was around 6'0" at 200 pounds.

"What's going on?" Officer Wesson asked.

The officers could see that the vehicles were badly damaged. Another male was seated in Thomas Wayne's SUV.

Thomas Wayne became nervous as the officers started to talk to them. He immediately calmed down and told the officers that everything was okay.

"No, everything isn't okay," the other man said. "My name is Toby Ballard. This man, Thomas Wayne Cartwright, stole $1,000 from me."

"What makes you think he stole $1,000 from you, sir?" Officer Wesson asked.

"He's sleeping with my sister, and last night, when he was over to her house, he stole the $1,000 I had given her for rent."

"He's crazy, officer. I'm married and hardly the type to cheat on my wife," Thomas Wayne said convincingly. "This man hit my SUV for no apparent reason. I just need to get my insurance information out of my car."

"That's fine, sir," Officer Wesson said.

The officers continued to listen to Mr. Ballard's ranting.

Thomas Wayne walked a few feet away. When he noticed that one of the officers had gone around to the front of the building and that the other officer was trying to calm down Mr. Ballard, Thomas Wayne motioned for his friend to get out of the SUV. They walked away unnoticed and disappeared.

A few minutes later, the officers realized that Thomas Wayne had never come back, and they looked around for him.

"Milburn, I don't see Mr. Cartwright."

"Stay here, sir," Officer Milburn said to Mr. Ballard.

They walked over to Thomas Wayne's SUV and peeked through the windows. They noticed a lot of items in the back seat and cargo area. Officer Wesson opened the driver-side car door and started to look around under the seat and console. He saw what looked like bags with white powder under the driver seat and called his dispatch to send out narcotics detectives.

The narcotics detectives arrived. They retrieved a plastic bag containing four plastic bags which appeared to be both crack cocaine (three bags) and powdered cocaine (one bag) which equaled about 40 grams. They asked Officers Wesson and Milburn about the owner of the vehicle.

"We were called out about a disturbance," Officer Wesson stated.

While he was talking, the narcotics officers looked in the glove compartment and found a 9mm firearm marked "Law Enforcement Use Only" and 9mm hollow-point ammunition.

Back at the house, the officers informed Trevor that they would contact him once they found out something concrete. After they left, Trevor walked Mr. Whitehouse back to his house.

Trevor wanted to call Uncle Bert to update him on everything that had been happening, but he knew it was too late. He would call him in the morning.

He decided to cut up a large box and tape it to cover the area where the window had been broken on the back door.

The following morning, Trevor tried to reach Uncle Bert, but he did not answer at any of his numbers.

Trevor went to retrieve a broom, a bucket, and a mop out of a storage cabinet in the kitchen. He needed to get the mud off the kitchen floors. He filled the bucket with water and added soap to it.

Melissa called as he was about to get started, "Hi Trevor. Have you spoken with Thomas Wayne or Uncle Bert?"

"Hi, Melissa," he responded. "No, not yet. Both he and Uncle Bert are missing in action."

"I can't believe you're at home on a Saturday morning. I thought you'd be teaching a class somewhere or running."

"Actually, I'm at Grandma's house. Someone broke in last night, so I decided to stay."

"Broke in!" she shouted. "No!"

"Yeah, the police came and took a report. Someone took stuff out of the garage and some appliances out of the house."

"Do they have any idea about who might have broken in?"

"No, they don't. They dusted for fingerprints, so we'll see if that turns up anything."

"I sure hate to hear that. The reason I was calling..." she paused, and Trevor could tell she was distracted by something.

"Everything okay?"

"Yes, one of my girlfriends sent me a message on Facebook. But, anyway, the holidays are coming up, and I wanted to get a head start on some sort of planning."

Trevor sat down on the sofa, surprised by what he was hearing.

"I know everyone is doing their own thing with their families for Thanksgiving, but I was thinking we, the cousins, could get together sometime after Thanksgiving and before Christmas, maybe after the half-marathon. I told Claire I wanted to volunteer. She sent me the contact information, so I called the race organizers."

"That sounds great!" Trevor said, happy. "By the way, how's school going?"

"It's going. It's a lot different going back at fifty-something. I'm only taking one class, Introduction to Accounting. Since I've been an accounting clerk for so long, I'm familiar with a lot of the curriculum like bookkeeping, financial statements, trial balances, worksheets, special journals, adjusting entries, and closing entries."

"That's good, right?"

"I had to start at the entry level. Next semester I'll take more classes, at least three," Melissa said. "I'm excited about the fact that I even decided to go back to school to get something I've always wanted."

"It's never too late."

"Right. Well, I hope you get in contact with Thomas Wayne. I plan to go by the Center this afternoon to visit Edward."

"I know he'll appreciate that."

"We'll talk more about planning something for the holiday. I'll talk to you later, Trevor."

"Okay."

Trevor proceeded with cleaning the floors. Then he called a company about fixing the back door.

On his way home, Trevor stopped by the grocery store to get some food to cook. While standing in line to checkout, he surveyed the baskets of the people in line around him.

The man behind him had a basket filled with an assortment of food items. Trevor obscurely inventoried the man's grocery basket. It contained two packages of breakfast sausages, five boxes of Pillsbury's frozen breakfasts, two boxes of Hostess muffins, three bags of tortilla chips, two packages of Oscar Mayer deli meat, three boxes of Totino's Party Pizzas, two packages of beef franks, two packages of hot dog and hamburger buns, a package of ground beef, a gallon container of whole milk, two packages of Nabisco Oreo cookies, and a case of beer.

A lady in front of him was placing her groceries on the carousel. He noticed a box of Goldfish snack crackers, three boxes of Tony Chachere's side dishes (cheddar broccoli, Alfredo, and jambalaya flavors), three Chef Boyardee microwave bowls, Oscar Mayer

Lunchables, two boxes of Pop Tarts, a box of Cheez-It crackers, a carton of whole milk, five different varieties of two-liter soft drink bottles (Sunkist, Dr. Pepper, Sun Drop, Big Red, and Canada Dry), two packages of Hostess Snack Cakes, a bag of Tostitos, and cheese dip.

He thought, *If I wasn't afraid of getting cursed out, I'd tell them to put it all back and start over. Look at what I have in my basket and copy it; bananas, cantaloupe, oranges, broccoli, yogurt, ground chicken, whole grain pasta, sweet potatoes, Kashi cereals, soy milk, and fresh wild-caught fish. You, too, can eat healthy. It's not more expensive. It's just about redistributing your dollars.*

Trevor laughed at himself as he began to place his items on the carousel.

He looked back at the man. He was around 6'6" at 280 pounds. He said, "Looks like you're having a party."

The man frowned and said, "Nope, not a party. My kids are visiting for the weekend, so I needed to get some food for them. I've got a lot of their favorites, but I know they'll eat the Oreo cookies and milk before anything else."

"I see," Trevor responded. "How old are they?"

"The boy is thirteen, and my girls are eight and ten."

"Do they favor you?"

The man smiled, "They sure do. The boy looks just like me, and he's already 6'0". Probably going to be a pro football player. Just need to get him on track with his grades. My girls are going to be tall, too. Right now, they're short and stout like their mom."

The cashier was ready for Trevor. She started to scan his items.

After he paid, Trevor turned back and wished the man a great time with his kids.

Walking to his car and wondering about the man's kids, Trevor thought about the growing number of overweight and obese kids. He had written numerous articles about obese children and adolescents and their risks for health problems during their youth and as adults.

He thought, *There is just no need for kids to be faced with risk factors associated with cardiovascular disease (like high blood pressure, high cholesterol, and Type 2 diabetes). Whether overweight or thin, parents and guardians should be making sure their children eat healthy foods that are low in trans and saturated fat, sodium, cholesterol, and refined sugar.*

Trevor sat in his car, looking at a text he had just received from his Uncle Bert.

The text stated, "Hi, Trevor. I know you have been trying to contact me. Just know that I'm okay. I'll be in touch soon. I'll be out of pocket, but I'll contact you around the holidays. Just know that I love you and your cousins."

Trevor sent a text back and said, "I love you, too, Uncle. Hope to talk to you soon."

Trevor had never received a text from Uncle Bert. He thought it was odd that he was doing so now.

Two weeks passed, and Trevor had finally located Thomas Wayne's wife, Joanna. She and their kids were staying with her sister. Trevor had called and asked if he could stop by to see her.

"Can I offer you something to drink," she asked.

"I'm good."

"Have a seat."

Trevor sat at the bar and said, "Thanks for letting me come over."

"I haven't seen or heard from Thomas Wayne in months. I guess you're wondering about some things."

Trevor stared at her and said, "Yes, that's right. I haven't been able to get in touch with him for weeks. About a month ago, our grandmother's house was broken into, and one of the neighbors thought he saw the Escalade driving away as the security alarm was going off."

"He told me about you and your Uncle Bert. I thought the two of you would be able to get him back on track. I found out in May that he had lost his job. He was fired in January for using drugs."

"Using drugs?" Trevor said, acting surprised.

"For years he'd occasionally smoke marijuana. Like a good wife, at least that's what I thought, I turned my head. As long as it didn't interfere with our life, I dismissed it. I didn't realize that he had probably increased his usage until a couple of years ago. And, whatever it initially did for him, it wasn't working anymore. He started confiding in me about his childhood and how much he loved me for being the kind of mother he never had. He was in so much pain."

Joanna paused, showing her reluctance to continue, "At the time, I worked as a nurse at a clinic. He asked me to get him some prescription drugs—handlebars."

Trevor interrupted her with a frown and asked, "What are handlebars?"

She continued and said, "It's the street name for Xanax, a drug used to treat anxiety, panic, and stress disorders. At first I thought I was helping him, but he started wanting more and more pills. Plus, he was drinking more and more. When I got laid off, I didn't have access to the pills anymore."

"Were you getting the pills illegally?" Trevor asked.

"He was my husband, and he needed help with the pain," Joanna stressed. "I thought I had to get him functioning. So much was at stake—the house, the cars, private school for the kids. But things got really crazy when the access to the drug went away. Then, one day, I realized that I wasn't helping him by supplying him. The issues he was dealing with ran too deep. He needed professional help. I was able to convince him to go to his supervisor at work to ask for time off. His supervisor granted him time off to enter into a drug treatment facility. When he came home, I was so proud of him. He had overcome his addiction. For a while, he was a better husband and father. I was able to get another nursing job and things were good. I was working. He was working."

"So something must have happened," Trevor looked puzzled.

"I estimate that things started changing last summer when he went to see his mom. Normally we'd go as a family, but for some reason he went by himself. When he returned home, there was something different about him. He was solemn and distant with me and the kids. I couldn't get him to talk about what may have been bothering him. Then, he started working a bunch of extra jobs. I didn't think anything about it because that's what law enforcement folks do, but I noticed how erratic his behavior had become. He was increasingly restless and irritable, never sleeping, no appetite. I know you probably haven't seen him in while, but he literally dropped sixty pounds in a matter of months. I just thought he was doing some weight loss product that he didn't want to tell me about. I know he wasn't pleased with his size. Once again, I turned my head."

"Do you have any idea of his whereabouts?" Trevor asked.

"No, I don't," she confirmed. Her eyes started to tear up. "He was with the Sheriff's Department for nearly twenty years. I found out that when he got fired, he withdrew his retirement and placed it into a separate bank account. For months, he transferred money to our joint account as though it was a paycheck. Between whatever drug addiction he has and transferring money to the joint account, he ran out. I guess that's when he started borrowing money from everyone. But Edward was calling him all the time about money he owed him. Things started missing around here. I just knew it was bad, again."

"When's the last time you heard from him?" Trevor asked.

"The last time I saw him was when me and my kids were being evicted from the house. He assured me everything was going to be okay. We were up to our eyeballs in debt. He told me how much he loved me. He made me promise that I wouldn't leave him. He was going to make everything right. In one conversation, he said he had all he needed because he had me. But moments later, he talked about the money his Uncle Bert was giving you all and that I just needed to be patient. Me and the kids drove away in my car, and he drove away in the Escalade."

"Do you have any idea where he could be?" Trevor stressed again.

"I imagine some drug house," Joanna said coldly. "That's all he knows now."

Trevor's head dropped.

"He really wanted that money, but not for the right reasons."

Trevor stood up to leave. "I'm looking for him, Joanna. When I find out something, I'll let you know."

He hugged Joanna tightly.

❖

Chapter 21

❖

The Perils of Family Secrets

The Sunday before the Thanksgiving Holiday, Trevor stood looking in his bathroom mirror, thinking about all of the things he was grateful for. He remembered a comment made by his Pastor, *"You can't fill your hands with new things until you let go of old things."* For years, he couldn't connect his decisions and actions with his past. But, once he made a decision to let go, his life changed.

He tightened his red, silk, pleated necktie that had tonal crystals. Rubbing the crystals on his tie with his fingers, he was grateful for clarity. When he finished, he walked into his bedroom and picked up his black Dolce & Gabbana martini jacket that matched his martini tux pants. He proceeded to the kitchen and laid his jacket across one of his bar chairs. Just as he opened his refrigerator door to get a carton of yogurt, his cell phone rang.

The man on the other end asked, "May I speak with Trevor McElroy?"

"This is he. Who's calling."

"This is Officer Calhoun," he stated. "Me and my partner met you at your house on Kittridge Street. We took the report regarding the burglary of your house."

"Yes, hi, Officer Calhoun," he said. Trevor was excited that the officers might have recovered items from the house. He leaned against his bar in anticipation of good news. "Did you find my items?"

"No, Mr. McElroy."

He interrupted, "Call me Trevor."

"Trevor, I really hate to tell you this over the phone," the officer said.

"Tell me what?" Trevor's expression changed. He sat down on his bar chair.

"We've found your cousin, Thomas Wayne Cartwright. The fingerprints from the window glass on the ground at your home were finally analyzed. They matched up with your cousin's fingerprints that were already in the system due to him being a deputy sheriff."

"Great! Where is he?" Trevor asked with enthusiasm. "I've been waiting to hear something about my cousin's whereabouts. I need to go and get him."

"Mr. McElroy, I need for you to come to the morgue on Old Spanish Trail to identify your cousin."

"The morgue? Identify him?" Trevor shouted.

"Trevor, his body was found in an alley near Prairie Oaks, an area known for high drug trafficking."

Realizing that Officer Calhoun was saying that Thomas Wayne was dead, Trevor stumbled back, standing unsteadily, and grabbed the back of his bar chair.

Officer Calhoun yelled out, "Trevor, are you okay! I'll meet you at the morgue."

Trevor walked into his living room and sat on his sofa.

With tears welling up in his eyes, Trevor could only murmur, and he said, "Officer, I'll be there in twenty-five minutes."

Trevor met Officer Calhoun at the entrance of the Harris County Medical Examiner's office. Officer Calhoun and a morgue assistant hastily escorted Trevor to the area where he could identify his cousin.

Officer Calhoun explained that it appeared as though Thomas Wayne died of a drug overdose. High levels of cocaine and Xanax were found in his body.

Leaning over Thomas Wayne, Trevor looked tearfully at his broken body. The officer had omitted telling him that Thomas Wayne had been shot in the head at close range.

"What happened to my cousin," Trevor asked angrily.

His body was badly damaged.

"The forensics revealed that a car repeatedly ran over him, and then he was shot in the head," Officer Calhoun replied.

Trevor closed his eyes and took a deep breath. He rubbed his hand across his forehead.

"When was he found?" Trevor asked with sadness.

"Yesterday morning."

"I'll call his wife," Trevor said, as he started to walk from the room, sorrowful.

As Trevor walked out the door, Officer Calhoun said, "I'm so sorry, Trevor."

Trevor headed out the front door of the building. Walking down the steps, he held onto the railing, tightly. Unable to move any further, he knelt down and sat on the bottom step.

Officer Calhoun came out the door. He sat beside Trevor.

"Trevor, I have no idea what you're going through. To have a relative die in the manner like that of your cousin is a hurt I can't comprehend, but you appear to be a spiritual man. If so, I know you know that his death was a part of God's plan for his life. Now, it's up to you to accept it."

Trevor slowly stood up and walked toward his car. He opened the door and sat inside. He buried his face in his hands and cried profusely. He sat in his car for nearly twenty minutes with his head against the steering wheel.

Officer Calhoun watched him from the steps of the building.

Trevor thought to himself, *How did I miss it? I knew your pain was deep-rooted, but... I am so sorry, Thomas Wayne.* Tears rolled down his cheeks.

Trevor knew he needed to contact Joanna. He started to search for her number through his cell phone.

He called her number. No one answered, so he left her a message. He called her sister's number. No one answered, so he left her a message as well. He decided to call his Uncle Bert. He received his voice mail.

He knew arrangements needed to be made, but he had to wait until Joanna was contacted.

Trevor decided to drive to his grandma's house. Consumed with thoughts of failure and regret and thinking that he could have done more, he blamed himself for the way Thomas Wayne's life had ended.

Trevor arrived at his grandma's house. He walked inside and stood in the middle of the living room, looking around. He walked over to the wall that had framed photos of him and his cousins. There was the one of him and Thomas Wayne. Thomas Wayne was holding the bucket filled with sand.

He thought, *It'll be up to me to love and protect his children, to be an example to Jeremy, teaching him how to be a man. One day he will be a husband and father. I'll teach him about taking care of a family. I'll lay the foundation for how Pamela should expect a man to treat her. She'll see herself as a queen of femininity and deserving of someone who will treat her with respect, courtesy, and dignity.*

Trevor was startled by a knock at the door.

He walked to the door and opened it. Uncle Bert stood in front of him, awkwardly.

"Uncle Bert!" Trevor shouted. He grabbed his uncle and held him tightly. "Where have you been? I've been trying to find you. Where have you been? Why haven't you contacted me?"

Trevor stood back to look at his uncle. He looked tired and weary.

"Come in," Trevor said.

"I am so sorry I haven't been accessible. So much has been going on…"

"It's okay, Uncle. You're here now."

"I received your last voice mail. It sounded urgent."

Trevor started crying.

"They found Thomas Wayne, dead."

Uncle Bert sat in a chair.

"What?" he asked in disbelief.

"Yes, sir. He was found in an alley, drug overdose, shot in the head." Trevor was distraught. "I can't get in touch with Joanna."

As Uncle Bert sat, listening to the words Trevor was saying. He stared at the wall. His breath started to come quickly. Then, tears emerged from his eyes. He slowly slid down into the chair. The grief and defeat that overcame him was apparent.

"What are we going to do, Uncle Bert?"

Uncle Bert sat motionless.

"Uncle Bert," Trevor shouted with tears streaming down his face. "What are we doing to do?"

"I'm sorry. What did you say?"

"I can't get in touch with Joanna. What are we going to do?"

"Son, we'll find her."

Uncle Bert sat with his head bowed, shaking it over and over again. He thought about how Thomas Wayne had never gotten over his mother leaving him. He thought to himself, *She was supposed to be a role model, someone he could count on, a mother who would love and protect them. A mother who would never hurt or discard him like a bag of trash.*

"Uncle Bert, I tried to help him," Trevor said sincerely. "I did everything I could to reach him."

"I know you did, son."

Uncle Bert stood up and walked toward the front door. He turned and looked at Trevor and said, "I'll find Joanna, and we'll give Thomas Wayne a great home going."

The death of Thomas Wayne left his cousins in a state of shock. They were infuriated by the local newspaper's account of his death. Once celebrated as a decorated deputy sheriff, the newspaper articles cast him as a disgrace and habitual user of illegal prescription drugs and cocaine who was eventually fired.

Trevor had invited his cousins over so they could go to church together. When he heard a faint knock at the door, he walked across the living room and opened it with a cup of freshly brewed coffee in his hand.

"Hi, Trevor," Erin said.

"Hey, cuz."

"Hey, Trevor," Dillard said.

"Hey."

"You have a cup for me?" Erin asked.

"I sure do. Come on in the kitchen."

Dillard sat down and picked up a newspaper Trevor had been reading. He looked inside, sighing. Erin seated herself next to him and drank her coffee. Suddenly, Dillard saw the article in the paper and became upset. He threw the newspaper aside, raised up, and walked angrily into the kitchen.

Erin picked up the newspaper. She found the article about Thomas Wayne.

She began to read, "A deputy sheriff was found dead in an alley at the 1600 block of Prairie Oaks. He was run over several times with a car and then shot in the head. His death in November was a shock to friends, colleagues, and family, none of whom had any idea he was addicted to illegal prescription drugs and cocaine. It has been reported that his wife was his supplier."

Dillard abruptly interrupted Erin and said, "Stopped reading that, Erin!"

She laid the newspaper on the coffee table and placed her arms around Dillard.

Trevor sat down in front of them.

"Come on, guys," Trevor said. "Claire and Melissa are going to meet us at church."

They all walked out together.

Chapter 22

An Anchored Spirit

More devastating news for the cousins was just around the corner. It was four weeks after Thomas Wayne's funeral and one week after the half-marathon that Trevor, Claire, Melissa, Edward, Erin, and Dillard all received a text from Uncle Bert to read their email. It was the Saturday before Christmas.

Trevor was preparing to leave his home to go and conduct a fitness seminar at his church. Melissa was online, enrolling in her spring classes. Dillard was cooking breakfast for his kids. Erin had just hopped out of bed to get ready for an early-morning walk. Claire was in bed recovering from her infusion, and Edward was at home preparing to meet Trevor; he was going to share his story about the stroke with the seminar attendees.

Each one of them made a concerted effort to access Uncle Bert's email. They were curious about what he had sent. They knew there was an inheritance. Now they all wondered about what it would entail.

Trevor sat upright in the chair at his desk and positioned his hands to log into his computer.

Having a mental debate on which accounting classes she would enroll in for the spring semester—Computerized Accounting

Applications or Oil and Gas Accounting—Melissa selected her email icon to retrieve the email message.

In the process of boiling quinoa for the cinnamon apple quinoa he was preparing for breakfast, Dillard asked his son to go and get his laptop.

A reoccurring problem with plantar fasciitis had prompted Erin to get a bottle of frozen water out of her freezer. She had started to rub her right foot with the bottle when she heard the text message indicator on her cellular phone. Her computer wasn't working, so she called Dillard. He lived in an apartment complex down the street. He told her to come over so they could read the email together.

Claire was in a full flare. She was unable to sit at her computer. She was dehydrated and weak, and she was suffering from severe joint pain. Unable to eat, her husband had brought her a can of Ensure to drink. She asked him to get his laptop and read Uncle Bert's email to her.

Edward didn't have a computer. He called Trevor and informed him that he would get to his home early so he could access his Yahoo account.

Trevor knew it would take Edward at least twenty minutes to get to his home. He decided to go ahead and read his email. Destined by faith, Trevor, Melissa, Dillard, and Claire's husband read their email at the same time.

Trevor opened the message from his Uncle Bert. He sat in front of his computer and began to read, "Trevor, you have turned out to be an amazing man. I am so proud of you. Because of you, I've witness a transformation that transcends through transparency. I know you were hesitant when I asked you to help your cousins. But, because you put your past behind you, you put aside your personal feelings to help your cousins mend years of tension and conflict. For that, I will be eternally grateful to you. They have removed significant obstacles that were standing in the way of their emotional well-being, healthier lifestyle habits, and a generational blessing. A new horizon of purpose and spirit of faith will serve them and their families for generations to come."

Trevor sat at his desk, bewildered by Uncle Bert's email. Distracted by the ring on his cellular phone, he reached to answer it. It was the outreach minister at his calling about the room set-up for the fitness seminar.

Claire's husband started to read, "Life is uncertain and unknown. You don't get to choose how it happens. The good thing, though, is that you get to choose how you respond to it. You're living a life of purpose. You didn't let your disease consume you. You made a decision to do something that would help others, and, I'm proud of you for that. Aside from the good that you're doing, you need to reconcile with your mother. Forgive her withholding the identity of your biological father. She only did what she thought was right to protect you."

Mark paused and looked at Claire.

He continued, "My accountant will direct you and your cousins on the acquisition of my business. May God continue to direct your path and bless you abundantly in spirit. By the time you read his email, my life will have changed dramatically. I pray that God will give you the comfort, strength, and courage you need. My wish for you is that you have a full life, one of significance and purpose, a life that will have an impact long after you've gone away. Smile, always smile, even when you're in pain, brokenhearted, or frustrated because things aren't going the way you'd like, or when someone disappoints you... smile! Always remember that I loved you and your cousins more than my life."

Dillard instructed Tiffany and Walter on mixing the ingredients. He sat down at his kitchen table and opened up his son's laptop. After he logged into his email account and retrieved his message, he read silently, "You've faced what was preventing you from forging ahead. The demons of your past have gone away.

You're living a life of purpose and I'm proud of you for that. A bank account has been established in your name at the Bank of America. I want you to take the money in the account and make a difference. Start with getting a home for you and your children. Set up a college fund for them and make sure they finish. My accountant will direct you and your cousins on the acquisition of my business. May God continue to direct your path and bless you abundantly in spirit."

Uncle Bert ended in the same manner as he did with Claire.

Dillard looked up, puzzled. Tiffany and Walter where eating their breakfast.

Moments later, there was a knock at the door. Dillard could see through their living room window that it was Erin. He got up to open the door.

"Hi, Erin," Dillard said as he opened the door.

"Hi," she said, looking confused. "Why do you have that strange look on your face?"

"I just read Uncle Bert's email. I have an eerie feeling."

"Let me read the email he sent me," she said, sitting down at the table. "Hi, Tiffany and Walter."

Dillard's kids said hello as they started to clear their dishes from the kitchen table.

She read, "You decided to let God touch your life in a brand new way. Now, your brokenness has been healed. You're living a life of purpose, and I'm proud of you for that. My accountant will direct you and your cousins on the acquisition of my business. May God continue to direct your path and bless you abundantly in spirit."

Uncle Bert ended in the same manner as he did with Claire and Dillard.

Erin looked over at Dillard. He was washing dishes.

"What are you thinking?"

Her eyes widened. She said, "What does he mean, 'By the time you read this email'?"

Melissa started to read her email, "I can't imagine the trauma of being raped as a young girl, the shame you must have felt for so many years. But, you've moved forward and settled your past, the memories that haunted you and held you captive. Now, you'll never be content. You'll always be pursuing. In spite of everything you've encountered, you have transformed your life mind, body, and spirit. You're living a life of purpose, and I'm proud of you for that. As promised, you and your cousins have been given leadership over and the responsibility of making decisions for Spencer Security Services. My accountant will direct you and your cousins on the acquisition of my business. May God continue to direct your path and bless you abundantly in spirit. Above all, I pray that you stay focused and be an example of someone who has been delivered."

Uncle Bert ended in the same manner as he did with Dillard, Claire, and Erin.

Melissa stared straight ahead as a tear rolled down her cheek. She knew something about Uncle Bert's email wasn't right.

Trevor was still on the telephone when Edward arrived. He opened the door and acknowledged that he was on the phone with someone. The look on his face was one of anxiety. His eyes keep shifting between the outreach minister and Edward.

Edward nodded as though he understood Trevor. He walked into Trevor's office to log into his email account. He started to read, "I know firsthand that a terrible thing happened to you and your siblings as young children. I regret standing by from afar and watching how your lives crumbled. And, for that, I apologize to you. My life was different back then. You see, I had a daughter who I didn't acknowledge and ignored. Before her mother died, she tried over and over to get me to be a part of my daughter's life. But, I had other things that were more important than being saddled with the responsibility of a child. Growing up poor and alone, I was determined to be rich by any means necessary. Having been teased as a boy about having to use wire as shoelaces, no one was going to prevent me from achieving greatness. Along the way, I've taken a shortcut or two. Just like you, I was an angry man and blamed God for all He allowed to happen to me. I acted out in fear, and I saw that same fear in you. Over time, I learned how to appreciate my long-suffering, and so have you. The hurt I caused my daughter was so unbearable that she committed suicide at the age of fifteen."

Edward became shaken by the words he was reading.

"Despite all that has happened, you have learned to confront and resolve the underlying root cause of your anger, hurt, pain, resentment, and blame. I don't know if your stroke had a hand in that awareness, but you have transformed your life, mind, body, and spirit. You're living a life of purpose, and I'm proud of you for that. My final wish for us is that you reconcile with your mother. Go to Manchester. It's time."

Edward looked away from the computer screen. Uncle Bert ended in the same manner as he did with Dillard, Claire, Erin, and Melissa.

Trevor finished his call. He walked over to his desk and started to write a note.

"That was a strange email, Trevor," Edward commented as Trevor was writing.

"I need to finish reading mine," Trevor said.

Edward got up so Trevor could sit down.

Trevor toggled back to his email and read silently, "I only wish the outcome would have been different for Thomas Wayne. I know everyone can't be saved, though. I know you've heard me say that people make mistakes. That's why they put erasers on pencils and now pens. Smile. Not necessarily intentional, I've made some grave mistakes that cannot be corrected, but I'm not willing to pay the price for them. I never wanted to ever disappoint you—I had to make a decision that most people will never understand. The one good thing I wanted to make sure of was that you and your cousins would be taken care of for life. The legal battle and fees probably would have wiped me out, and then there would not have been anything left. My accountant will direct you and your cousins on the acquisition of the business. May God continue to direct your path and bless you abundantly in your quest to empower people and change lives. You are leading a full life, a life that will leave an impact long after you're gone. And, I pray you continue to do so. By the time you read his email, my life will have been ended. I can feel your sadness. Just know that I left you all in peace."

Trevor ran into the living room where Edward was sitting.

"What's wrong, Trevor?"

"I don't like the tone of that message."

Trevor started to dial a number on his cell phone.

"Who are you calling?"

"Uncle Bert!"

Only a voice message sounded.

Trevor turned slowly away from Edward and crossed the floor deeply in thought. Abruptly, his fearful eyes encounter something on the floor. He quickly stooped. It was a signature pen Uncle Bert had given him last year. Trevor stared at the pen.

"Is there anyone else you can call?" Edward asked.

Trevor placed the pen on an end table and started dialing again.

"Who are you calling this time?"

"I'm calling his office," Trevor responded.

There was no answer.

"Are we still going to the church?" Edward asked.

Trevor looked at his watch.

"Yeah, we'd better get there. Call Erin, Dillard, Melissa, and Claire while I drive and tell them to meet us there."

"Okay."

Edward call his cousins as Trevor asked. Claire informed him that she was in a lot of joint pain and couldn't move.

❖

Trevor and Edward arrived at the church. They hurried to the room where Trevor would use Edward to deliver his message on choice and change.

About thirty people were waiting for Trevor. After the introductions, he started to speak, "According to the Center for Disease Control and Prevention (CDC), chronic diseases like cardiovascular disease (primarily heart disease and stroke), cancer, and diabetes are among the most common, most costly, and most preventable of all health problems. They are considered preventable because they are tied to our lifestyle choices, choices that we have the power to control."

He spoke firmly, raising his voice loudly and showing a certain wariness.

"It seems like every day I hear something that attempts to encourage and cause me to make healthier choices," a lady commented.

"Absolutely! You see tips on TV, hear them on the radio, read them in the newspaper and our favorite magazines—they even pop up while we're surfing the Internet," Trevor said. "Can anymore tell me why these messages are so prevalent?"

A man sitting next to his wife looked at Trevor and made a face.

Trevor looked directly at the man and said, "Sir, what is your name?"

The man, dressed in army camouflage pants and a T-shirt, was around six feet and weighed 180 pounds.

"Miles."

"Any thoughts, Miles?"

"No, I'm not here to participate. I just brought my wife."

His wife looked over at him, embarrassed.

"It's because our neighborhoods, our communities, our cities, our states, and our nation are saturated with diseases and illnesses that have our healthcare system in a financial bind," Trevor said.

Erin, Melissa, and Dillard entered the room as Trevor was speaking.

"The CDC states that the medical care costs of people with chronic diseases account for more than 75% of the nation's $2 trillion medical care costs. Most of us will see the direct impact as health insurance co-pays and out-of-pocket expenses continue to rise. And in many cases, choices and care are limited. So, the question now becomes: How are you going to respond to these messages? You see them. You hear them. They're everywhere."

Two ladies look at each other with opposition. One of the ladies shrugged.

"For months, during the president's campaign, we heard a message that resonated throughout this country. It was, 'Yes we can!' It was a statement of possibility, a statement of hope, a statement that caused us all to believe. Well, in your own personal lives, you can keep that statement alive. You can make it your own by saying 'Yes I can!' You can even add to it and say, 'Yes, I can change and make better choices!' "

A man who had been observing Trevor with skepticism noticeably had a change in his demeanor.

"How are we supposed to do that?" the man shouted out. "There is no hope with the state of our nation—the dismal economy, the high unemployment rate, people struggling to put food on the table or maintain their health care coverage, and/or struggling to stay in their homes."

"I disagree, sir," Trevor said. "With all of the changes that are underway, it's critical that we do our part, and a good place to start is with our own health and fitness."

Edward thought about how he had dismissed the connection of his lifestyle habits and the healthcare crisis.

A lady raised her hand to speak.

Trevor acknowledged her and nodded his head.

"Now, I think about my father who recently had a massive heart attack that costs somebody—Medicare, the insurance company—over $150,000. I think about the costs associated with my debilitating arthritis that primarily stems from my excess body weight. I think about my cousin's stroke that caused paralysis on her left side. I think about my aunt's leg amputation due to diabetes. I think more and more about how our unhealthy lifestyle habits are contributing factors that lead to our health predicaments," the lady commented.

Trevor shook his head in agreement and said, "Today, one of my cousins is here. He recently recovered from a stroke that left him unable to speak."

He motioned for Edward to come to the front of the room.

"Tell everyone your story, Edward."

"A few months ago, I was on a job doing some electrical work. I was fine the day before, but while working, I became really tired. I didn't think anything about it. I had been working twelve hours on this construction project, over 70 hours a week. I never would have suspected that anything medically was wrong with me."

Edward paused.

"I remember starting to talk to one of the guys about wiring in a particular location, but when I started, all that came out of my mouth was gibberish. He looked at me strangely. The only thing I could say was 'fine'. I started thinking that something was strange, but I just attributed it to tiredness. On my way home, I started to feel fine and made it into my apartment. My friend, Lonnie, called me about going to get a beer. I noticed that my speech was off. I couldn't get out more than a word or two at a time. Lonnie said to me, 'Man something is wrong with you. I can't understand a word you're saying. Sounds like you've already been drinking.' I managed to assure him that I had not been drinking. 'I'm coming over to take you to the hospital'."

Edward paused again to collect his thoughts.

"While waiting on Lonnie, I sat still on my sofa. There was a bill on my coffee table that was due. I knew I needed to write out a check. I would have Lonnie drop me by the mailbox on the way to the hospital. I reached for the bill and my checkbook. I tried to write on my check, but my pen kept falling out of my hand. It was like my hand was asleep. I was concerned that whatever was going on with me was serious and I didn't have any insurance. What was I going to do?"

Trevor realized that Edward needed to sit down. He looked winded while talking. Trevor went and got a chair to place in front of the room.

Edward continued as he sat down, "I had pretty much decided that I was not going, but, Lonnie was adamant about me going to the hospital. When we arrived to the hospital, I literally couldn't say anything that made sense. Lonnie spoke to a lady at the emergency room desk. I kept thinking about not having any medical insurance and filling out a bunch of forms. Lonnie informed the lady that I was having trouble speaking. She called for a wheelchair, and I was immediately taken to a room and connected to a bunch of machines. It was later determined that I'd had a stroke, and as a result of the stroke I developed aphasia."

Trevor interjected and said, "They don't mess around when they think someone is having a stroke."

"What is aphasia?" a lady asked.

"It's a disorder that results from damage to portions of the brain that are responsible for language," Trevor said.

"Never in a million years would I have thought I was having a stroke," Edward said. "I did remember some of the things Trevor had told us about different medical conditions like a stroke, things such as sudden numbness of the face, arm, or leg, especially on one side of the body, sudden trouble seeing in one or both eyes, sudden trouble walking, dizziness, loss of balance or coordination, or sudden severe headache with no known cause."

Trevor interrupted and said, "Sudden confusion, trouble speaking, or trouble understanding speech."

"Right," Edward smiled. "I'm just so grateful to Lonnie for taking me to the hospital when he did."

"It's been a long journey for Edward," Trevor said. "It's a blessing that he does not have to take any prescription drugs."

"And, although I've gone through months of speech therapy, I am not disabled," Edward said, gratefully. "I have to admit that all the while I was in rehabilitation, I knew God was punishing me for a life of wrong-doing and my mean spirit. But, it was Trevor's prayers and messages of redemption that touched and changed me. I was able to let God come into my life."

"Thank you, Edward," Trevor said. "The bottom line is, we all have the power of choice, and it's our responsibility to implement healthy choices, not only for ourselves but for those in our lives. It's our responsibility to include the neighborhoods, communities, states, and the nation which our unhealthy lifestyles now impact."

"Wow! I can't help but think about some of my food choices for lunch last week. On Monday, I had a barbecue pulled pork sandwich on a sub roll with a 21 ounce soda and a bag of chips. On Wednesday, enchiladas served with refried beans and Spanish rice with tortilla chips and salsa. Fried fish, fries, and coleslaw with hush puppies on Friday. All of which were separate and apart from my breakfast, snacks, and dinner," another lady confessed.

"It's important that you gain a better understanding of why those food choices which contain a large volume of calories, saturated fat, trans fat, cholesterol, and sodium can have monumental consequences," Trevor said. "The best way we can help with curtailing the challenges of our healthcare system is by increasing our knowledge and taking the advice of the medical professionals. If we do our part by maintaining a healthy weight, practicing healthier eating habits, and engaging in routine physical activity, we will see a reduction in chronic diseases and illnesses like heart disease and diabetes, and consequently better management of healthcare costs. Best of all, you'll be able to elevate your statement from 'Yes I can' to 'Yes I did.' "

Chapter 23

❖

Stewards of Brokenness

After the fitness seminar, Trevor and his cousins drove to their grandma's house. He was frantically trying to find someone who knew his uncle's whereabouts.

He called his uncle's executive assistant. She had been with Uncle Bert for nearly twenty years.

She answered her telephone.

"Hi, Ms. Simmons, this is Trevor McElroy, Bert Spencer's nephew."

She screamed and yelled when she heard Trevor's voice.

Trevor couldn't understand her ramblings and was trying to get her to slow down.

"He loved you so much. All he wanted was for you to be free."

"Ms. Simmons, is everything okay?"

"Turn on your news," she cried out. "Channel 13. Now!"

The telephone went dead.

Trevor and his cousins were pulling into the driveway. He jumped out of his car and ran into the house. Edward followed slowly behind and waved for the other cousins to hurry.

Trevor went into the backroom where there was an extra television and brought it into the living room. He set the television on a table, plugged it into the wall, and turned it on.

The cousins walked inside and sat down, watching Trevor. He tuned the television to Channel 13.

In a breaking news report, a news reporter said, "Shortly before 12:00 P.M., Houston Police Captain Michael Manning in the homicide unit confirmed the death of state representative and prominent business owner Bert Spencer. Earlier this morning, Representative Spencer took a handgun and shot himself in the head. We're at the beginning stages of the investigation and far from getting the results of toxicology reports. The medical examiner will determine the cause of death which will probably be suicide. Mr. Spencer was found dead around 8:15 A.M. in his office by police officers. His administrative assistant, Beverly Chappell, called 911 because she knew something was wrong based on a telephone call she'd had with him. She called him at eight o'clock that morning to let him know she would be arriving to the office late. He told her that by the time she arrived, he would be dead. The trail of news reports raising questions about emails, contracts, and security guards and equipment was closing in on Representative Spencer. It's apparent that he decided to end it all himself."

Trevor was stunned, horrified, and visibly grief-stricken.

Melissa jumped up and ran out of the room.

Dillard walked out the back door, his head down.

Claire and Erin began to cry. Trevor sat on the sofa between the two and placed his arms around them.

Edward walked to the hall of frames to look at a picture of their Uncle Bert as a young man standing in front of their grandma's house. He bit his lip as tears welled.

"The one thing I am sorry for is that I didn't tell Uncle Bert thank you," Edward said with chattering teeth.

Hundreds gathered on a Wednesday at The George R. Brown Convention Center for the funeral of Texas State Representative and prominent businessman, Bert Spencer. As Trevor listened to the expressions of praise and tribute made by Uncle Bert's colleagues, business associates, friends, and employees, his attention was interrupted by thoughts of his support and encouragement to Erin, Melissa, Claire, Dillard, and Edward.

Fighting to regain his focus, he zoomed in on the minister's final words of tribute commemorating Uncle Bert's life, comments filled with celebratory accounts of his Uncle Bert's energy and passion toward the countless number of constituents in the community he served over a career that had lasted nearly four decades.

The prayer of one of his friends who was a pastor comforted those in attendance. He said, "Our Father who are in Heaven, Father of our Lord and Savior, Jesus Christ. Master, we come in the precious name of Jesus Christ, praying for this family, for Bert's constituents, his colleagues, and all who knew him and have suffered a great loss. We pray that You give them strength to endure his unexpected death. God, make them to know that all things work together for the good of those who love You and who are called according to Your purpose. God, let them be a witness of Your goodness and mercy toward them."

When the pastor completed his prayer, others came forward to make comments.

"He is loved around the capitol for his dazzling spirit, meticulousness, and ability to work with all legislators on very important issues facing our state. I will miss Bert deeply," a colleague said.

"Bert Spencer dedicated his life to service and making the Kashmere Height's community a better place. As a state representative, he served the people of the 155th District with reliability and courage, and his sudden passing is a tremendous loss," another colleague said. "He has left an incredible legacy for us to follow, and I'm going to be more representative of his strength and dedication to add value."

"Bert was a pro at adapting to life's upheavals that he encountered throughout his journey. He was a great contributor to society. I pray a decision that we'll never understand doesn't overshadow his accomplishments," a friend said.

"He never avoided an opportunity to tackle the pressing challenges he met at the capitol or his business. He showed us all how to make the trade-off between the 'easy' way and the 'right' way."

As the minister concluded his message, a cloud of sadness came over Trevor and his cousins as they stared at the premium stainless steel casket. The funeral directors approached the front, opened the casket, and arranged the tailored gray velvet interior with matching pillow and throw. The old familiar hymn "When We Get to Heaven" led the recessional, and those in attendance stood and began marching around the casket for a final viewing.

Whispers about Uncle Bert's suicide spilled over from the sanctuary to the church corridors as the crowd awaited the processional to the burial grounds. Praises of a person who loved life, his constituents, family, and the purpose he was placed on Earth to accomplish resonated in the minds of those assembled for the going home celebration. The last order of business was a twenty-minute drive to Uncle Bert's family burial ground. Upon approaching Bert's earthly resting place, Trevor admired the silhouette of cedar and maple trees blanketed in peacefulness that surrounded his grave.

At the conclusion of the graveside service, his pastor, Pastor Bryant, spoke an unforgettable prayer. He concluded by saying, "In sure and certain hope of the resurrection to eternal life through our Lord Jesus Christ, we commend to Almighty God our brother, Bert Spencer. We commit his body to the ground, earth to earth, ashes to ashes, dust to dust. The Lord bless him and keep him. The Lord make His face to shine upon him, and be gracious unto him, and give him peace. Amen."

❖

Two month later, the cousins met at Grandma Saddie's house to celebrate nearly a year of truth, healing, and love.

"It has been a tumultuous year," Melissa said.

"I know that's right," Erin agreed.

Dillard said, "For months, you put up with our disrespect and contempt toward you and one another. We rejected you and what you were trying to get us to see. I know it was God that brought you back to us and out of the wilderness. And, I know I speak for Melissa, Erin, Claire, and Edward, as well, that we'll always be grateful to Uncle Bert for loving us enough to…" He started to cry.

Trevor walked over to the sofa. He sat next to him and hugged him while saying, "I know, Dillard."

Whimpering, Dillard said, "You could have easily traded insults with us, but you never wavered."

"I could tell he was irritated a lot of times with us," Claire said, laughing.

Dillard wiped his eyes.

"My constant prayer for all of us was to have peace," Trevor said, looking at his cousins.

A silence echoed through the room.

Claire said, "My flare-ups are under much better control now. My last one was a couple of months ago. I used to have severe flare-ups at least every 3 months. I know stress is a big cause of my flare-ups. Now I'm doing a better job of managing any stress."

Erin quickly interrupted and said, "Some information I received at the half-marathon provided detailed information about flare-ups."

Claire continued and said, "Yes, my first indication of a flare-up is that all my joints will start aching, and then the next day I will start developing diarrhea. If I happen to have diarrhea without the joint pain, I know that it is not Crohn's related and is something that will pass. Now, even at my best, I still have five to seven bowel movements a day. Every time I urinate, I will have a bowel movement. Some people do go into remission for years. I have not gotten to that point yet, but I think I'm getting closer. But, even if it doesn't, I know there's value in what I must come through."

Erin said, "Brian is doing much better managing his diabetes. He has to measure his blood sugar before he eats, in the mornings, and before he goes to bed. He's getting better with the routine. He's eleven now, and I don't have to monitor him as closely as before. I am working on letting him be more responsible. He's still the typical boy, sneaking in sweets when he thinks he won't be caught. I know he will eat these things, so I just try to remind him to cover the carbohydrates. I'm confident that even though he's a type I diabetic, he can and will live a healthy life."

"What about Chanitah?" Trevor asked.

"It's a struggle because she wants to eat like her friends—pizza. She and her friends love some new barbecue pizza," she paused and shook her head, "and bread sticks, hot wings, chili cheese hot dogs, onion rings, chicken nuggets, and milkshakes. I can't get her to eat fruit and vegetables consistently. She volunteered with me at the half-marathon, but she wasn't fazed by seeing the other kids who actually walked and ran in the event."

Erin had never talked much about her ex-husband. He was out of jail and trying to win over his kids.

"I don't know about the other parents, but for me it's very difficult to compete with this age of electronics and gadgets. He doesn't pay child support, but for Christmas, Nick purchased a flat-screen television and a Nintendo system with an array of games for Chanitah and Brian. Chanitah spends most of her time in her bedroom watching television or playing video games. A couple of weeks ago he brought her a cell phone. Now, I'm seeing the effects of the cell phone. All she does all day is sends text messages to her friends."

"Erin, always remember that you are the parent. You must implement blackout times for video games, computer usage, and TV watching, and schedule regular exercise time periods," Trevor hesitated before continuing, "Children and teenagers spend many hours on their computers, watching television, playing video games, sending texts, and chatting with their friends online. With school assignments and possibly participating in extra-curricular activities (non-fitness related), so much is vying for their attention. But, it's a parent's responsibility to schedule time for their child to engage in some sort of physical activities (whether it's inside or outside). You don't have to compete. You set the rules!"

"I know that's right!" Melissa exclaimed.

"The one thing you don't want to do is force your child to do a physical activity he or she is not interested in. Parents who push kids into organized sports or some boring routine will turn kids off early to a lifetime of physical fitness. But, you do need to make it clear to Chanitah that physical activity is good and needs to become an integral part of her daily life. Always make exercise fun—never as a duty or as a punishment."

Edward sat quietly listening.

"Are you okay, Edward?" Trevor asked.

"Just thinking," Edward stated. "I can remember vividly all the times I wished I had an automatic turn off button that would turn you off." Edward smiled. "I'd think that you were just a show off, Uncle Bert's pet," he said. "But, like Dillard said, you never wavered. You stayed with us to create the drive and determination among us all so we'd have the alliance needed for a shared purpose."

"Because of you, we've discovered our sense of purpose," Melissa said.

"Okay, guys, I wish I could take all this credit you're wanting to give me," Trevor said, grinning. "Most often, our lives are plagued with so much discord, conflict, and chaos (and that can be between others or ourselves) that we're unable to pursue the sort of life that

God would like for us to experience with passion and enthusiasm. We allow so many things to distract us and take the steering wheel from us and drive us in a direction contrary to what we really need and most often want. And, more than likely we end up at a place where we're burdened and overwhelmed, which will impact the way we think—our minds, feel—our bodies, and act—our spirit. Although it took some time, you began to realize that you had a choice."

Trevor continued to smile.

"You'd choose whether you'd allow discord, conflict, and chaos to overtake your life, whether you'd allow the pain of your past to keep you from pursuing your purpose, whether you'd choose to allow food to be your escape—your coping mechanism."

Chapter 24

❖

Lessons From The Broken Ones

A year later, it was time for the cousins to receive their inheritance. They had made great strides to fulfilled their uncle's stipulations to live healthier and with purpose.

Trevor had summoned his cousin to their grandma's house on a Saturday morning for the reading of Uncle Bert's will. While waiting for Uncle Bert's attorney, Mr. Sasser, and his accountant, Mr. Castillo, they talked about the things going on in their lives. All of them looked noticeably different in appearance and spirit.

Erin, Dillard, and Edward sat in the living room, facing each other.

"I went to visit my mother last month," Edward said abruptly.

Erin and Dillard looked surprised.

"You went to Manchester, New Hampshire?" Dillard asked.

"Yes, I did," Edward said proudly.

Melissa walked out of the bathroom and said, "Did I overhear you say you went to Manchester?"

Edward nodded slowly and said, "Uh huh."

"That's wonderful, Edward."

"It was a good meeting," he said as he bowed his head. "She's not in the best of health. Thomas Wayne's death really affected her. She blames herself." He paused. "I'll be going back."

Trevor and Claire walked in from the kitchen and joined the conversation.

"Great," Trevor said as he sat down. He started to peel an orange.

"That is wonderful," Claire commented.

They sat in silence for a few moments, waiting for someone to say something. They were nervously anticipating the reading of Uncle Bert's will.

"I've been walking in the mornings," Erin said to keep the conversation going.

"In the mornings?" Dillard said, surprised.

"Seeing all of the walkers and runners while volunteering at the half-marathon inspired me. I saw big people, little people, tall people, and short people all striving together to accomplish a goal," Erin stated.

"Yeah, I know. I was one of those big people," Dillard said, laughing.

"I realized it was time for me to do something. But, because of my size, I wasn't comfortable attending Trevor's classes, joining a fitness club, or even walking down the street or at the park. I was self-conscious and embarrassed, and I didn't want anyone to see my fat. Knowing that I needed to do something, I started walking around the neighborhood in the mornings at five o'clock when no one would see me. And, Trevor, I've even mixed in some running."

"Scary as you are, I can't believe you were outside walking that early," Dillard said.

"Believe me; I wear my mace for protection," she commented. "I walk at least three times a week for about an hour."

Trevor looked at her and said, "I am so proud of you. Now we have you, Dillard, and Claire walking and running."

"All I need to do now is get rid of this sagging fat," Erin commented.

"Those leg lifts and sit-ups Trevor showed us have really helped me," Melissa said.

Erin raised her arm to show them the amount of sagging skin. "It's more than what I want," Erin said.

"When you make a decision to start exercising, you must consider both some sort of cardio activity as well as what is known as resistance training or strength training. I'm sure you have seen someone after they've lost a large amount of weight quickly?"

"A lady a work," Melissa said, "had a lot of sagging fat."

Trevor said, "She could have lost her weight through nutritional changes or doing a lot of cardio activity. Both can result in a lot of excess skin at the end of this weight loss process. The point I want to make is that cardio is necessary for losing weight and increasing your metabolism (the rate at which your body burns the food you eat). But, as you've heard me say, resistance training is essential. You need to do both, because doing a lot of cardio will lead to a loss in water, fat, and muscle."

"That's what we want, right?" Dillard asked.

"You want to build muscle, not lose it," Trevor answered. "You build it through resistance training. The goal is to progressively lose weight where the skin has an opportunity to keep up with the weight loss. When you lose a lot, say 50 to 100 pounds in a short period of time, your skin can't keep up with the loss in body mass. That's when you typically hear about people having to get the excess skin surgically removed."

"Right," Edward chimed in.

"So, during your process of weight loss, you have to think about your skin's elasticity."

"What is that?" Erin asked.

"Elasticity is the extent to which skin is able to stretch and then recover back to normal once the need to stretch is removed—as in the case of weight gain and loss. The more fat that sits beneath the skin and the longer it remains, the less accommodating the skin becomes. For this reason, skin is less likely to shrink in cases of extreme and rapid weight loss because elasticity is diminished. In cases where skin is permanently stretched, people who have lost a lot of weight may be left with excess skin."

"I guess my dance classes mixed with resistance training has helped me in that area," Melissa stated.

"Most definitely," Trevor said. "There is something I want to mention before Mr. Sasser and Mr. Castillo arrive."

"What Trevor?" Melissa asked.

"A friend of mine, Diane Proud, is having her Run Proud for Dessert 5K Race in a couple of months, and I would like for all of you to participate."

"Is the race benefitting a cause or something?" Edward asked.

"In early 2009, Diane was diagnosed with amyotrophic lateral sclerosis (ALS), often referred to as Lou Gehrig's Disease. It is a progressive neurodegenerative disease that affects nerve cells in the brain and the spinal cord. With voluntary muscle action progressively affected, patients in the later stages of the disease may become totally paralyzed. The money raised from the race will go toward research."

"Is your friend paralyzed?" Edward asked.

"She's not totally paralyzed, but her health has declined. Based on my last email communication, her cervical spine muscles are weak, so she has trouble holding up her head."

"Wow!" Erin said.

"Was she unhealthy?" Dillard asked.

"Actually, she has been an athlete for a great majority of her life, winning all sorts of awards, plus she is a certified USA Triathlon Coach who has traveled all over the world."

"How does someone like that end up with such a devastating disease?" Dillard asked.

"Who knows? Genetics? The bottom line is that none of us know our destiny," Trevor stated. "As I've told you all before, you can do everything right and still end up with some disease or illness. We just hope that our healthier lifestyles will help to lessen the impact."

"So sad," Melissa commented.

"Sad to some, but a blessing for others. She didn't lie down or retreat into some corner. She created the Run Proud for Dessert event to bring awareness and raise money for amyotrophic lateral sclerosis (ALS)."

"It goes back to what you told us early last year. That is, how God allows things to happen in our lives for His purpose. Being a rape victim, I never would have thought like that. Now, because I'm involved in a rape support group for young girls, I understand I had to encounter what I did to be of benefit to others," Melissa said.

"Absolutely!" Trevor exclaimed. "And, like Claire and Dillard running for causes, like Claire bringing awareness to and raising money for research to help those impacted by Crohn's and Ulcerative Colitis, and, like Erin and Edward sharing how they've overcome the anger, resentment, and pain they harbored for so long against their parents, and in Erin's case, against her husband, and, in addition, Edward, like in your case, your stroke and its impact on your life and how you've learned to forgive."

"All I need to do is be healthy like you," Erin said.

Trevor hesitated and said, "Last year, my doctor informed me that I had high cholesterol."

"You!" Erin shouted.

"Yes, me," Trevor said, calmly. "It just reinforced how I needed to be even more diligent in making sure I was eating healthy."

"How does someone like you end up with high cholesterol?" Dillard asked.

"Who knows? Genetics?" Trevor answered and continued, "It's odd, since I don't eat a lot of meat, dairy products, or fried foods. But, it did cause me to consider my increased intake in potato chips. So, I had to completely cut them out."

"I'll be happy to walk in the event for your friend," Erin said.

"Me, too," Melissa seconded.

"I'm there," Dillard said.

"Me, too," Edward joined in.

"I wouldn't miss it," Claire said.

"Great! Then, we'll start the discussion about all of you participating in the Houston Chevron half-marathon."

There was an intentional silence as they smiled at Trevor.

"Thank you," Trevor said. "The inspiration to live healthier today, tomorrow, and forever comes from understanding what's at stake and a desire to do things differently. I thank God for the way He has touched and made a difference in your lives, the way you've opened up, your transparency, and your pursuit of a purpose. So many people walk around every day pretending that things are okay and they never resolved their lives. I pray that you all stay focused, not get lazy or comfortable, and, that you continue to give Him all of the honor, praise, and glory for how your life has changed and evolved over the past year."

He paused.

"I know you want to enjoy the journey you're on. Just remember that it's a journey of many paths you'll take. As much as we'd like to prepare for the journey, we can never prepare for and know what we'll run into. Along the way, you're subject to hit a pothole that gets you out of alignment; drive into a ditch because your vision becomes blocked; hit a tree because you lose control, or get stuck at a dead end because you took a wrong turn. As long as you keep your perspective intact, you'll be able to manage life's inevitable mishaps and uncertainties."

Trevor paused and looked around.

"I want us to take a few minutes to pray," Trevor said.

"I'll do it," Edward said.

His cousins looked surprised. Trevor nodded in agreement.

"God, thank You for Uncle Bert and Trevor, for sending them to us, Your modern day good Samaritans for showing us mercy, for using them to make us aware of Your word and its application for our life. Thank You for forgiving us for every wrong we've done and for all of the sins we've committed. We thank You, God, for Your faithfulness to us, Your mercy, and Your grace. We thank You for the time we had with Uncle Bert and pray that his soul is at rest. While I pray that me and my cousins are good stewards over the inheritance Uncle Bert has left us, the greater inheritance is how we now view ourselves and one another. I pray that we will always cherish the latter. I pray that You guide me on how to be a good role model for my brother's children."

Mr. Sasser and Mr. Castillo arrived. They were ready to reveal the wealth Uncle Bert had passed on to his great-nieces and nephews.

"Me and your Uncle Bert were good friends for many years," Mr. Sasser started out saying. "We met while I was a legal intern and he was a security guard in the building where I worked. The day he made his decision to quit being a security guard, we were eating hot dogs in the cafeteria. He turned to me and said 'Today is the day. I'm going to start my own security business, Sasser.' He knew he had greatness inside that needed to be unleashed. From the moment he received the first security services contract, his business soared, but working day and night to build it wasn't good enough for him. A few years later he announced that he'd run for state representative. Although he wanted to make a lot of money so he could help those in need, he also wanted to be in a position where he could make a difference in the community he grew up in."

Mr. Castillo commented and said, "For many years, he knew he hadn't been there for his own family, namely, his sister, Saddie."

"And that's when he decided he wanted to pass on his legacy to you all," Mr. Sasser said. "He chose you all to continue his legacy because in his heart he felt that if you had the right intervention, you would do even greater things than he had accomplished."

Mr. Sasser motioned for Mr. Castillo to speak.

"Trevor, as you are aware, Bert named you as the executor of his estate to include the power to run his business. The charitable bequests in the will include one million for the Kashmere Heights Library, one million for the Crohn's and Colitis Foundation, one million for the American Diabetes Association, and one million for the American Heart Association. The remainder of the estate, after the distribution of $30 million in a trust for Erin, Dillard, Melissa, Claire, Edward, and Thomas Wayne's wife, is to go to create a charitable organization in his name."

Dillard looked stunned.

"Five million for each of us!" Dillard shouted.

"Yes, five million for each of you," Mr. Castillo stated.

Erin, Melissa, and Claire sat in disbelief.

"Are you sure?" Melissa asked, looking at Mr. Castillo.

"I'm sure."

"You're sure I'm included in the figure?" Edward asked with doubt.

"I'm sure, Edward."

They all looked at Trevor for confirmation.

He smiled and nodded his head, acknowledging that it was true.

Instantaneously, Trevor's cousins jumped up out of their seats, screaming, as tears started to cover their faces. They descended on him with hugs of joy and gratefulness.

Melissa started breathing heavily.

"Are you okay?" Mr. Sasser asked her.

"I'm okay," she said while crying. "I just need a moment to process it all. I never would have imagined . . ."

"Your uncle loved all of you so much," Mr. Castillo said.

Mr. Sasser looked down at his clipboard and said, "We have more to cover."

Trevor motioned for his cousins to have a seat.

Mr. Castillo continued, "It was important to your uncle that you didn't get caught up with money like so many people do when they inherit a large sum."

Erin, Melissa, Claire, Edward, and Dillard stared at Mr. Castillo curiously.

"Bert stipulated that each you are to find lots in Kashmere Heights and build a modest home, no more than 4,000 square feet, for you and your family, and purchase one American-made car of your choice. You will receive a monthly allowance of $5,000 for living expenses for the rest of your life. The monthly allowance may be increased if warranted. The monthly allowance will continue as long as each of you demonstrates a consistency with living healthy and with purpose."

"The money in your trust will be used to fund any community and charitable organizations you create and/or support. I will serve as the administrator and advisor as related to your involvement," Mr. Sasser said.

Mr. Castillo said, "If Bert were here today, his first question to each of you would be, 'What are you going to do with the five million you have inherited?' It will not be given to you all at once, but in stages, as needed for your projects upon completion of my and Mr. Castillo's research and joint approval."

"So, that is the question each of you must answer. What are you going to do with your portion?" Mr. Sasser said.

"Each of you will need to meet me and Mr. Sasser at ten o'clock Monday morning to provide your plans for your portion."

Two days later, they met Mr. Sasser and Mr. Castillo as scheduled. They had appointed Edward as their spokesperson.

Edward looked at his cousins and said, "We are committed to continuing the legacy of our uncle. There's nothing more important to us than making him proud that he took a risk and chose us."

Trevor patted him on back.

"We all have our individual missions, but collectively we want to rebuild Kittridge Street. First, we want to purchase and renovate foreclosed and abandoned homes and give them away to individuals who may otherwise never be able to experience purchasing their own home. They would be required to maintain the home's interior, exterior, and the yard areas, to ensure upkeep of the street and neighborhood. We would work with existing homeowners or renters on the street to remodel their homes, update fencing and landscaping, paint over graffiti, and remove refuse/trash from the various vacant lots."

"We're confident that the two of you will help us establish the qualifying criteria for people to get one of the free renovated homes," Erin said.

"My cousin, Edward, counted approximately fifteen foreclosed and abandoned properties," Melissa said.

Both Mr. Sasser and Mr. Castillo nodded and smiled.

Trevor looked at Melissa.

She was nervous and excited.

"I haven't gotten an ounce of sleep thinking about what I'd like to do with my portion," Melissa said, smiling at her cousins. "Years ago, when me and my children had to live in a homeless shelter, I knew I'd never want anyone to experience what we experienced."

Melissa looked at Mr. Sasser and Mr. Castillo, teary eyed and grateful. "I want to buy the Sahara Motel over on Brady Street and turn it into a homeless shelter. Right now, it's a haven for thugs and their illegal activity, prostitutes and their guests, and drug addicts getting high. I want to transform the approximately thirty units into quality living quarters for homeless individuals and families. I envision having a community and social service center attached to the property."

"She wants the shelter to position people to get into permanent housing. The two of you may be able to help her find government grants to refurbish the property," Trevor said.

"Most definitely," Mr. Sasser said.

"A homeless shelter is really needed in our community," Melissa added. "Not just from a shelter perspective, but to offer people who have hit rock bottom every opportunity to succeed and get off the streets."

Mr. Sasser looked at Mr. Castillo and said, "That will be a great project. We have resources we can tap into where you can partner with organizations to provide spiritual counseling, food and clothing, drug and alcohol treatment, assistance for skill development and job readiness training, and medical treatment services."

They both nodded their heads in agreement.

Erin and Dillard looked at one another, signaling it was their turn.

Erin started out and said, "Me and my brother would like to use our portion to build a community wellness center on the grounds of the Kashmere Heights Park. It would provide an array of education, support, and wellness programs to help our community to live healthier."

"Our project will also include renovating the park, the basketball courts, the softball field, and the playground."

"It's a shame how the city has allowed the park to deteriorate. They don't even keep up the landscaping," Erin commented.

"It'll be great! Our kids need a decent park and playground," Trevor said.

"We hope to attract some of your health and fitness friends, Trevor, to lead support groups, educational workshops, nutrition and exercise classes, and stress reduction seminars, so our residents can be exposed to the essentials for living healthier."

"Absolutely."

"As me, Erin, and Dillard discussed last night—with all of the rehabilitation, redevelopment, and revitalization that has been talked about and targeted, there's no reason why I couldn't purchase Faulkner's Liquor Store and turn it into a health food store and restaurant," Claire said.

"That is something that's much needed in our neighborhood," Trevor agreed. "I believe in supporting our neighborhood food establishments like the soul food restaurants, chicken shacks, barbecue and burger joints, but our community needs and wants the ability to purchase healthy items without having to travel across town."

They burst out in laughter, clapping their hands.

While the content of all of the cousin's lives had changed significantly, the height of Edward's transformation clearly set him apart from the others. He had joined Trevor's church and had become an active in the men's ministry. He had started a *Meet Me: Morning Fitness on Your Corner* walking initiative in his neighborhood. He was researching assisted living centers and making plans to move his mother back to Texas.

"For starters, I want to take all of the residents living on Kittridge Street on a vacation. Before I went to visit my mother, I had never traveled outside of Houston. While in Manchester, I visited some amazing tourist sites and drove to Boston where I toured Martha's Vineyard and Cape Cod. So much history I experienced..."

Claire gave him a loving smile.

"It was such an awesome adventure. Last night, I had flashbacks about the ways the trip affected my life. And I want people who probably couldn't afford to travel there to do so."

"So many people have never been outside of Kashmere Heights, Edward," Trevor said. "I think it's wonderful what you're wanting to do. Only one stipulation, though."

Edward looked puzzled and said, "What?"

"You are responsible for Mr. Whitehouse."

They all started laughing.

Edward looked at each of them and said, "I spent most of my life driving around in circles on life's freeway, passing exit after exit after exit, and looking at the same scenery (pain, fear, disappointment, anger, resentment) over and over again. When I finally made the choice to get off and took an exit, my life changed. And, I apologize for the pain, insults, and grief I caused all of you."

"Your uncle would be so proud of all of you and your contributions to the community," Mr. Sasser said. "Me and Castillo will be working closely with Trevor and each of you to get your projects in motion. We need to do research and planning related to the allocation of financing. Give us a month to sort through everything we need to consider. The difference you are going to make in Kashmere Heights is going to be paramount. I believe it's only fitting the community wellness center be named the Bert Spencer Community Wellness Center."

They all smiled and nodded in agreement.

Recipes

Every attempt possible has been made to ensure the nutrition information provided for the following recipe items is accurate. However, the author of this book does not guarantee the accuracy of nutritional information. When food items are freshly prepared and "handmade", the actual values may vary; ingredient and nutrition content of foods may vary due to changes in product formulation, recipe substitutions, portion size, and other factors. The intent of the nutritional information provided in this book is to encourage the reader to review and analyze the food content of their meals for purposes of obtaining healthier eating goals.

❖

❖

Recipes

By Angela M. Collier
Certified Personal Trainer, Nutritionist
www.hhealthy.net

❖

❖

Breakfast

❖

Breakfast Egg & Vegetable Pita

Low Fat, Diabetes Friendly, Low-Carb,
Low Cholesterol, Healthy Weight

Ingredients

½ whole-wheat pita bread
¼ tsp olive oil
½ cup diced portabella mushrooms
4 large egg whites
1 small diced tomato

Directions

Begin with heating 1 tsp of olive oil in a skillet on medium high heat. In a medium bowl, scramble egg whites and set aside.

Dice mushrooms and dice tomatoes (For a time saver, you can also use any salsa.). Add vegetables first to the skillet, allow to cook for 2 minutes, then add egg whites, and scramble mixture to combine.

Cut the pita in half and stuff one half of the pita with vegetable scramble.

Tip: Be gentle with opening the pita because they tear easily. Also, save the other half of the pita for another day!

Nutrition Information Per Serving:

Serving Size - 1 serving
Calories: 244
Total Fat: 9 grams
(Saturated Fat 3 grams,
Monounsaturated Fat 4 grams,
and Polyunsaturated Fat 1 gram)

Cholesterol: 18 mg
Sodium: 481 mg
Total carbohydrate: 16 grams
(Dietary Fiber 4 grams, Sugar 6 grams)
Protein: 22 grams

Cinnamon Apple Quinoa Breakfast

Low Fat, Diabetes Friendly, Gluten Free, Cholesterol Free,
Low Sodium, High Fiber, Healthy Weight

Ingredients

2 cups water
1 tbsp ground cinnamon
¼ cup sliced almonds
1 cup uncooked quinoa
1 tsp ground nutmeg
2 apples

Directions

Begin with boiling quinoa in a large pot with water. Once at a boil, simmer and cover pot for 10 to 15 minutes, or until all water is absorbed by the quinoa.

While water is boiling, remove core of apple and dice with the skin still on. Place the apple to the side until quinoa has completed cooking. (Feel free to add lemon juice to prevent browning of apples.)

Mix in diced apple, almonds, and flaxseed. Add fresh cinnamon and nutmeg. Remove pot from heat, and re-cover with lid.

Serve while hot; 1/2 cup in bowl. Also goes great with fresh fruit on the side, and herbal tea.

Tip: Great recipe to make ahead of time! Pre-portion size out to 1/2 cup servings for quick on-the-go grab for breakfast!

Yields – 4 servings

Nutritional Information Per Serving

Serving Size - ½ cup
Calories: 242
Total Fat: 7 grams
(Saturated Fat 1 grams,
Monounsaturated Fat 3 grams,
Polyunsaturated Fat 2 grams)

Cholesterol: 0 mg
Sodium: 2 mg
Total carbohydrate: 39 grams (Dietary Fiber 7 grams and Sugar 7 grams)
Protein: 8 grams

Fruit, Oats-n-Yogurt

Low Fat, Diabetes Appropriate, Low Cholesterol,
High Fiber, Healthy Weight

Ingredients

½ cup oats
½ cup plain or vanilla yogurt (fat free or low fat)
½ cup fresh or frozen blueberries (Any favorite fresh or frozen fruit can be substituted)

Directions

In a small to-go container, mix yogurt, oats, and blueberries well.

Yields – 1 serving

Nutrition Information Per Serving:

Serving Size - approximately 1 ½ cup
Calories: 264
Total Fat: 3 grams
(Saturated Fat 1 grams,
Monounsaturated Fat 1 grams, and
Polyunsaturated Fat 1 gram)

Cholesterol: 2 mg
Sodium: 97 mg
Total carbohydrate: 47 grams
(Dietary Fiber 6 grams and Sugar 10 grams)
Protein: 13 grams

Good Morning Egg White and Vegetable Frittata

Low Fat, Diabetes Appropriate, Gluten-Free

Ingredients

8 egg whites
1 diced tomato
1 cup diced portabella mushrooms
1 cup fresh or frozen spinach
1 tbsp olive oil
¼ cup skim milk
1 tsp black pepper
¼ tsp salt (optional)
1 oz. part-skim mozzarella cheese, shredded

Directions

Begin with pre-heating broiler on high.

Lightly coat a medium-sized skillet with olive oil. Place the skillet over medium heat. When skillet is hot, add spinach and mushrooms, cover skillet with lid, and let vegetables steam for about 2 minutes.

When spinach looks slightly wilted, add scrambled egg white and milk mixture. Pour over vegetables.

Add diced tomatoes, salt, pepper, and top with cheese.

Continue to cook in skillet until the edges begin to brown.

Remove from skillet, then place skillet under the broiler. Broil until frittata is golden and slightly crisp on top.

Remove from heat and let set for about 5 to 10 minutes. Then cut into 8 slices to serve.

Tip: This recipe can be made ahead of time for a grab-and-go breakfast! This recipe can be enjoyed for breakfast, brunch, or even as a snack! You can add 1 cup of fresh fruit and 1 cup of low fat or fat-free yogurt!

Yields – 8 servings

Nutrition Information Per Serving

Serving Size - 1 slice
Calories: 65 calories
Total Fat: 4 grams
(Saturated Fat 1 grams,
Monounsaturated Fat 1 grams,
and Polyunsaturated Fat 0 grams)

Cholesterol: 5 mg
Sodium: 125 mg
Total carbohydrate: 3 grams
(Dietary Fiber 1 grams, Sugar 1 gram)
Protein: 6 grams

❖

Lunch

❖

Black Bean and Mango-Veggie Pita

Low Fat, Diabetes Friendly, Cholesterol Free, High Fiber,
Low Sodium, Low Calorie, Healthy Weight

Ingredients

1/2 Organic Whole-Wheat Pita Bread
1/2 cup Black Beans
1/2 cup Spinach Fresh
3 slices Avocado
½ cup fresh mango, diced
Cilantro (optional)

Directions

Begin by cutting pita completely in half. Gently open pita (If necessary, place pita in oven or microwave to heat slightly to make opening the pita without tearing easier.).

Gently stuff each pita with spinach, then beans, avocado (3 slices in each pita), diced mango, and chopped cilantro if desired

Serve with 1 cup of fresh fruit, 1 cup of spinach or garden salad, or 8 ounces of carrot juice.

Tip: This vegetarian dish requires no cooking, is great for on the go, and to pack in any lunch for kids or a kid at heart! This super healthy but super tasty meal is low fat, includes a great source of protein, and contains all kinds of other nutrients such as vitamin A, vitamin C, vitamin K, folate, and calcium. This dish is also great served with 1 cup of fresh fruit, 1 cup of spinach salad with lemon and olive oil, or 8 ounces of carrot juice.

Nutrition Information Per Serving

Serving Size - 1/2 pita
Calories: 136
Total Fat: 2.7g (Saturated Fat 0.5g)
Cholesterol: 0mg

Sodium: 241mg
Total Carbohydrate: 23g (Dietary Fiber 5g, Sugars 3.5g)
Protein: 6.23g

Mediterranean Quinoa Salad

Diabetes Appropriate, Gluten Free, Low fat, healthy weight

Ingredients

- 1 cup dry quinoa
- 2 cups water
- 2 cups sliced cherry tomatoes
- 1 cucumber, peeled and chopped
- 3/4 cup queso fresco
- 1 can organic black beans
- 1 1/2 T extra virgin olive oil
- 1/2 lemon, juiced
- 1 tsp dry oregano
- 1 tsp salt
- 1/4 tsp black pepper

Directions

Combine the water and quinoa in a medium-sized pot and bring to a boil. Reduce heat to simmer and let cook for about 15 minutes or until the quinoa has absorbed all of the water. Fluff with a fork and set aside to cool.

In a large bowl, combine the sliced tomatoes, black beans, and cucumber. Add quinoa and spices and mix well. Drizzle olive oil and lemon juice on top and add cheese.

Toss everything together. Serve immediately or store in the fridge until serving.

Yield – 4 to 6 servings

Nutrition Information Per Serving

Serving Size - ½ cup
Calories: 278
Fat: 12 grams

Carbohydrates: 31 grams
Protein: 11 grams

Spinach Chicken Salad with Honey - Lemon Zest Dressing

Low-Fat, Diabetic Friendly, Great source
of protein and omega-3 fatty acids

Ingredients

2 cups Spinach, Raw
1/2 cup Mandarin orange
3 oz Grilled Chicken

Directions

Begin with laying a bed of spinach on a plate
Then top with grilled and sliced or chopped chicken
Top with mandarin oranges and queso fresco

Tip: This salad is a great salad to celebrate spring and summer! This salad is not only packed with vitamins and minerals but also give a punch of protein and great flavor!

Nutrition Information Per Serving

Serving Size – the entire salad
Calories: 257
Total Fat: 9 grams
(Saturated fat 2.1 grams)
Cholesterol: 60 mg

Sodium: 505 mg
Total Carbohydrate: 22 grams
(Dietary Fiber 2.3 grams, Sugars 18.25 grams)
Protein: 23.12 grams

Honey-Lemon Zest Salad Dressing Recipe

Ingredients

1/4 cup Lemon Juice
1 tsp Lemon Zest
1 tbsp Honey
1/2 tsp Thyme, Fresh
1/4 cup Extra Virgin Olive Oil

Directions

Combine all ingredients.
Whisk, shake, blend, or mix until all ingredients are combined and smooth.

Tip: Creating your own salad dressing is not only fun but can also be tastier than the bottled fare you buy at the grocery store! Making your own salad dressings can also be much cheaper with getting ingredients for pennies and putting them together yourself rather than spending $4-$5 on dressing! This dressing goes perfectly with the Spinach Chicken Salad with Honey - Lemon Zest Dressing.

Nutrition Information Per Serving

Serving Size - 2 tbsp
Calories: 54
Total Fat: 5 grams
(Saturated fat 0.8)
Cholesterol: 0 mg

Sodium: 0 mg
Total Carbohydrate: 1 gram
(Dietary Fiber 0 grams, Sugars 1.6 grams)
Protein: 0 grams

❖

Dinner

❖

Easy Spicy Shrimp and Mango Ceviche

Cholesterol Free, Weight Control, Heart Healthy
High Fiber, Low Calorie, Low Sodium

Ingredients

1 lb. Cooked Shrimps (cleaned, rinsed, drained, and dried)
1 cup Pico De Gayo
1 1/2 cups mango, diced
1 med Avocado
3/4 cup Lime Juice
1 tbsp Taco Seasoning
1/4 cup Cilantro
Cucumber, diced (optional)
Serrano peppers (optional)
10 Baked Corn Tortilla Chips (see Homemade Tortilla Chip Recipe below)

Directions

In a large bowl, combine Pico de Gallo, mango, shrimp, avocado, cilantro, cucumber, lemon and lime juice, taco seasoning, and sea salt to taste. Add Serrano peppers (if desired). Combine well.

Homemade Tortilla Chips: Preheat the oven to 350 degrees. Cut 2-3 corn tortillas in quarters. Place on cookie sheet, and bake for approximately 15 minutes or until the edges are browned.

Before serving, add a little cilantro, cucumber, avocado and tortilla chips to garnish.

Tips: The avocado in this recipe provides a healthy fat called Omega-6 Fatty acids (linoleic acid) that helps to stabilize blood sugar levels and is also rich in the antioxidant vitamin E. Avocado also provides vitamins B1, B2, B3, B5, C, K, folate, copper, iron, phosphorus, zinc, and fiber.

Yields - 4 servings

Nutrition Information Per Serving

Serving Size 1 cup and 8 baked chips
Calories: 277
Total fat: 8 grams
(Saturated fat 1.5 grams)
Cholesterol: 0 mg
Sodium: 222 grams
Total carbohydrate: 42.17 grams
(Dietary Fiber 6 grams, Sugar 7 grams)
Protein: 4 grams

Ginger Chicken Stir Fry

Gluten Free, Low Cholesterol, Heart Healthy
Healthy Weight, Diabetic Friendly

Ingredients

5 Garlic Cloves, diced
2 tbsp Ginger Root, diced
2 tbsp Extra Virgin Olive Oil
4 cups Mixed Vegetables, frozen
1 lb Chicken Breast, diced or sliced
1/4 cup Chinese Rice Wine Vinegar
1 cup Quinoa, uncooked

Directions

Begin with boiling 2 cups of water in a large pot. Once at a boil, add quinoa, continue to boil for about 10 minutes, and then reduce heat and cover. Allow to cook for an additional 15 minutes or until quinoa has absorbed water. Drain excess water if needed.

In a large skillet or wok, heat olive oil over medium-high heat.

Begin with sautéing garlic and ginger, add diced chicken breast.

Add frozen vegetables to mixture and Chinese rice wine vinegar. Cover to allow vegetables to steam for about 5 to 8 minutes. Season to taste (optional).

Serve on top of 1/2 cup of bed of quinoa.

Tips: Ginger is great for the digestive system. It also benefits by heating the body boosting circulation and metabolism! You can use ground ginger root, but fresh ginger root that you chop yourself is best.
Yields 4 servings

Nutrition Information Per Serving

Serving size – quinoa ½ cup, and stir fry 1 cup
Calories: 445
Total fat: 10.5 grams
(Saturated fat 1.65 grams)
Cholesterol: 68 mg

Sodium: 185.5 mg
Total Carbohydrate: 45.6 grams
(Dietary fiber 6.13 grams, sugar 6.1 grams)
Protein: 36.31 grams

Fiery Bean-n-Turkey Chili

Low Cholesterol, Low Fat, Healthy Weight, High Fiber

Ingredients

1 pound ground turkey (Lean)
1 chopped onion
1 chopped garlic
1 chopped tomato
1 can black beans (drained and rinsed)
1 cup of fresh or frozen corn
1 can of tomato paste (6 ounces) (For gluten free - mix the tomato paste and add 1 cup of pureed tomatoes instead.)
2 cups water
1 tbsp chili powder
1 tbsp paprika
1 tsp salt (To cut salt, do not add to recipe.)
1 tsp black pepper
1 tbsp olive oil

Directions

Begin with heating a large soup pot on medium-high heat. Add olive oil and begin to brown onion and garlic.

Add turkey meat to brown.

Add beans (drained and rinsed) and corn into the pot.

Add tomato paste and 2 cups of water. Mix well.

Bring entire contents to a boil for about 10 minutes and then reduce heat. Add tomatoes and seasonings.

Tips: Black beans are rich in minerals and fiber. They are also great sources of iron and protein, important for energy production and metabolism.

Nutrition Information Per Serving

Serving Size – 1 cup
Calories: 315
Fat: 11 grams
Cholesterol: 5 mg

Sodium: 691 mg
Total Carbohydrate: 3 grams (Dietary fiber 10 grams)
Protein: 24 grams

❖

Snacks

❖

Energy Snack Bars

Low fat, low carb, healthy weight,
diabetes friendly, cholesterol free

Ingredients

1 cup no sugar added applesauce (For gluten free, substitute with 1 cup of mashed bananas.)
1/3 cup rolled oats
1/4 cup flax Seed
1/8 tsp ground Cinnamon
1/8 tsp nutmeg
1/8 tsp salt
1 cup fresh or frozen blueberries
1 cup shaved almonds
2 tbsp Canola Oil

Directions

Preheat oven to 350° F. Line an 8x8-inch baking pan with parchment paper, overlapping at the sides.

Pulse oatmeal in a food processor or coffee grinder until fine.

Combine oatmeal powder with flax seeds, shaved almonds, cinnamon, sea salt, and nutmeg. Stir well to combine.

Whisk together canola oil, applesauce, and blueberries.

Pour into dry mix and mix well to combine.

Transfer to the baking dish, spreading into an even layer, and pushing into sides and corners of the pan. You can use a rubber spatula to do this or the back of a wooden spoon.

Bake in center of oven 30 minutes until deeply golden. Remove from oven and let cool in pan until room temperature.

Place in fridge for about 2 hours to set.

Remove from fridge. Lift out of pan by grabbing firmly by the parchment on both sides of pan. It should lift right out. Cut into quarters, then cut quarters into three bars each, for a total of 12 bars. Store tightly covered in the fridge.

Tip: This snack is perfect to pack for pre or post workout! Or anytime you need a quick pick me up!

Yield 12 bars

Nutrition Information Per Serving

Serving size – 1 bar
Calories: 122
Total Fat: 8 grams (Saturated Fat < 1 gram)
Cholesterol: 0 mg

Sodium: 28 mg
Total Carbohydrate: 11 grams (Fiber 3.5 grams, Sugar 4.5 grams)
Protein: 3 grams

Angie's Going Green Smoothie

Gluten Free, low-fat, healthy weight,
Diabetes Friendly, high fiber, low sodium

Ingredients

1/2 cup Pineapple, raw
1/2 medium Banana
2 oz Protein Powder
2 tbsp Ground Flaxseed
1/2 cup Skim Milk
1 cup Spinach

Directions

Combine pineapple, banana, spinach, protein (if desired), ground flaxseed, and milk in a blender. Other milk options (almond milk, soy milk, coconut milk, or rice milk).

Blend for about 60 seconds.

Pour into a glass or "to-go" container.

Tip: Having a smoothie as a snack or meal replacement makes it easy to fit in your vegetable and fruit servings all in 1!

Yields: 2 (8 ounce servings)

Nutrition Information Per Serving

One 8 ounce serving
Calories: 218
Fat: 4 g (Saturated Fat < 1 gram)
Cholesterol: 1 mg

Sodium: 178 mg
Total Carbohydrate: 22 g (fiber 6 grams, sugar 12 grams)
Protein: 11 g

Almond-Mint & Raspberry Vanilla Yogurt Parfait

Low-fat, low-cholesterol, healthy weight

Ingredients
1/2 cup fat free or low fat vanilla yogurt
2 tbsp Sliced Almonds
1 tbsp Raspberry Preserves

Directions

You will need a wine glass or goblet, martini glass, or dessert serving dish to prepare each parfait.

Begin with 1/4 cup of yogurt, then a small layer of almonds, then raspberry preserves.

Continue to make layers. Garnish with mint leaves.

Tip: Trying to ward off those sweet cravings? This recipe can cure any sweet craving while filling you up with nutritional goodness!

Nutrition Information Per Serving
Serving Size - 1 parfait
Calories: 200
Fat: 6 grams (saturated fat .5 grams)
Cholesterol: 0 mg
Sodium: 45 mg
Total Carbohydrate: 24 grams (Fiber 1.5 grams, Sugar 21 grams)
Protein: 14 grams

Recipes

By Private Chef H.D Harris
Chef Services Inc.

❖

Breakfast

❖

Bran Muffins with Flaxseed

Ingredients

1 cup wheat bran
1/2 cup ground flax seed
1 cup whole wheat flour
1 tsp baking powder
1 tsp baking soda
1/4 cup raisins
1 cup 2% milk
2 tbsp canola oil
1/2 cup molasses
1 medium apple peeled and grated or 1/2 cup apple sauce
2 eggs

Directions

Preheat the oven to 400 degrees.

Combine wheat bran, flax seed, flour, baking powder, and baking soda. Stir in raisins.

In a separate bowl, whisk milk, oil, molasses, apples, eggs. Add to dry ingredients and blend until moistened.

Spoon into greased muffin tin and bake for 15-20 minutes.

Servings Per Recipe: 12 muffins

Nutrition Information Per Serving

Serving Size: 1 muffin
Calories: 319.2
Total Fat: 23.4 g
Cholesterol: 28.7 mg

Sodium: 169.6 mg
Total Carbs: 27.3 g
Dietary Fiber: 5.1 g
Protein: 4.8 g

Easy Egg White and Salmon Breakfast Frittata

Ingredients

8 egg whites
1/2 tsp salt
1/4 tsp black pepper
1/2 can Pink Salmon (drained of oil) separated with a fork
1/4 cup chopped green onion
1/4 tsp minced garlic (not the jar kind!)

Directions

Whip egg whites until frothy, about 3-4 minutes.

Preheat 10-inch omelet or sauté pan with non-stick spray.

Pour egg whites in pan, sprinkle salmon, green onions, and garlic over the whites. (Experiment with your other favorite small diced vegetables.).

Place in oven preheated at 375 degrees and cook until eggs are set, about 10 minutes.

Remove, slide out of pan, and cut into slices.

Number of Servings: 8

Nutrition Information per serving

Serving Size: 1 slice
Calories: 425.4
Total Fat: 17.7 g
Cholesterol: 160.5 mg

Sodium: 425.2 mg
Total Carbs: 0.5 g
Dietary Fiber: 0.1 g
Protein: 61.9 g

❖

Lunch

❖

Easy Turkey and Spinach Wraps

Ingredients

4 ounces cream cheese

2 tbsp Dijon mustard

1 tsp honey

2 green onion chopped

1 ½ cup baby spinach

1 large carrot peeled and grated

1 small tomato diced

½ tsp salt

¼ black pepper

¾ lb thin sliced deli turkey

1 cup fat-free grated cheddar cheese

6 medium whole wheat tortillas

Directions

Mix cream cheese, mustard, and honey until smooth.

Spread each tortillas with about 2 tablespoons of the cream cheese mixture, almost to the edge of the tortilla.

Place two tablespoons of spinach mixture on cream cheese mixture.

Place 2-3 slices of turkey over spinach and add 2 tablespoons of cheese.

Roll each tortilla up very tight and cut diagonally across the middle.

Number of servings: 6

Nutritional Information Per Serving

Serving Size: 1 wrap
Calories: 320.4
Total Fat: 10.3 g

Cholesterol: 49.1 mg
Sodium: 918.8 mg
Total Carbs: 32.2 g
Dietary Fiber: 5.4 g
Protein: 25.4 g

Twice a Week Salad

Ingredients

  1 bag baby spinach
  1 small red onion sliced
  1 large tomato chopped
  1 large shredded carrot
  1 large sliced cucumber
  1 small bag sunflower seeds (about 1/4 cup)

Directions

Twice a week, prepare the above items and place separate in small airtight containers.

Experiment with your favorite low-fat ingredients and fresh vegetables.

On a daily basis, take a small amount from each container to make a quick, fresh salad.

Add your favorite low-fat, low-sugar dressing. Avoid creamy dressings.

This can be eaten on a daily basis and will only take about 4 minutes or less to assemble. NO MORE EXCUSES!

Number of Servings: 2

Nutrition Informational Per Serving

Serving Size: 1 cup
Calories: 177.1
Total Fat: 8.9 g

Cholesterol: 0.0 mg
Sodium: 96.8 mg
Total Carbs: 21.4 g
Dietary Fiber: 7.3 g
Protein: 7.8 g

Fresh Basil Salad Dressing

Ingredients

> 1 medium tomato
> 1/4 cup olive oil
> 1 tbsp Italian seasoning
> 1 tbsp fresh basil
> Juice of 1/2 lemon
> 1/4 tbsp salt

Directions

Blend above ingredients in a blender and serve with your daily salad.

Number of Servings: 4

Nutrition Information Per Serving

Serving Size: 2 tbsp
Calories: 128.9
Total Fat: 13.7 g

Cholesterol: 0.0 mg
Sodium: 148.6 mg
Total Carbs: 2.9 g
Dietary Fiber: 1.0 g
Protein: 0.5 g

❖

Dinner

❖

Halibut in White Wine

Ingredients

4 medium halibut fillets

1/2 tsp salt

1/2 tsp pepper

1/4 tsp garlic powder

1/2 cup bread crumbs

1 tbsp Dijon mustard

2 tbsp minced red onions

3/4 cup white wine (not sweet)

Directions

Sprinkle halibut with your favorite seasonings.

Mix the next four ingredients and spread evenly over fish.

Place in baking dish and pour wine in the bottom.

Bake for about 20 minutes or until fish is flakey.

Number of Servings: 4

Nutrition Information Per Serving

Serving Size: 1 medium halibut filet

Calories: 536.8

Total Fat: 10.1 g

Cholesterol: 130.4 mg

Sodium: 731.4 mg

Total Carbs: 10.8 g

Dietary Fiber: 0.8 g

Protein: 86.8 g

Italian Chicken and Tomato Casserole

Ingredients

3 chicken breasts cooked and chopped or 1 pkg ground turkey

1/2 cup cooked brown rice, cooled

1/2 large zucchini

1/2 cup celery finely chopped

1 small onion chopped

2 garlic cloves minced

1 tbsp Italian seasoning

1 tsp salt

1 tsp pepper

1-28 ounce can whole peeled tomatoes chopped, drained

1 egg

1/4 cup olive oil

1/4 cup chicken broth

Directions

Mix all ingredients and pour into sprayed casserole dish and cook for 35-40 minutes. Let it stand for about 15 minutes.

Number of Servings: 6

Nutrition Information per serving

Serving Size: 1/2 cup
Servings Per Recipe: 6
Amount Per Serving
Calories: 186.3
Total Fat: 10.7 g

Cholesterol: 51.6 mg
Sodium: 486.3 mg
Total Carbs: 12.4 g
Dietary Fiber: 2.4 g
Protein: 11.3 g

❖

About the Author

❖

Fitness coach Bridgette Collins is the owner of Total Innovative Wellness Solutions, LLC, a consulting firm that provides individuals and organizations with strategic solutions for implementing and sustaining healthy lifestyle habits. Through MAC Fitness and Origins Publishing Company, subsidiaries of Total Innovative Wellness Solutions, LLC, she introduces innovative and creative resources for achieving well-being and physical fitness to help her clients gain traction on disease prevention and management. Coach Bridgette is also the author of two books, *Destined to Live Healthier* and *Imagine Living Healthier*, which have educated and empowered many through the collection of fictional stories that tell of real life challenges with weight, health, work, marriage, and lack of self-love. She is also featured in *The Ultimate Runner* by Ultimate HCI Books, publisher of the *Chicken Soup for the Soul* series.

Bridgette has worked as a certified personal trainer, both privately and for Bally's Total Fitness, and she holds a personal trainer certification through the Aerobics and Fitness Association of America. Combining her fitness training and passion for healthy living with over ten years of human resources management (most recently as an Assistant Human Resources Director for Dallas County), and program development experience, Bridgette delivers practical and actionable health and fitness solutions. From women's groups and church ministries to half-marathon training programs, Bridgette has inspired and motivated thousands with her ten essential habits for living a healthy lifestyle.

As a motivational speaker, Bridgette travels throughout the United States, delivering a message that empowers audiences to make positive lifestyle choices. She writes healthy lifestyle columns for various print and online magazines, and has also served as a fitness coach for an Internet radio station. Understanding that the quest to incorporate a healthy lifestyle is often hampered by daily demands and obligations, she equips her readers and audiences with a collection of lifestyle tools that helps to close the gap between understanding how to implement healthier lifestyle habits and reduce their risk of disease and illness.

An avid runner for more than 15 years, Bridgette has participated in numerous 5K and 10K races and has completed five marathons and a host of half-marathons. In an effort to share the benefits of a consistent running program, she has coached several group training programs to provide beginner walkers and runners weekly instruction for improving their fitness level both privately and for national organizations like the Crohn's and Colitis Foundation.

A native of Houston, Bridgette resides in Grand Prairie, Texas, where she is an active member at Golden Gate Missionary Baptist Church. She enjoys running, watching football, traveling, and going to movies and stage plays. She has a degree in business administration.

Bridgette would love to receive your feedback on *Broken in Plain Sight*. To contact her, please write or email:

Bridgette L. Collins
P.O. Box 542671
Grand Prairie, Texas 75054-2671
bridgette@bridgettecollins.com